Still My
Aching Heart

Still My Aching Heart

Kay Rizzo

When tragedy breaks her heart, old dreams return. Is it time for Chloe to make peace with her past?

Pacific Press Publishing Association
Boise, Idaho
Oshawa, Ontario, Canada

Edited by Bonnie Widicker
Designed by Tim Larson
Cover photograph by Sinclair Studios
Typeset in 11/13 New Century Schoolbook

Copyright © 1993 by
Pacific Press Publishing Association
Printed in the United States of America
All Rights Reserved

Library of Congress Cataloging-in-Publication Data:

Rizzo, Kay D., 1943-
    Still my aching heart / Kay D. Rizzo.
       p.   cm.
   ISBN 0-8163-1136-6 paper
   ISBN 0-8163-1157-9 hardcover
   I. Title.
  PS3568. I836S7 1993
  813'.54—dc20
                                 92-43699
                                     CIP

93 94 95 96 97 ● 5 4 3 2 1

Contents

From Rags to Riches

Ba-ba-ba-boom! The windows rattled, and dust fell from the rafters. Rags ran barking through the two-room cabin, looking for the invader. Dropping the carrot I'd been peeling, I shook my paring knife over my head and cried, "I hate this! Will I ever get used to this?"

Ba-boom! A second explosion. At the breakfast table, James had warned me they'd begin dynamiting a new entrance into the mountain that morning. But I'd never imagined . . .

Until James could build his own stamp mill, three mule teams carried the Renegade ore to the railhead in Hahn's Peak. From there it was shipped, under guard, to Steamboat Springs, the nearest processor. When Jamie came home and told me about the sad, scrawny little beasts, I decided to save my peelings and my leftovers for them. I diced the last carrot and tossed it into the large pot of vegetables simmering on the stove, then collected the peelings in my colander, threw my cape over my shoulders, and headed for the door. The moment the door creaked open, Sunshine dashed around my skirts, out of the cabin, and across the clearing toward the woods.

I minced my way toward the stables, hopping from snow mound to snow mound to avoid the mud created by mine traffic and melting snow. A fine mist of dust filtered down from the work site. I glanced over my shoulder at the opening to the mine high up on the side of the mountain and the cable tramway connecting it with the camp itself.

I passed the mining office and supply shed. As I approached the rear of the stable, I heard the mules braying and a man shouting. Timidly, I inched along the side of the building and peered around the corner.

A man, his back to me, stood with whip raised over the back of a braying mule. The mule tugged at the rope around his neck, trying to pull away from the stinging whip. A second man, of Chinese origin, lay on the ground nearby, his shirt slashed to rags.

My Irish soared. Dropping my colander in a pile of hay, I slipped between the corral post and the building. One look at me, and the Chinese mule skinner leapt to his feet and dashed out of sight. Bounding through the mud, I shouted, "What are you doing to the poor animal?"

Without thinking of the consequences, I grabbed the wrist holding the whip. The man growled and lifted me off my feet. Certain he intended to toss me over his shoulder to the ground, I screamed, "Let go! Let go this instant!"

He obeyed, and I plopped seat first into the mud. "What in the devi . . ." The man whirled about, fire darting from his eyes. The beard and bushy mustache didn't disguise his evil eyes. Shivers of fear skittered up and down my spine. "You! You're the peeping Tom!" I shouted. "Who are you? What are you doing here? How dare you beat my husband's animals!"

His menacing gaze made me scramble to my feet. He curled his lip into a snarl. "Yes, Mrs. McCall, we have met before, but we have not been properly introduced." He swept his hat from his head and extended his hand. "Otis Millard Roy at your service."

"You?" I backed away from his outstretched hand as I would a coiled rattlesnake. "You're the manager of the mine?"

"The one and the same." While he grinned through stained and missing teeth, his beady black eyes narrowed. "Sorry to hear about your fire. Lucky no one was hurt . . ." His words trailed off into an ambiguous silence.

I swallowed back a lump of fear growing in my throat. "I appreciate your condolences, Mr. Roy, but you still haven't answered my question." I walked over toward the injured mule. The animal backed away as far as her tether allowed. "Why were you beating this animal? And why did you beat the poor mule skinner?"

"The mule bit me, that's why! The Chink? You're worried about a Chink?" A fresh anger flared up into his eyes. "And why am I explaining myself to you, a woman? Get back to your knittin', lady — before you lose more than your pretty curls."

"How dare you threaten me! You best listen well to me." I planted my hands on my hips and glared. "If I ever catch you mistreating one of my husband's mules or one of his employees again, I'll have you out of here in nothing flat. Do you understand my warning, Mr. Roy?"

We stared into one another's eyes for several seconds, both of us uncertain what to do next and unwilling to cry "uncle."

"What's going on here?" I recognized the voice behind me. Relieved, I whirled about to face James.

"Sorry, Mr. McCall." The manager dipped his head humbly to one side. "But your little lady here and I had a misunderstanding. She thought I was beating the mule when I was only showing the coolie how to train the beast."

My eyes snapped with anger; my mouth flew open. "James, the man threatened me."

The look on Otis's face was one of hurt and disbelief. "I'm so sorry, Mrs. McCall. You misunderstood my intentions. Sir, I was trying to warn her of the dangers around a working mine." He shook his head condescendingly. "A mine is no place for a woman. You know how superstitious the men are about women jinxing the operation."

James took my arm. "We'll talk more about this at home tonight. In the meantime, why don't you go back to the cabin."

Through clenched teeth, I snarled, "And tend to my knitting?"

James started at my vehemence. "Fine, if that's what you want to do." If I hadn't been so furious, I would have laughed at the look of bewilderment on his face. Coated with mud from my hem to my waist, I stomped across the corral, mud spatting with each step. At the fence, I picked up my colander, dumped the vegetable skins on the ground, and called over my shoulder. "You may want to check on one of your mule skinners. His back needs doctoring!"

I'd barely changed into clean clothing when I heard James open the front door. Still seething with anger, I took my time buttoning the bodice of my dress; I had no intention of rushing to his side like an adoring, repentant wife.

The bedroom door opened. "Chloe?" James peeked around the door at me. I eyed him with disdain. "I need your help out here. Mihn Ho has serious lacerations."

I grabbed my medicine bag from the corner and marched past him. The frightened mule skinner sat at the table. "Don't be afraid, sir. I'm not going to hurt you." When the man replied with a blank stare, I turned to James. "Does he speak any English?"

James shrugged.

"Well, don't you know anything about your men?" I snapped.

James bristled, strode over to the stove and picked up the teakettle. "You'll be needing sterilized water, I suppose."

"If you could, please." Carefully lifting away the strips of soiled flannel from Mihn Ho's back, I sickened at the sight of deep lacerations. "Also, I need the jar of wheat-germ ointment for these abrasions. It's in the cold cellar."

James disappeared out the front door and returned quickly with the requested potion. I used my father's recipe of wheat-germ oil, honey, and comfrey leaves to soothe inflammation and aid the body in restoring damaged skin.

After treating the mule skinner's injuries as best I could, I then covered them with clean gauze strips. I tied the last strip and straightened. "Make sure he comes back tomorrow so I can change the bandages."

James helped the man to his feet. "You can go now. Come back tomorrow."

The man nodded and bowed repeatedly, but I sensed he didn't really understand what either of us had said. After Mihn Ho left, James helped me clean up. "Chloe, I didn't mean to be abrupt with you—"

I turned slowly to face him, my body rigid with fury. "Abrupt?"

"I did what I had to do."

"Yes, dear, I'm sure you did, dear." My words dripped of sarcasm.

James ran a distraught hand through his hair. "All right. Sit down. It's time you hear the whole story."

I straightened my back and jutted my chin. "I prefer to stand."

He sighed and sat down at the table. "Suit yourself; just hear me out. Roy is one of the two men I suspect of high-grading gold ore from the mine. The other is the mine foreman, Paddy O'Sullivan."

Reluctantly, I sat across from James. "What is high-grading?"

"Skimming. The culprit pockets gold ore as he inspects the mine. Only a foreman or a manager would have access to the mine when no one was around. The miners themselves are carefully searched going and coming."

James sighed. His shoulders sagged. "Under the previous owner, the mine produced $50,000 a year. During the first six months since Ian purchased it, the output has dropped. And if the trend continues, at the end of the year, it will have produced less than $30,000."

"Couldn't there be reasons other than theft?"

He nodded. "That's why we're here. I've been taking ore samples to the assay's office in Steamboat Springs instead of the one in Hahn's Peak, in case the discrepancy is due to the quality of the ore or the honesty of the assayer. So you see, I couldn't afford to antagonize Roy until I know who, if anyone, is to blame for the loss."

I folded my arms and eyed my husband. "My money's on Otis Roy, I'll tell you. I've never met someone so ornery, beating a poor defenseless mule like that!"

James chuckled. "I did talk to him about that. But when it comes to you, he does have a point."

My jaw jutted forward again. "I beg your pardon?"

He reached across the table and captured my hands in his. "The men are superstitious about having a woman around the mines. Why do you think I've never suggested you tour the area?"

I hadn't thought about it. *Superstitious? Of all the . . .*

I promised to stay away from the operation in the future, but only after I made James vow to do his best to keep Otis Roy's streak of cruelty in line.

"I'll put Indian Pete on it," James said.

When Jamie returned from school that evening, he asked about Sunshine. That was the first I realized I hadn't seen her since the morning explosions.

"She'll return to us, son," I assured him.

The next day the Chinese mule skinner and three friends with varying physical complaints showed up at my door immediately after breakfast. One had a stomach pain; the second, a boil. The third complained of an ear pain. I treated them as best I could. As they left, they bowed and kissed my hands. While I couldn't understand most of what they said, I caught two words, camp angel.

When I asked James about the title, he groaned. "I was afraid this was going to happen. Now you'll never get rid of them. A camp angel is a woman who — well, she's like a missionary to the heathen, easing their pains and listening to their troubles."

After seeing the "fancy women" in Hahn's Peak and Steamboat Springs, I had to know. "Do they mean it in respect?"

He laughed. "Absolutely. Some of them left home before they could shave and have never returned. These men are homesick for their mamas."

Word spread throughout the camp, and before the end of the week I was caring for the sick miners as well as the mule skinners. My practice consisted mostly of coughs due to lung infections, black eyes, cut lips, and broken bones from Saturday-night celebrations at the bars in Hahn's Peak. With Christmas a week away, a few miners asked me to write letters home to sweethearts or mothers in Ireland and in Wales.

I was so busy caring for the miners' needs that I failed to notice Jamie's. He missed Sunshine. Each morning before leaving for school and immediately upon returning, he went calling and searching for the big yellow cat. When Sunshine appeared at Ula's front door, mewing for milk, Ula volunteered to give the animal a good home.

"You can come and visit her whenever you please," Ula assured Jamie. Jamie seemed content with the arrangement.

One morning I stood at the kitchen sink washing the

breakfast dishes. Since dawn, the men had been blasting on the side of the mountain. When I saw Pete running toward the house, I knew something was wrong and I hurried to open the door. "Pete! What's happened? Is James all right?"

"There's been an accident. Grab your medicine bag and come. Where do you keep the bandages? We'll need all you got."

"Look in the wooden crates by the sink." I rushed into the bedroom and grabbed my bag and cape. Back in the living room, my hand flew to my head. "My hat!"

"Forget your hat. Come on!" He grabbed my arm with one hand and the stack of bandages with the other and hauled me from the house. I'd never seen him so distraught.

"James? Is James all right?" I jogged along at Pete's side. He averted his eyes but urged me to run faster.

That's when I knew. James had been injured. Hiking my skirts to my knees, I bounded ahead of the startled man. "Where is my husband? What has happened to him?"

We reached the mining office, and Pete pointed toward the mine entrance. At the foot of the tramway, I shaded my eyes and saw the ore buckets inching down the side of the mountain on the cable. As the first one drew closer, I could see arms and legs sticking out.

Pete held my arm until the cable stopped and two miners lifted the victim from the bucket. I lunged forward. "James!"

Pain etched my husband's face, but he tried to smile. "A dislocated shoulder, that's all. Let Pete patch me up while you help the men."

The rest of the morning I treated the injured. Except for the Croatian with the broken back and the Hungarian with crushed legs, the injuries were surprisingly minor. Interestingly, Otis Roy was nowhere in sight, but the foreman, Paddy O'Sullivan, stayed close by to carry out my every request. I knew there was little I could do for the man from

Croatia. He'd lost all feeling in his feet and legs. I stopped the bleeding and splinted the Hungarian's legs, but I suspected they would have to be amputated. After making the two men as comfortable as possible, I suggested that they be taken to a doctor in Steamboat Springs.

Jamie had returned from school before I managed to get home to James. There I found him propped up in bed, sipping a bowl of hot chili beans. "My men? Are they going to be all right?"

Jamie sat at the foot of the bed; Pete sat beside James, holding the bowl.

"They're as good as can be expected. What happened up there? And where did you find the chili beans?"

Pete laughed. "You think you're the only good cook around here? My mama taught me how to cook a tasty chili stew."

James grinned up at me. "It is mighty good."

I tossed my cape on a chair. "Well, I hope you saved me some."

Pete nodded. "Plenty where that came from, probably more than you can stand. I always make more than needed so I don't have to cook so often."

James interrupted. "The men? Did they all make it?"

I told him about each injury I treated and about the two men I sent to Steamboat Springs. "Tomorrow I'll see that the injured men get triple their usual pay." James leaned back against his pillow. "Pete, did you see what happened up there on the mountain? What went wrong?"

"It was no accident." Pete's eyes darkened. His mouth narrowed into a frown. "I was up top when she blew. I saw Otis Roy leave the mine and disappear into the woods seconds before the explosion. The man was in a mighty hurry to get away, I can tell you that."

Puzzled, James asked, "Did he take the tram?"

Pete shook his head. "No, he just disappeared into the

woods. I ran inside and called down to you. Once the rescue team got underway, I went for Chloe."

"And you're sure no one was killed?" James frowned.

I nodded my head. "Everyone is accounted for except Mr. Roy."

Pete stood and carried the empty chili bowl to the door. "Why don't you let me do a little scouting for information? Someone always knows something."

James pursed his lips. "I hate to continue with the explosives until I know what went wrong. Besides," he massaged his injured arm, "I'm in no condition to work up there. What if I gave the miners a holiday bonus and closed the mine over Christmas? Would that help the investigation?"

Pete thought for a moment. "Good idea. I'll postpone my trip to Utah and hire four men I trust to guard the mine around the clock while I snoop, both here at the mine and in Hahn's Peak, since that's where most of the men will spend their money."

"Why guards?" I asked.

Pete frowned. "With all the accidents that have been happening, I wouldn't want to take chances."

I glanced toward my husband. "Accidents? What accidents, besides this one?"

The two men exchanged glances. Then Pete spoke. "The heavy equipment has been mysteriously breaking down. And I have reason to believe that your cabin fire in Columbine was arson. I found a burned kerosene can outside where the kitchen window had been."

Jamie heaved a sigh of relief. I whipped about to face James. "You knew this and didn't tell me?"

He grinned sheepishly. "I didn't want to worry you."

"Worry me? Do you know how many times in the last few weeks I've tried to figure out what I did that might have started the fire?"

"I'm sorry," James mumbled. "It seemed like a good idea at the time to keep you from worrying, what with the baby and all."

"Men!" I cast my gaze toward the ceiling.

"You know," James's eyes twinkled as he grinned at me, then over at Jamie, "we could accept the Putnams' holiday invitation, shop for a few pieces of furniture, clothing to replace what we lost, maybe buy a napoleon or two. And on the way, I can stop at Steamboat Springs to find out how my men are doing."

The next morning I helped James dress and walk to the office while Pete assembled the miners. Again, Otis Roy was nowhere around. When James announced the vacation and the bonus pay, the men whistled and cheered. "The Renegade mine will reopen on January fifth. If any of you know something that will help me figure out what went wrong yesterday, please come see me before you leave for town."

No one came.

The next morning, the day before Christmas, Pete drove us to Hahn's Peak to the railhead. We had no luggage. Any personal items we might have valued were destroyed in the fire. In Steamboat Springs, after sending a telegram to the Putnams regarding our arrival, we located the town's doctor. He directed us to a hotel, where he'd taken the injured men. Though James gave them each a generous settlement for their injuries, I couldn't help but wonder how much money could compensate for the suffering they would endure the rest of their lives.

After paying the men's doctor bills, we hurried back to the railroad station. James gave Jamie a nickel to spend in the small shop while we sat down on one of the long wooden benches inside the depot to await the train.

"What more could I have done?" Had James read my mind, or was he speaking his own thoughts? "There's no way to remove the gold ore without risk. Every man who walks into the mine knows he might not come out. It's just the way it is."

"Honey, I understand." I checked his sling to be certain the arm was being held at the correct angle. "Don't torment yourself about it."

James massaged his injured shoulder. "I can't help it. Until I know the cause . . ."

A sense of freedom swept through me as the train wound its way through the mountains toward Denver. When the train finally pulled into the Denver station, I cringed when I thought of Gladys Putnam meeting us in her highly polished curricle with the matching pair of bays and tried to slick down Jamie's hair with my hands. Tucking my uneven strands of hair under the bonnet, I could only imagine the horror on the woman's face when she first glimpsed us.

But my fears were groundless.

The moment we stepped onto the platform, we were instantly engulfed by our host and hostess. If I'd been draped with diamonds and ermine furs, I couldn't have received a warmer welcome.

"Oh, you poor dear, you're shivering," she gushed as she led me to the waiting carriage. "That cape isn't warm enough for this weather. I have just the coat at home for you. It's a little number I picked up on my last visit to New York City."

I started to protest.

"Nonsense, that shade of green turns my skin a ghastly yellow. With your hair . . ." She paused, removed my bonnet, and inspected my shorn locks. I reddened under her scrutiny. "Hmm, have you seen the latest issue of *Ladies Home Journal*?" When my hair stylist gets done with you, your hair will be in the height of Paris fashion."

Gladys barely paused to take a breath. "When James

telegraphed the news of the fire, I was beside myself. Why didn't you come right away? And the baby."

I glanced at James. He responded with a shrug.

She continued. "Even though it's the holidays, you need to take it easy, my dear. That's why I canceled tomorrow's big dinner the moment I heard you were coming. A little sit-down dinner for twenty will be much more cozy, don't you think?"

Overwhelmed, I nodded.

"And don't worry about what you will wear; I had a delightful afternoon shopping. I hope you like everything. Phineas, let's take the long drive home so Jamie can see the decorated houses along Seventeenth Avenue."

Phineas nodded and told the driver of the change of plan.

"You won't believe the extravagance of these nouveaux riches."

I chuckled to myself. After living in a mining camp for a few months, I understood why miners who struck it rich would spend the money foolishly.

Lights glowed over the frozen pond as the carriage came to a stop in front of the guest cottage. Once inside, Gladys and Phineas wished us a good night's sleep and left. The clothing they had purchased fit each of us as if it had been hand tailored, and on our beds we found brand new nightwear.

After seeing Jamie to bed, I had one thought in mind— a hot bath. As I undid the buttons on the faded calico dress Ula had given me, I asked James, "Why would Gladys go to all this trouble and expense for us?"

James paused from pulling off his boots. "Three years ago, their only daughter died in a boating accident while attending a girls' finishing school in Europe. Phineas says that you're the best thing that's happened to Gladys since. He's thankful to see the sparkle returning to her eyes once again." James reached over and put his good arm around my shoulder. "Like it or not, she's adopted you."

As I sank into a tub full of hot water and soap bubbles, weeks of roughing it were eased from my memory. A wash tub on the bedroom floor couldn't equal the pleasure of a genuine bath, bubbles and all. I was forever spoiled. I called to my husband. "We've got to do something in return for all Gladys has done. What can we buy that she doesn't already have?"

James peeked around the bathroom door. "Buy? Honey, this woman can buy the likes of us, five times over. The best gift you can give is yourself. For a woman like Gladys, a true friend is the rarest jewel of all."

I thought of Ula and the other women in Columbine. "For any of us, wouldn't you say?"

He grinned, scooped up a handful of bubbles, and dotted my nose. "Are you going to hog that tub all night, or do I get a turn?"

I sneezed and brushed the bubbles from my face. "There is a second bathtub, you know, in Jamie's room."

"I thought you'd say that," he grumbled and left.

Christmas morning was unbelievable. A giant fir tree ablaze with tiny white candles occupied the center of the Putnams' parlor. Hand-crafted, imported baubles decked each bough, and garlands of evergreen with red-velvet ribbon were draped over the mirrors and doors.

Gladys and Phineas Putnam carried generosity to the extreme. Jamie, especially, had never enjoyed such abundance, even back in Boston. When I gently scolded our hostess for such extravagance, she smiled guiltily at me. "I know I went overboard, but do you know how long it's been since I could shop for a child?"

I hugged her and whispered, "You're going to spoil him rotten."

With the authority of a blue blood, she said, "Well, if you

ask me, he deserves a little coddling after all he's been through during the last few years."

The small Christmas dinner for twenty left me speechless. The table groaned with an abundance of tastefully prepared dishes from around the world. But when I thought of our friends in Columbine and the spartan meals they'd be enjoying, I found it hard to indulge in the exotic pleasures. As we lounged in front of the fireplace during the evening, our every whim supplied, I imagined the wind howling through the chinks in log cabin walls. We listened to the voice of Enrico Caruso over the gramophone and played charades, a parlor game popular with European royalty since the 1700s.

By that evening snowflakes had turned the estate and the city into a fairyland. We bundled into the Putnams' sleigh and drove through the city park.

The week between Christmas and New Year's passed quickly, with fittings and shopping for the essentials lost in the fire. As for my shorn hair, when Gladys's stylist finished, soft curls haloed my face. At first glance in the mirror, I felt like a Parisian strumpet. Gladys finally convinced me I was a trendsetter.

I thanked God many times over that the important things—our wedding photo, my silver dresser set, my wedding gown, and James's grandmother's brooch—were safe in my trunk in Kansas. More than ever, I looked forward to returning to the ranch come spring.

The evening of the Putnams' New Year's Eve celebration, I pampered myself with a long bubble bath, then sat down at the dressing table to style my hair. "What am I going to do?" I wailed.

James stuck his head out of the bathroom, his face covered with shaving lather. "With what?"

"My hair! All the women will have elegant coiffeurs—

and mine? Mine looks like a, a show girl or a street urchin from Paris."

He laughed. "Either way, you'll be a hit."

"That's not funny." I threw my brush at him. He ducked, and the brush bounced off the doorjamb. James reached down and picked it up. With a twinkle in his eye, he sashayed toward me. I reached for the brush, and he snatched it back. "You want your brush?"

I pretended a sigh of exasperation. "We don't have time for games."

"Here, take it." Again I reached for the brush, and again, he retreated.

"James, we're going to be late."

"So . . ."

I smiled innocently. He leaned forward and kissed me, leaving a glob of shaving lather on my face. "James," I sputtered, wiping the soap from my mouth. My hand darted toward the brush.

"Uh-uh-uh," he teased. "You forgot to say please."

"Please," I hissed.

"No-no-no. You've got to mean it."

I lunged for the elusive brush again. "I mean it. I mean it!"

"No, you don't." The foamy lather couldn't hide the wicked grin on his face.

I folded my arms and tapped my foot threateningly on the Persian carpet.

"All right, I'll be good." He turned me around to face the three-way mirror. "Look at yourself. Really look at yourself. You've never looked so beautiful." He caressed my face. "Every woman there will envy the natural glow in your complexion. I've never seen your hair so shiny and alive. Contrasted with the towering wigs and faces matted with powder, you are a breath of fresh air."

My eyes grew misty. "You really think so?"

He turned me to face him. "Think so? There's no doubt."

He kissed my cheek and handed me the hairbrush. With his other hand he wiped away the splotch of lather left by his kiss. I frowned. Something was different. "Your arm? You can use your arm."

"Yes, it's feeling a lot better. I'm not planning to wear the sling tonight."

"What—and lose the tender ministrations of every damsel at the party?" I poked him in the ribs. He blushed and returned to his shaving.

Keeping his warm sentiments in mind, I fluffed my hair, adjusting a few ringlets, then pinned the camellia that James had given me in place. I stared at my reflection for a moment. *He's right. I've never had so much color in my cheeks. I guess happiness is the greatest makeup.*

I felt like a little girl playing dress-up as I slipped into the blue satin gown and matching shoes Gladys insisted I wear for the occasion. Jamie knocked on the door. I called, "Come on in, honey."

"I'm leaving now." He'd been invited to the children's party next door.

"Come here; your tie's crooked." He obeyed, scowling. "I can't wait to get home. I hate wearing starched shirts and stiff collars."

"You know something," I whispered. "I feel the same way. If you think that collar is bad, imagine pouring yourself into this straightjacket."

I sucked in my stomach to emphasize the constricted waistline. The exaggerated bustle on the dress and the whale-boned undergarments projected the top half of my body dangerously forward. "I can't even stand straight."

He frowned and shook his head. "Why do you wear it?"

I shrugged. "I don't know. Maybe to look beautiful for your dad."

"Hey," James stuck his head around the doorjamb, "don't blame me. I love you in calico and flour sacking, remember?"

Chills, Thrills, and Red Velvet

A bank of potted ferns and feathery palms surrounded the orchestra seated in the atrium. In the parlor and dining room, soft light from the Venetian chandeliers reflected off the mirrored walls and off the jewels of the party-goers as they swirled to the music of Johann Strauss. I used my condition as an excuse for not dancing; actually I didn't know how because dancing was frowned upon in the primarily Baptist community of Shinglehouse. James hovered protectively by my side.

Furtively, I watched the hands on the clock inch their way toward midnight. At 11:45 my husband put his arm around my shoulder and whispered in my ear. "Come, I want to show you something."

After stopping for my coat and his leather jacket, we slipped away to the gazebo beside the pond. Though a biting wind whipped around the enclosure, inside, a different world engulfed us—one of solitude and beauty.

Taking my hands in his, James led me to a marble bench.

"I didn't want the crowds and the laughter to intrude on our celebration of the new century." Gently, James tousled the curls beside my face, then reached inside his jacket and pulled out a box. "Happy New Year, my darling. I know how much you've missed having your own since the fire."

Taking the box from his hands, I lifted the lid. Through misted eyes I gazed at the black leather Bible with my name printed in gold leaf in the lower right-hand corner.

When I lifted the Bible from the box, the book fell open to Proverbs 31, the passage marked with a gold chain. In response to my questioning look, James took the book from me and asked me to reach into his jacket pocket. The small velvet jewelry box I withdrew contained an engraved gold watch.

"Turn it over," he urged.

Engraved on the back were the words, "To CMM. Eternal Love, JEM."

Tears trickled down my cheeks. "Oh, James, it's beautiful. Thank you so much. But I didn't get you anything. I'm sorry."

He kissed me tenderly. "These last four months together have been four of the happiest months I've ever known. You've brought joy back into my life. I'll always love you for that."

On New Year's Day Gladys and I spent the afternoon together while the men took Jamie ice-skating for the first time. Because of the scare we'd had almost losing our baby, I agreed with James that ice-skating for me would have to wait until another year.

Gladys and I discovered a major common interest—we both loved reading. "Would you mind if I sent you books and magazines from time to time? They pile up around here so quickly."

Suspicious of her excuse, I nevertheless appreciated her offer. The most difficult adjustment I'd had to make in moving to Columbine—outside of giving up my copper bathtub at the ranch—was the lack of reading material.

Once ignited, Gladys became a ball of fire. "Let me sort through the books and magazines I have on hand now. I'll have our butler pack them in time to take with you."

With uncharacteristic hesitation she asked, "You've told me about the poverty in Columbine. Would your friends be insulted if I packed a few things they might be able to use?"

"I don't know. They're proud and independent people." How could I turn down the woman's generosity? On the other hand, could I risk insulting my friends with Gladys's castoffs?

She brightened. "I know you'll find a way to handle the situation delicately."

The next morning boxes, crates, and bundles of every size waited at the train station to go home with us. When Gladys had done her sorting and packing, I could only guess. We had kissed our friends goodbye and turned to climb on board when Phineas called Jamie aside.

"Your mother said something about a problem with rats in the camp." The man reached inside his cashmere over-coat. "Do you think Hector might help eradicate the problem?" He handed Jamie a gray-and-white striped kitten, its eyes barely open.

I stared at the bundle of fluff. *How in the world will we get that kitten safely home?*

Gladys read my mind. She called to their driver, and the man handed me a covered basket, lined with a soft towel. We boarded the first passenger car amid a profusion of thanks and admonitions to keep in contact. As the train pulled from the station, Gladys and Phineas dabbed at their eyes. But then, so did I.

The snow crunched beneath our feet as we deboarded the train in Hahn's Peak. Jamie handed Hector and his basket to me to carry while he scooped up a handful of snow to make a snowball. The powder filtered through his gloved fingers. I'd never seen snow so dry that it evaporated rather than melted in the late-afternoon sunlight.

While James went to the livery stable to get our horse

and wagon, Jamie and I strolled along the uneven board-walk on Main Street. A girl of fourteen or fifteen, her brassy yellow hair frizzed, her eyelids darkened with makeup, waved at us as we passed. Next door in Whitey's Bar, the evening's action had already begun. Gamblers hunched over gaming tables, staring expressionless at their cards and their opponents. Miners bellied up to a mahogany bar, hoisting shots of whiskey to the new century.

By midnight, grubstakes would be lost, and the "bully boys" would be shooting up mirrors, windows, and bottles— "havin' a little fun," as the local newspaper editor would call their wanton behavior in tomorrow morning's edition. As we strolled past the open door, the pungent aroma of cigar smoke, stale alcohol, and sweat accosted my nostrils. A tinny rendition of "Sweet Liza Jane" from a player piano accosted my ears.

The saloon keeper, his white canvas apron stained with layers of spilled drinks and grime, leaned against the doorjamb, smoking a cigar. The man smiled and tipped his felt hat. I smiled politely and accelerated my pace. I had difficulty understanding why, in mining towns, the bar owner was considered the highest on the social ladder, with the banker and newspaper editor coming in second and third respectively.

James met us with the wagon outside the general store. Evidence of Gladys's generosity crammed the wagon bed. I stared first at the mountain, then at James. He shrugged. "There's more. I'll have to come in after the rest tomorrow."

As James and Indian Pete unloaded the contents of the wagon into our little cabin, Jamie and I celebrated Christmas all over again. Finding the three crates of books and magazines, I could have stopped unpacking right there except for the chaos. One narrow pathway led from the door to the kitchen sink and to the bedroom.

James scratched his head and stared. "What will we do

with all this stuff? We don't have use for most of it, let alone storage space."

I laughed and plopped myself down on one of the trunks. "You told me to be nice to Gladys, to let her smother me with love." I gazed about the cabin. "Well, this is an expression of Gladys's love."

James shook his head. "Seriously, what are we going to do with this stuff?"

"Seriously?" I giggled. "I don't know. I have enough books alone to start a lending library."

"And enough ladies' attire to open a dress shop!" he groaned. "And Jamie, how many pairs of breeches does a growing boy need?"

"Hmm, you're right. I like the idea of the lending library. Why not? As for the dress shop, I'd rather give away what we don't need instead of charging my friends for it."

"Fine, do it." James strode into our bedroom and closed the door.

I turned toward Jamie, who had already immersed himself in an adventure story. "Jamie, I need your help. First, we'll put all of your things in one pile, your dad's in another, and mine in a third. Then, we'll set aside everything we want to keep."

Groaning at the interruption, he put the book down and helped carry out my instructions. The hardest for me was choosing the books I'd keep and the books I'd give away. The magazines like *Ladies Home Journal*, *McClures*, *The Atlantic*, and *Harper's Bazaar*, I stored under our bed. The next day, before James drove into town for the second load, I wrote out invitations to the women in town, inviting them to the first meeting of Columbine Ladies' Club.

Ula was the first to arrive at the cabin. Jamie greeted her at the door, then escaped outside. She gazed wonderingly about the room. "What happened here?"

"Good question." As the other women arrived, their reaction mirrored hers.

"This," I waved toward the trunks and boxes, "is part of the reason I asked you here today. I need help." I told them about Gladys's largess. "But now I have a problem, and you're here to help me solve it. First, the books. Gladys will be sending more in the future, I'm sure." I handed a couple of the leather-bound volumes to the women to examine. "I'd like to propose that we start a lending library in town. Any ideas where?"

"At least until spring when the men can build a library, it seems that the jail and the mercantile are the only places big enough," Mrs. Jones suggested.

Ma Bovee threw back her head and laughed. "Better make it the mercantile. Those bully boys your husband houses each Saturday night couldn't read if their lives depended upon it. Besides, I'm not into prison reform."

Beth Walsh enthusiastically agreed. "I like that. Then the children can borrow the books too." The women responded positively to Ula's suggestion that we start a literary society to discuss the books we read.

"Now, for the next part of my problem." I opened one of the trunks and held up a dark-blue serge traveling dress with lighter blue piping trimming the jacket. My friends gasped appreciatively. "This is just one of many. There are satin ball gowns, calico everyday dresses, crinolines, camisoles, chemises, corsets, blouses, skirts, bloomers—you name it. Most of the garments have never been worn.

"Now, don't be getting prideful with me. If I had to swallow my pride and accept Mrs. Putnam's generosity, you can too. I wanted to offer the clothing to you, my friends, first, before I took it to the crib girls in Hahn's Peak." Another gasp passed around the room. I knew how they hated the loose women in Hahn's Peak. *If that doesn't break down their reserve, nothing will.*

I pointed to the other side the room. "Over by the ladder are boys' clothes; there by the fireplace is men's wear. So help yourselves." I pulled out a soft dimity dress and dropped it in Beth Walsh's hands. "I thought this pink one could be cut down for Molly, your daughter."

The woman stared in stunned silence. *Oh, no, what if I've offended them? Should I apologize?* Ula eyed me for a moment, then lifted the lid on the trunk nearest her and held up a cinnamon-colored cashmere woolen cape with a muskrat collar. "I've been needing a warmer coat since the lining gave out on my old one."

Then the stampede began. Within minutes the room was chaotic with chatter and laughter and squeals of excitement. It was such fun. Dresses flew from one side of the room to the other as the women recommended outfits for one another.

Tears glistened in Ma Bovee's eyes as she examined a red velvet ball gown several sizes smaller than her ample build. "If I let it out a little here in the seams . . ."

Recognizing her happiness, we all agreed. Ula tossed Ma a cape of the same fabric. "This will go beautifully with the dress. Or maybe you can use it for the fabric when you restyle the dress."

When James came home from the mining office at noon, I met him at the door with a sandwich and a cup of herbal tea. I handed him the food and kissed him. "Perhaps you'd better come back a little later. It's a circus in there."

The noises coming from the cabin reinforced my statement. Muttering "Deliver me," he turned and strode back toward the office.

I accepted my friends' gratitude with the same graciousness I'd received from Gladys. "I'm just thankful you can use this stuff. Obviously it was more than we could use in one lifetime."

Beth said she'd arrange for her husband to pick up the

books the next day. "But I don't know the first thing about sorting and arranging them," she admitted.

"No problem," Ula assured her. "I'll be glad to help out. Libraries and I used to be good friends before Noah and I moved to Columbine."

The biggest surprise for me came after the women left and I opened the first trunk, then the second and the third. In each, I discovered clothing for the crib girls of Hahn's Peak. I hadn't been serious when I threatened to take the clothes to the "painted hussies," as they were commonly called, but my friends had been. We'd all seen the squalor some of the girls endured in mining camps. Only the big-city ones sashayed around in satin and lace.

I consolidated the clothing into one trunk and slid the others against the kitchen wall until we could figure out what to do with them. Then I stacked the wooden crates against the back wall; they would make great bookshelves. All in all, I was satisfied with the day's accomplishments.

When James and Jamie returned home, I was mixing a batch of biscuits for supper, and a pot of potato soup simmered on the back of the stove. Both peered into the cabin, apprehensive about entering. "They're all gone." I laughed.

"I hope so." Jamie entered cautiously. "You wouldn't believe the caterwauling that went on in here today, Dad."

"Caterwauling?" I huffed. "You mean like the noise you and your friends make during recess at school?"

Jamie grinned sheepishly. "Just teasin', Mama."

"You'd better be if you expect some supper." I picked up a wooden spoon and turned toward James. "And what are you grinning at?"

He threw up his hands in defense. "Not a thing, my love, not a thing."

"Seriously, you've never seen such happy women. They were like little girls, laughing and giggling. You'd never guess from Ma Bovee's behavior that the poor woman has buried three out of seven sons." I scraped the dough into a pan and carried it to the oven. "Gladys would have loved seeing it."

Jamie hung his jacket on one of the wooden pegs behind the door. "Guess what, Mama. Daddy and Indian Pete promised to take me down into the mine tomorrow before the men get back to camp."

I looked up, my eyes dancing with excitement. "Really? Tomorrow? Oh, I'd love to go too."

James sighed and shook his head. "Chloe, when will you remember that you're pregnant? Camp angel or not, if the miners find out that a woman went down into the mine, they're likely to quit."

"Honey, my being pregnant has nothing to do with going into the tunnel. It doesn't take strength or skill to ride the cable down. As far as the miners are concerned, who's going to tell?"

Answering objection after objection, I continued my barrage throughout the evening. The next morning, I picked up where I'd left off until I wore down James's resistance. "I always said you'd be a fabulous wife except for your impetuous and relentless nature."

I lifted one eyebrow. "Actually, I believe you included my Irish temper in that unwarranted character assessment."

He shook his head and carried his breakfast dishes to the sink. "You'd better change into a pair of my work pants and one of my cotton shirts before Pete arrives. I can only imagine what he'll think when I tell him you're coming along!"

I glanced out the window at the sunlight reflecting off the snow. "It's below freezing out there. Wouldn't it be better if I wore something more substantial?"

"Not down in the mine. Wear a coat, of course, until we reach the mine entrance."

A knock sounded at the door. I could tell by Pete's expression that he wasn't at all pleased to learn that I was going along on the expedition, but he kept silent.

It was agreed that we'd hike up to the mine entrance instead of using the tramway, and Pete would man the machinery that would lower the three of us into the shaft.

By the time we reached the mine entrance, I panted from the exertion. Frozen mud crunched beneath my boots as I stepped inside the shaft house, excitement coursing through my veins. A clutter of machinery filled the small building. I leaned forward to hear James explain the process to his son.

"It looks more complicated than it is. See the gallows frame? It carries the hoisting cable up through the windlass." I gazed up at the steel cable and gears atop the wooden scaffold mounted over the shaft. Pete took his position behind the machine and set the creaking, grinding gears in motion. Muscles bulged as he turned the lever that would roll the cable on a huge spool raising the ore bucket.

"By next fall," James explained, "I want to install two elevator cages for the miners. Until then, the miners must rely on this cable and the hoistman for their safety. A single error on Pete's part could send us crashing to our deaths."

As I grasped the ghastly facts, my stomach heaved and I blanched. Maybe inspecting the underground operations of the Renegade Mine wasn't such a great idea after all. The idea of climbing into the ore bucket and dropping through the five-foot-wide hole in the shaft-house floor into unknown depths suddenly terrified me.

"Normally, the roar of the machinery below would prevent you from hearing my voice. Drills, air hoses, water hoses, sinkers, sledgehammers, moils, picks, shovels, blowers, the pump, and the clanging of ore cars make communicating impossible."

James glanced toward me and arched one eyebrow.

"There's no need to be afraid, Chloe. Pete knows what he's doing. However, if you'd rather not go . . ."

If it hadn't been for his smug grin, I would have changed my mind then and there. He turned toward Jamie. "Are you ready to go below, son?"

"Yes, let's go," responded the eager child.

"Good. First, I'll go take your mama down, if she still wants to go. When we come back up, it will be your turn." Turning to me, James instructed, "The thing to remember is don't look down."

Although James had said the ore bucket, or the skip, as it was called, regularly carried eight men—two inside, four on the rim, and two on the cable ring—it looked terribly small swaying at the end of the heavy cable. I peered over the edge of the hole.

"You don't have to do this, you know," James whispered in my ear. "There's nothing to prove."

"I—I know." I barely choked out the words. "Except to me."

"In you go, then." He lifted me from the floor and swung me out over the shaft. "No matter what, don't look down."

Don't look down? How can I not look down? Where else should I look? My eyes fixed morbidly at the abyss. My heart leapt to my throat. For an agonizingly long second, I hung suspended over the yawning hole, my life cradled in James's arms. I squeezed my eyes shut and prayed. *"Oh, dear Father, pleee—"* My eyes flew open as he dropped me firmly into the ore bucket. The impact of my entry caused the skip to crash against the far wall of the shaft. Instinctively I clutched the rim of the ore bucket. Without warning, my knees buckled.

"Chloe! Don't faint on me," James growled, shaking me sharply. "You could topple out and be killed!" With one hand gripping my upper arm, he grabbed hold of the massive cable above our heads, stabilized the gyrating skip, and stepped in beside me.

Against my will my gaze returned to the darkness beneath my feet.

"Chloe, stop looking down! Didn't I tell you not—" James jerked me into his arms, burying my face in his broad chest. In a calmer voice, he soothed, "If I let you go, will you promise not to look down again?"

"Yes." His freshly washed cambric shirt muffled my reply. Slowly he released me, but he kept his hands poised, ready to grab me if I broke my promise. I fought the wild, incredible urge to look down by focusing on his face. "You're doing fine now," he encouraged. "Keep your eyes on me. I'm going to signal Pete to start lowering us into the shaft. We'll drop rapidly, but don't worry. The windlass cable is secure. Brace yourself against the sides, but keep your body well inside the bucket. The rocks jutting out of the wall are sharp."

Nauseated with fear, I wanted more than anything else to leap out of the swaying bucket onto solid ground. Only sheer terror kept my feet rooted in the bottom of the bucket. *I must be utterly insane doing this. How could James have agreed to take me in the first place? "Oh, dear Father, forgive me for being so insistent." Pa always said my stubbornness would be the death of me.*

"Steady yourself," James shouted into my ear, wrapping his arms, like steel cords, about me. The skip swooshed past glistening wet walls at an alarming rate of speed. Steam blurred the air around the bucket as the atmosphere changed from damp and chilly to hot and muggy, the farther we descended into the mine. From what James had told me previously, the steam rose from a pool of water at the bottom of the shaft, heated to more than 150 degrees by the earth's molten core.

By the time the ore bucket thumped to a stop, I was drenched in sweat and gasping for breath in the stifling, motionless air. James struck a match and lighted a lantern, then helped me out of the bucket. Removing a handkerchief from his hip pocket, James wiped away the sweat trickling off my forehead into my eyes.

James removed his shirt and tossed it into the ore bucket. "You might want to remove your shirt too. In these temperatures, it would be easy to suffer heat stroke."

Numbly I unbuttoned my shirt and handed it to my husband. My chemise clung to my body. Lifting the lantern over his head, James took my hand. The flickering lantern light reflected off metallic particles on the walls and ceiling of the tunnel.

"Is that gold?" I whispered. My voice echoed throughout the tunnel.

"Pyrite, fool's gold."

I heard a squeak by my right boot, followed by tiny feet scurrying away in the darkness. I leapt into James's arms. "What? What was that?"

"Rats. Their erratic behavior warns the miners if a cave-in is imminent," he explained. I shuddered.

Deeper in the mine's interior, massive timbers shoring up the walls and ceiling, the main tunnel broke off into shafts and secondary tunnels, a maze of cross-cuts and drifts going several directions. "Be careful as you step," James warned. "There's gumbo ahead."

A few steps later my boot gushed into a clay muck.

"That's one of the conditions we have to remedy before we blast much deeper in this shaft. I don't believe in cutting costs on the men's safety."

Except for the constant dripping of water and the chattering of rats, we were enveloped in a tomblike silence. James moved the lantern closer to one wall. "Paddy believes we are within weeks of hitting the mother lode. That's why we tried to blast in from a different direction."

We made our way along a drift, a horizontal passage that

followed a vein of gold ore. "See this ribbon of ore?" James pointed to a narrow streak along one wall. "Paddy suspects it leads to the mother lode."

"You depend a lot on Paddy, don't you?"

"And Pete, of course."

"What if Paddy's the thief?"

James paused. "I've thought of that. I'd much rather believe it is Otis, however."

I shuddered. "Me too."

"Seen enough?" he asked.

I nodded. "Thank you for bringing me down here." He squeezed my hand and led me back to the main shaft. Once there, we climbed into the skip, James rang a bell to signal Pete, and we inched upward.

On top, I waited with Pete while James gave his eager son the same tour. The muscles in Pete's shoulders and back strained as he turned the crank that lowered the skip to the base of the shaft. After the bucket touched the shaft floor, he relaxed against the wall to await the bell indicating James was ready to return.

"Why would any human willingly go down into the bowels of the earth day after day?" I asked.

"Greed. As you know, they come from different parts of the world, hoping to get rich in America. And a few do strike it rich. The rest . . ."

I thought about the men I'd treated since coming to Columbine. Each had dreams of fabulous wealth, of bringing a wife and family over from the old country, of building a mansion to rival the mineral kings of Denver.

"Mining gets in your blood. It's getting to James's, you know."

I snapped my head toward Pete. "What do you mean, 'It's getting to James's'?"

"I mean life on a cattle ranch will be boring after the excitement of mining ore. The closer we come to the mother lode, the less he's going to want to leave, come spring."

"That's ridiculous! Ranching is his life." I knew my husband better than that.

Pete shrugged. The clang of the bell at the bottom of the shaft ended our discussion.

That evening, the miners returned from Hahn's Peak, many sporting painful hangovers. Otis Roy was among them.

Throughout the next week, Pete's words haunted me. *What if he's right? What if James does choose to stay in Columbine instead of returning to Hays? No, no, it won't happen.*

Two letters arrived that week, one from Joe and the other from Ian. I opened Joe's letter first.

Dearest Chloe,

Best wishes for the holidays. New Year's Eve brought with it many surprises. First, Cy married his debutante, the illustrious Pamela Rochelle Vandersmith. That's quite a mouthful to swallow. (So is she!) Phillip announced his engagement to a young woman he met while in New Orleans. And I, your brother, have met the most engaging green-eyed brunette. Her name is Cathy Patton. I can't wait to have you meet her. You will love her, Chloe . . ."

Don't be too sure, little brother. I'm already green with jealousy. She'd better treat you well!

The other good news is, Mr. Chamberlain telegraphed through the money so I can buy the horse ranch I've been admiring across the bay . . .

Ian's letter brought mixed news. First he announced

the birth of Ashley Elizabeth McCall. Then he went on to say, "Dru is experiencing what Minna calls 'new mama blues.' Minna promises that it will pass. Drucilla cries all the time; even Minna can't lift my wife's spirits. And whenever I mention Colorado, she goes into hysterics. I know this is an imposition, with Chloe pregnant and all, but please, James, can you stay in Columbine a little longer, until I can get Drucilla settled down?"

On Friday, four men appeared at the cabin door. A Welsh miner named Furnam insisted that his tooth had to come out. The other men came along to hold him down while I performed the extraction. One look at the angry gums surrounding the abscessed tooth, and I agreed with this diagnosis. Gently I tapped the surface of the tooth with a metal spoon handle.

"Get on with it, Mrs. McCall," my patient growled.

I located the bottle of rubbing alcohol from beneath the sink and poured the liquid into a bowl as one of the men went for James's toolbox, which he stored in the back of the wagon. When the man returned with the wooden box, I located a pair of pliers and dropped them into the alcohol. After washing my hands, I told the men to hold down their friend. I clamped the pliers around the man's abscessed tooth and yanked as hard as I could. The tooth didn't budge. The man's eyes glassed over with pain, but he didn't make a sound.

Bracing my foot against the chair, I got another grip on the tooth and pulled. This time the roots broke free, and the diseased tooth popped out of the man's mouth, blood spraying in every direction. The patient sat up, spit into his handkerchief, and grinned. Thanking me for my service, Mr. Furnam pressed a coin into my hand.

I shook my head and handed back the coin. "No, I don't need the money."

The man's lips tightened. "I can't be beholden to you, ma'am. I ain't beholden to anyone."

I thought for a moment, then smiled. "You and your friends take special care of my husband when he's down in the mine, all right? I'd like that more than any amount of money."

The man grinned, shook my hand, and left.

The days on the calendar passed—January, February, March. The snows melted, leaving ankle-deep muck in their wake. Whenever I broached the subject of returning to the ranch, James put me off with, "We're almost through to the mother lode."

One evening in April when he used that excuse, I turned my profile toward him. Placing my hands on my stomach, I said, "So am I, if you've noticed recently."

He glanced up from the mining ledgers spread out across the table. "Of course I've noticed. And I've decided to send you to Gladys next month, until the baby arrives."

I planted my hands on my hips and glared. "You decided what?"

James sighed and shook his head. "Now, don't fight me on this, Chloe. Under the circumstances, it's the best I can do."

"And what about Jamie? He has to finish out the school term."

Patiently my husband explained, "I've talked with Ula. She and Noah have agreed to let him stay with them until school's out. Then he'll take the train to Denver also."

My Irish fury boiled up. I knew that if I spoke now, I'd say the wrong thing. Storming over to the sink, I pumped out a glassful of water, took a sip, then turned toward my husband.

"Once you have both of us out of your way, what will you do?"

"Out of my way?" James pushed his chair back from the table. "Do you think I want to send you to Denver, to have our first child born without my being present?"

I blinked back my tears. "I honestly don't know." I drank the rest of the water and strode into the bedroom.

"Chloe, I'm doing it for you."

Miner and Not-So-Minor Emergencies

I slammed the iron down on the hot stove to heat. Picking up a second iron, I pressed it with a vengeance onto James's favorite cambric shirt. *You know he's right. Stop being so pig-headed! You don't want to have this baby out here in the wilds. You're acting just like Pa, refusing to back down when you're wrong.*

I admired my father for his intellect, for his compassion, and for his decisiveness. It was his inability to bend, to admit to being wrong and to forgive that rankled me. And here I was—behaving just like him. Hanging James's pressed shirt on the back of a kitchen chair, I strolled over to the door and opened it. When it came to onerous tasks, ironing was right up there with scrubbing burned baking pans and disinfecting the outhouse.

The May sunlight danced on the puddles left by April's incessant showers, and tiny lavender and white woodland flowers blossomed around the cabin. I walked out onto the front steps and massaged my lower back. Backaches had become a regular occurrence for me during the last several weeks. I was almost eager to go to Denver and be pampered by Gladys and her retinue of servants.

To my left I could hear the clanging and rumbling of the machinery at the mine. It had been too long since I'd stood on the back porch of our prairie farmhouse and heard the

43

songs of goldfinches and the creaking of windmills. As I turned to go back inside the cabin, Rags darted from behind a fir tree and into the house.

Hector, who'd been sleeping beside the hearth, bounded to greet his best friend. Instead of licking the kitten's face the way he always did, Rags growled and slunk into my bedroom. I bent down to pick up the surprised cat.

"What's wrong, Hector? Did Rags not want to play?" A spot of fresh blood glistened on the rug at my feet. I touched it, then examined it closer. *Yes, it's blood. But where . . .*

I followed the trail into the bedroom. I looked behind the chair and on my side of the bed, calling, "Rags? Rags, where are you?" Getting down on my knees, I peered under the bed. Two beady eyes stared at me out of the darkness.

"Rags, come here, boy. What's happened? Let me help you." I coaxed until the dog crawled forward to lick my hands. "What happened, little buddy?"

I gently eased the dog out from under the bed. "What in the . . ." A wound the size of a silver dollar lay open on his back, and blood trickled through his wiry fur. Examining the injury further, I noticed a flap of skin. He whimpered and tugged at my sleeve to get me to leave the wound alone. "How in the world did this happen, boy?"

Grabbing a sheet I'd ironed and folded that morning, I carried him out to the kitchen table and placed him on the sheet. "It's all right, boy." The dog stayed on the sheet while I dashed about the cabin collecting the medical supplies I would need to clean the wound. I dabbed at the wound with gauze and alcohol. He whined but remained still. Lifting the flap of skin, I discovered a round lead ball—buckshot. *Someone shot him—purposely shot him. A fraction of an inch deeper, and the poor animal could have been paralyzed. Who would do such a thing?*

Furious, I removed the buckshot and cleansed the area, then wrapped his body with gauze. Laying him on the rug, I cleaned the mess and threw my coat over my shoulders. *I'm going to get to the bottom of this—no matter what.*

I grabbed the rifle off the wall and stormed down the muddy road to James's office. My eyes blazing with fury, I swung open the door so vigorously that it crashed against the wall. James's and Pete's heads popped up from the papers on the desks in front of them. "What kind of place is this that someone would shoot an innocent dog? What kind of reptile would do such a thing?"

James leapt from his chair and rushed to my side. "Chloe, calm down. Sit down and tell me exactly what happened."

I yanked my arm from his grasp. "I don't want to sit down. I want to find the brute who put buckshot into Rags's back!" I waved the rifle in the air. Pete ducked for cover behind the desk while James wrested the gun from my hands. My tirade continued through the struggle. "Who around here owns a shotgun? He needs to feel what it's like having a lead ball fired into his backside!"

"Chloe!" James stared at me, horrified. "Calm down. You're being irrational."

I glared at him. Out of the corner of my eye I saw Pete ease behind us toward the open door. If I hadn't been so angry, I would have laughed at the stunned expressions on the two men's faces.

"Well, the way I figure it, no judge would convict a pregnant woman of murder. And I am surely angry enough to . . ." My whole body shook with rage.

When I heard the door close, I glanced around. James and I were alone.

I allowed James to put his arm around me and lead me to a chair. I don't know where he'd put the rifle, but his soothing tones irked me further. "Now, tell me slowly, exactly what happened?"

I tried, but I could hold them back no longer. My tears of rage shifted to tears of frustration. "Don't you understand? The animal could die of lead poisoning."

After I quit sobbing, James dried my tears with his handkerchief, then helped me to my feet. "Should I walk you back to the cabin?"

I shook my head. "No, I'll be fine. You will try to find the coward who did this, won't you?"

"Yes," he repeated over and over as he guided me to the door. "I'm sure Indian Pete is on the man's trail right now."

James kissed me tenderly, then opened the door. I sniffed and minced my way down the steps. I looked up to find Otis Roy leaning against the corner of the building, smirking. "Be careful, Mrs. McCall," he murmured. "It can be dangerous around here for women, children, and pets."

"The same is true for cowards, Mr. Roy," I snapped and stormed past.

Pete met me halfway to the cabin, a shotgun in his hand. "I found this out by the stable. Now, if we can only find who owns it."

I gestured over my shoulder. "Personally, I'd start with Mr. Roy."

That evening, I asked James about the gun. "No one has claimed it. Pete suspects Otis. And when I asked Otis about it, he suggested that one of the Chinese mule skinners probably shot the dog for food."

"The mule skinners. You knew he'd put the blame on someone else." I folded my arms across my chest. "How long do you have to investigate the man? Isn't it obvious he's the thief and saboteur?"

James sighed deeply. "I wish it were that simple. Knowing it and proving it in a court of law are two different things."

Jamie, who'd been sitting beside Rags on the rug listening to the discussion, asked, "Can't you do anything, Dad?"

"I'm doing the best I can, son."

Then I made the mistake of telling James what Otis had said to me outside the mining office.

"That's it. I have to get you and Jamie out of here as soon as possible. If the culprit is Otis, the closer I come to unmasking him, the more dangerous he'll become."

I whipped about to face him. "And what about you, James? Aren't you in danger as well? Why can't we just sell this horrid mine and go home?"

He shook his head slowly and pushed his chair back from the table. "I'm seriously considering it."

I walked behind his chair and massaged the taut muscles in my husband's neck. "You're right about Jamie and me leaving until you clear up this mess. If I leave on June five, Jamie can come with me, and there will still be a good two, two and a half weeks before the baby is due. June five is less than a month from now."

James grasped my hands and kissed the palms tenderly. "I wish you could both leave tonight!"

I kissed the tip of his left ear. "Three weeks, that's all. What can happen in three weeks?"

Two weeks later, flour, sugar, molasses, and eggs sat on the kitchen table. I'd found a recipe in my month-old copy of *Ladies' Home Journal* for molasses sugar cookies, and I knew I had to have some. I scooped a teaspoon of dough from the mixing bowl, rolled it into a ball, and placed it on the ungreased cookie sheet.

Outside, the mine whistle brayed, once, twice, three times. I walked to the window and looked out. *It's not closing time. The sun's too high. Besides, Jamie's not home from school yet. Something's wrong. Something's very wrong!*

After hurriedly washing my hands at the sink, I rushed

into the yard. I could see miners scurrying in every direction, some climbing up the slope toward the mine shaft, others riding the buckets to the top.

Fear wrapped itself around my heart. I picked up my skirts and hurried toward the mine office as quickly as my eight-month pregnant body would allow. One of the miners ran past me, his eyes bulging with terror.

"What's happening? What's wrong?" I shouted.

"A cave-in! In the main shaft!"

The building was empty. *Of course, James would have been one of the first ones up there to help. James! At lunch, didn't he say something about going down into the shaft this afternoon?* That's when I remembered that he'd changed from his plaid flannel shirt to a lighter-weight cotton one.

I dashed across the wooden platform to the tramway operator. "Please, I've got to go up there. I've got to find out if my husband's all right."

"Thorpe," the operator called to the man preparing to climb into the next bucket. "Get her out of here!"

The miner grabbed my arm with an iron grip and led me, protesting, back into the office. "Lady, the last thing they need up top right now is a hysterical female. If you want to help Mr. McCall, you stay put, do you hear?"

"Just tell me, is my husband up there? Is he safe?"

He shook his head. "I'll be honest with you if you promise to control yourself." The grizzled miner stared into my eyes until I nodded. "The word is that the boss is down below. Which side of the cave-in he's on, I don't know."

"No!" I jerked free of his grasp and ran toward the door, straight into an iron bar of an arm.

"Ma'am, you said you'd settle down." He grasped my arm and led me to a chair. "Either you stay right here in this chair, or you go back to your home to wait. Do you understand?"

I nodded reluctantly.

"You promise, for that baby's sake?" He glanced down at my protruding stomach, then into my eyes.

I nodded again.

He leaned toward me, his face hard, his eyes piercing. "Can I trust you this time?"

"Yes," I whispered. "You can trust me. But, please, tell me the minute you know something."

He smiled through his droopy brown mustache. "I promise."

I shook my finger in his face. "Good or bad!"

"Good or bad."

As for sitting in the chair, the second the miner departed, I hopped up and stood by the window. A spyglass sat on the shelf below the window ledge. I focused on the movement around the shaft house. While I couldn't make any sense of what was happening up there, it occupied me to watch.

I shut my eyes, trying to erase the images of the steaming mine shaft, the pool of hot water, the tunnel, and the rats, always the rats. *James? James!* Suddenly I sensed my husband was in danger. He was on the wrong side of the cave-in. *Pete! Where are you, Pete? Are you trapped alongside him? Or are you helping to rescue him?*

I hated standing by, doing nothing. I strode to the door. My hand gripped the latch, then dropped to my side. *You promised.* Pacing from the door to the desk and back again, I paused only long enough to gaze through the spyglass. Back and forth I walked, my prayers becoming more insistent with each step.

"Oh, dear Father, this isn't happening." My words bounced off log walls. "You can't let anything happen to James. You just can't! He can't die. Do You hear me? You can't let him die!"

When the baby kicked, I caressed my abdomen. "I'm sorry, Father. I have no right telling You what to do. But, please, Lord, please protect James." I wiped my eyes on my soiled apron. "In Psalm 139, it says You are with us if we ascend to the heavens or make our beds in hell. That mine shaft, Lord, is as close to hell as any human can get." I knew I was arguing with the God of the universe, but I didn't care. I'd do anything to save my husband.

The door opened. It was Jamie. "Mama, what are you doing up here? Did you know Hector got into your cookie dough?"

I rushed to him and engulfed him in my arms. He struggled free. "What's wrong? Why are you crying?"

I took a deep, ragged breath. "There's been a cave-in, in the main shaft. I'm waiting to hear from your father."

Horror spread across Jamie's face. "You mean he may be trapped in the mine?"

"I don't know for sure. He could be part of the rescue team, helping to dig out the trapped men."

Jamie ran to the window. "Here." I handed him the spyglass. "This might help."

Minutes ticked by while the boy studied the movement by the shaft house, and I continued pacing and bargaining with God. Then a wagon pulled up outside. Ula was the first inside the mining office, the rest of the women following right behind.

Now that friends had arrived to support me, my control dissolved in an avalanche of tears. Ula wrapped her arms around me and held me close.

"I haven't heard anything for more than an hour. They don't know who's trapped yet. I'm positive James is safe. He's probably just down in the shaft helping with the rescue. . . ." I knew I was babbling, but I couldn't stop. Nor could I stop shaking. Ula let me talk myself out.

The air grew cool, and pinpoints of light from kerosene

lanterns dotted the mountain as the sun disappeared beyond the western peaks. When someone suggested that the rescuers must be hungry, Ula sent the ladies to the camp cook to volunteer their help.

"Thanks," I whispered as the room emptied. "I need to sit down. My back is killing me. This baby is getting bigger and bigger every day."

She led me to my husband's desk chair. "Open the bottom drawer and put your feet up for a while. Your ankles are badly swollen."

I glanced down at my feet. Drucilla's words came back to me. *Elephant lady.* I rubbed my lower back and stretched.

Ula eyed me strangely. "Let me take you to the cabin. You need to stretch out on a bed." She tipped her head toward Jamie. "It wouldn't hurt if he went home as well."

I shook my head vigorously. "No, I can't leave until I know James is safe."

"Chloe, the rescue attempt could go on for days. You've got to think of that baby now. It needs you."

What Ula said made sense. And I was exhausted; the pains in my back had intensified. I allowed Ula to talk me into leaving, but Jamie put up more resistance. Noah struck a bargain with the boy, allowing Jamie to stay at the mine for one more hour before returning to the cabin.

Ula walked me home and put me to bed. When I made a halfhearted gesture toward the cookie remains on the table, she assured me she'd handle everything.

As Ula tucked me into the bed, she said, "It looks like it's time for a cup of comfrey tea to help you sleep."

"I'll never be able to sleep until I know James is all right."

She patted my arm and smiled. "Let's give it a try, anyway."

Whether she made the tea, I never found out. For within seconds of my head touching the pillow, I was asleep, dreaming of a field of buffalo grass rippling in the summer breeze. I lay on the ground surrounded by brown-eyed susans and Queen Anne's lace. When a butterfly landed on my forehead, I lifted my arm to brush it away.

"Sh, it's just me."

My eyes flew open. James was leaning over me, brushing the curls from my forehead.

"It's you! You're safe." I threw my arms about his neck and cried. "Oh, James, I feared you were dead. I thought you were trapped in the mine."

He laid me back against the pillow and kissed my forehead, cheek, and nose. "I was." His voice rasped with emotion as he told me about the cave-in and the rescue. "All eighteen of us came out alive, a bit bruised and scratched, but, nevertheless, alive. And we can thank Pete's skill and determination for it."

"Oh, darling, I came so close to losing you." I pulled him down into my arms. He nuzzled my neck, then straightened.

"And how are you feeling?"

"Fine, what time is it?"

James looked at his pocket watch. "Around midnight."

"Is Jamie—"

"Sound asleep in his bed. Ula said you've been having back pains. You don't think the baby is coming sooner than we thought, do you?"

I scoffed at the suggestion. "That would be impossible. If this child arrives much sooner than June fifteen, I would have had to get pregnant on our honeymoon."

James chuckled. "Stranger things have happened, you know."

"James, I know what I'm talking about." I ran my hand over my stomach. "Just look at the size. As big as I am, I'm nowhere near as large as my sister was when she delivered her son."

James clicked his tongue. "Well, you could be right. You

do know more about the process than I, even if your knowledge is secondhand."

The sound of angry voices outside our bedroom window followed by a loud banging at the door shattered our quiet interlude. James hurried to the door. I felt a stitch in my side as I crawled out of bed. Ignoring the discomfort, I tiptoed to the door and listened. Rags bounded off the bed and pressed against my legs, growling.

"This is your man, James." Pete spoke in a firm, even tone. "He didn't know I was behind him when he kicked down a shoring at a spot weakened by the spring runoff. By the time it dawned on me what he was trying to do, the mountain had caved in on us."

"The man's a liar," Otis shouted. "Ya can't take the word of a lyin' Injun' over that of your own kind."

I heard James respond. "I don't consider you my own kind, Mr. Roy. Why would you want to kill seventeen of your own men?"

"Hey, it's my word against his. And while you might cozy up to a lyin' heathen, there ain't a judge in the country who would take an Injun's word over a white man's."

"You make me embarrassed to be a white man!" James snarled.

At the sound of scuffling and chairs overturning, I threw on my dressing gown and opened the door. Rags lunged at Otis. I called him away. Pete had pinned Otis's arms behind his back. James stood with his face inches from the prisoner's face. When James heard my voice, he turned and growled, "Go back to the bedroom."

A sardonic grin spread across Otis's face. "Ah, the mommy-to-be." He glanced down at the quivering Rags. "And how is that dog of yours?"

"Why you . . ." I started toward the arrogant man.

James caught me by the arms. "Take Rags and go back into the bedroom."

I started to protest when Otis scoffed, "Ya can't control your woman, McCall. How do you expect to control a mining operation? You and your silver-spoon brother."

James's head snapped around. "What do you know about my brother?"

"You think I'd tell you?" Otis sneered. "Look, either take me to Sheriff Jones and press charges, or make this redskin let me go."

I saw Pete's lips press together and his grip on Otis tighten. Then he looked toward James for direction.

James released my arms. "Let him go, Pete."

"James," I wailed, ignoring a stitch in my other side, "you can't leave him free to attack again."

My husband strode toward Otis. "I may not have the evidence necessary to hang you, Mr. Roy, but I can and will fire you. Pack your things and be out of here before dawn. If you show your ugly face around the mine again, I will have you arrested for trespassing and for suspicion of arson and attempted murder, do you understand?"

"You can't fire me. I quit!" Otis shouted, as he stormed out of the cabin.

I rushed to James. "Is he gone? Is he really gone for good?"

"As far as I'm concerned, he'd better be. I will carry out my threat." He walked over to our friend and placed a hand on Pete's shoulder. "Pete, I'm going to need your help managing the mine. Will you take the job?"

Pete grinned. "I think I can handle it."

James laughed. "I know you can."

"Well, I'd better be going. Someone needs to be certain Otis Roy leaves without causing more trouble." Pete tipped his hat toward me. "Good night, Mrs. McCall. Good night, boss. Thanks for the vote of confidence."

James shook his hand. "And thank you, dear friend, for saving my life today."

As Pete walked down the steps, James barred the door. Then he took my hand in his. "Well, it looks like the nightmare has finally come to an end. Once Pete and I can get the mine running smoothly, you and I can go home to Kansas."

I snuggled closer to his side and purred, "That would be nice. I'd like that."

The next morning after James left for the mine and Jamie for school, I lumbered around the cabin in a haze. The pain in my back had receded to a dull ache. Midmorning, I did the unthinkable—I lay down for a nap.

I awakened when James came home for lunch. Forcing myself to get up, I made him something to eat. He studied me as I shuffled around the kitchen. "Are you feeling all right?"

"It's just this dumb backache. It won't go away."

He eyed me suspiciously as he bit into his sandwich. "I'll be at the office if you need me."

I nodded and smiled. "I'll be fine, honest."

He stood to leave. "Should I stay here with you or send someone down later to check on you?"

"No." I straightened his collar. "When you leave, I'll lie down again until Jamie comes home. I think I must have strained something yesterday without knowing it."

James kissed me and left.

I didn't hear Jamie come home from school or James return from work. I awoke to the aroma of pancakes. Staggering out of the bedroom, I was greeted by two grinning faces and a table set for supper. James pointed the pancake turner at me. "Lo, what delicate creature appears from yonder cave?"

I glanced down at my swollen body and muttered, "*Delicate* hardly describes me, I'm afraid."

James laughed and tossed the spatula to Jamie. "Here, son, take over for me." While Jamie turned the hotcakes,

James swept me in his arms and waltzed me across the floor.

"La-la-la-la, la-la," he sang. "La-la-la-la-la, la-la." We swirled to the "Waltz of the Flowers."

"James, stop. James," I scolded. "That's hardly appropriate behavior in front of Jamie."

He took my hand and twirled me around in a circle, then clasped me in his arms again. "I'd say it's extremely appropriate behavior. What greater gift can we give him and our child-to-be than to demonstrate our love for one another?"

I looked deep into my husband's sparkling eyes. "You are incorrigible, Mr. McCall."

"And you are adorable, Mrs. McCall."

I threw back my head and laughed. Suddenly a pain gripped my abdomen; I groaned and doubled over.

"Chloe, what happened? Are you all right?"

I shook my head and shuffled blindly to the sofa and sat down in a heap. "It's—it's all right," I gasped. "I've been getting these stitches in my side for the last day or so."

"Why didn't you tell me?"

"You had enough to worry about. O-o-o-h!" I curled up into a ball. *Something's definitely wrong! Is it possible? Is this what labor feels like?* As the pain lessened, I sighed with relief. Even as my body relaxed, I suddenly knew I was well beyond the first stages of labor.

James hovered over me. "What can I do? Tell me what to do."

I struggled to my feet. "I think I'd better go lie down."

"What about your pancakes?" Jamie asked.

"Sorry, cowboy, I'd better not try any this time." Turning to James, I said, "You'd better get the birthing linens out of the trunk. Then you'd better send for Ula. I think this baby's coming tonight."

James leapt away from me as if burned by a hot coal.

"Tonight? No, the baby can't be born here. You've got to go to Denver."

I shook my head. "I don't think so. Help me to the bedroom, please."

James wrapped his arm around my shoulder and guided me to the bedroom, calling over his shoulder as we walked. "Jamie, you know where Pete's cabin is?" He didn't wait for a reply. "Tell him Chloe's gone into labor and to go for Ula."

The boy stared, frozen with terror. "Now, son, now!" James shouted. "Take Rags with you."

The child's head nodded as if connected to his shoulders with a spring. I could only imagine the memories of his mother going through his mind. "It's all right, cowboy," I assured. "I'll be fine, you'll see."

"So get moving," James growled.

Jamie grabbed his jacket off the hook by the door and dashed out of the cabin into the night, Rags barking at his heels.

"He'll be all right, won't he?" I whimpered. "No grizzlies have been sighted recently, have they?"

James lowered me onto the edge of the bed. "Woman, you think of the nicest things at the nicest times. Stop asking impossible questions and help me unbutton these infernal buttons and get you into bed."

I pushed his shaking hands away from my dress collar and undid the line of ivory buttons. I slipped out of my dress and petticoat. Pointing toward the dresser we'd purchased in Denver, I said, "I need my flannel nightgown." Another pain gripped my abdomen.

James's head snapped first one direction, then the other. "Right, nightgown, where? Where is your nightgown?"

I laughed in spite of my agony. "Look where I'm pointing."

He found the gown and helped me slip it over my head,

then lifted my feet onto the bed and pulled the covers up around my shoulders.

"You just stay right there and wait for Ula," he demanded.

I laughed and groaned simultaneously. "I'll wait, but I'm not sure this baby will."

"It will. It will," he insisted, hanging up my dress and petticoat.

New Beginnings

The contraction lessened. I fell back against the pillow to catch my breath before the next spasm.

"Just in case he or she doesn't wait, will you sit down here and listen while I tell what you'll need to do?"

The terror I'd seen earlier in Jamie's eyes now filled my husband's. All color drained from his face. While I explained the process, he shook his head from side to side, muttering, "I can't do this, Chloe. I can't do this."

"You can, and you wi-ow-ee-oo!" Another contraction arrived on the heels of the last. Now I was the one terrified. The labor was moving faster than it should for a first baby. I curled into a ball; the gripping pain erased all other thoughts from my mind. I could hear James's voice, but I had no idea what he was saying. *Mama, where are you? I need you. Please, help me!*

As the pain subsided, I fell back against the pillow, my face and neck bathed in sweat. "I've changed my mind. I can't go through with this. Please, please, I'm sorry, honey, but I can't go through with thi-i-i-s . . ."

"What? What?" James's face peered around the corner of the door. "You told me to boil water, didn't you?"

"Oh, no," I wailed, feeling moisture on the sheet beneath me. "Forget the water. It's coming. The baby's coming n-o-o-w-w-w!"

But I was wrong. My muscles relaxed again. And again I collapsed against the pillow. From the foot of the bed, James shouted, "I can see the baby's head." Tears streamed down his face. "I can see his head!"

"His head?" I gasped, laughing as tears streamed down my face. "From past experience, I would say your diagnosis is a little premature."

A new wave of pain swept through me, plunging me into a vortex of agony. None of the birthings in which I'd assisted had prepared me for this. I heard a woman scream and realized I was hearing my own voice.

Chloe, my rational mind scolded, *stop kicking up a ruckus. Childbirth is the most natural process in the world.* Even as I remembered the words I'd occasionally uttered to my more violent patients, I couldn't believe I'd been so insensitive and naive. *It's a wonder those women ever spoke to me again. And wait until I get my hands on the ladies who say they don't remember the pain afterward. I'll never forget this until the day I die, which just might be toni-i-i-ght. Pant, Chloe, pant. Stop pushing so hard. Now, now, push. Good. Don't quit. Push!*

A shout filled the air, followed by an infant's squawl. My body felt an overwhelming surge of relief from the pain. I fell back against the pillow, laughing and sobbing as James held a tiny wet body over the bed. Tears streamed down my husband's face.

"Look, a girl. We've got a baby girl. And would you look at her shock of red hair!"

Clenched fists flailed and angry feet kicked as our baby wailed out her displeasure. James cleaned the child and wrapped her in a flannel receiving blanket. "She's beautiful. She's utterly beautiful. Thank you, darling, for our beautiful daughter." He placed her in the crook of my arm before finishing taking care of me.

Gently, I unwound her tiny, perfectly formed fingers. My

husband was right. Our daughter was the most beautiful baby in the world. I couldn't take my eyes off her. "What shall we name her?"

I looked up at my husband, who was grinning broadly. "I'm partial to the name Chloe, myself."

I scowled. "They don't name daughters after their mothers, like they do sons after fathers."

He shrugged. "Why not?"

"Well, because—they just don't."

"Who's they?"

"I don't know."

James had just removed the soiled linen from the room when Ula burst through the front door.

"I hurried as fast as I could." She tossed her jacket on the sofa and bustled into the bedroom. "So what's that child doing arriving off schedule?" Ula stared at the bundle in my arms. "It's here? I rushed poor Indian Pete and ended up missing the party?"

I glanced beyond Ula into the next room. "Where's Jamie? He needs to meet his new sister."

I'd barely spoken the words when the front door opened, and Jamie burst into the cabin. "Mama, you're all right? Daddy said you're all right."

"That's right, son." I reached for his hand. "Come and meet your little sister."

James brought Pete into the room to meet our new family member. Like most men, Pete acted uncomfortable around our newborn and refused to hold her. "When she gets older, when she gets older. What do you plan to name her?"

James told everyone how he wanted to call her Chloe but I wasn't so sure. I don't know who suggested Chloe Celeste, but we all agreed the name fit her perfectly.

"We could call her CeeCee for short," Jamie suggested. He knelt down on the floor beside the bed and touched his sister's hand with his little finger. The baby wrapped her fingers around his and studied his face intensely. By the adoration in his eyes, I knew she had wrapped her fingers around his heart as well. He grinned up at his father. "She likes me."

James chuckled. "Of course she does, son. You're her big brother, just like Joe is your mom's. And you know how special he is to her."

Noticing how tired I looked, Ula urged the men to leave so I could rest. As much as I'd enjoyed their company, I was grateful. Reluctantly, Jamie withdrew his finger from his sister's hand.

After encouraging the newborn to nurse for a few minutes, Ula picked up the baby and adjusted the blankets around my shoulders. "You rest a while. I'll bring her back when she gets hungry. Oh, by the way, does James know where to find her diapers?"

I nodded sleepily. "Thank you for coming."

"You can rest now. You did a good job tonight. So did James."

"I know." I swallowed a wave of tears threatening to erupt. "I'll never forget the look on his face when he held CeeCee for the first time. We shared something special tonight."

The next few days, Ula and the other women dropped in to see our daughter. Though Ula tried to convince me that two weeks in bed would be wise, I assured her that wouldn't happen. My first day out of bed, I wrote a letter home telling my parents all about their precocious granddaughter.

". . . CeeCee has the sweetest disposition. She adores her big brother. And, Ma, it is so strange. One look at CeeCee's pink, round face, and I hardly remembered any pain at all. She's definitely worth it."

I also sent word of CeeCee's arrival to the Putnams. A week later a hand-carved cradle for CeeCee arrived on the train. The attached card read, "With our love, Gladys and Phineas."

We also received a letter from Ian saying Drucilla was pregnant again and insisted on returning to Boston before the end of summer. With the threat of Otis gone and the baby thriving in the clean Colorado air, James confessed that he'd like to stay in Columbine until fall. "We're so close to hitting the mother lode, I can't abandon the mine now. Once we do, I'll turn the operation over to Pete."

As he spoke, excitement sparkled in his eyes. Pete's prediction flashed through my mind. *Mining is getting to James. It's getting in his blood.*

I sighed. As beautiful as the mountains were, I missed the prairie. I missed our beautiful home. I missed the modern conveniences like the bathtub with hot-and-cold running water.

"Just until fall, right?" There was an edge to my voice.

He kissed me hard on the lips. "Just until fall."

During the month of June, I was so busy learning to be a mommy that when the next packages of books and magazines arrived from Gladys, I barely skimmed the titles and the lead articles, that is until I read the headline "U.S. Troops Sent to Quell Boxer Uprising." I read on.

Seven thousand U.S. troops were sent to aid the British in their attempt to put down the secret society popularly called the Boxers, who have vowed to drive all "foreign devils" from the continent. The state department is urging all U.S. citizens to leave China.

I glanced down at the sleeping infant in the basket by my feet. Even as she slept, her lips curled into a tiny smile. *How different my life would have been if I'd boarded that boat to China.* I couldn't imagine my life without James, Jamie, and CeeCee. I thought of the Van Dorns and wondered if they had returned home yet.

James read verses from the Bible at breakfast and at supper. Otherwise, I neglected that too. While he and Jamie continued to go to the weekly meetings in Columbine, I begged off. I told them, "The night air isn't good for CeeCee."

Occasionally I attended the ladies' club, mainly to have my friends ogle CeeCee. But mainly my interests circled around my little family. July passed, then August. If James hadn't remembered my nineteenth birthday with a new pink shawl he'd purchased on one of his trips to Steamboat Springs, I would have forgotten the day. In my next letter to Hattie, I told her that, any day now, I expected James to announce that we were packing up and heading home to Kansas.

For our first wedding anniversary, my husband treated the entire family to a day in Steamboat Springs. Since he had to make the trip to the assayer's office anyway, he suggested we go along. The best part of the day was dining at the only restaurant in town not associated with a bar and brothel. Eating someone else's cooking—ah! I savored every mouthful of the lumpy mashed potatoes, the mushy peas, the soggy carrots, and the stale bread. We all ordered tapioca pudding for dessert.

James paid the bill, picked up CeeCee's basket, and led us out of the restaurant. "The assayer said there was a holdup a couple of weeks ago on the Union Pacific, somewhere near Hugo, Colorado."

"I hope they caught the culprits."

"Me too, since we have a big shipment going out next week. He also told me that some foreigner tried to assassinate the president last week."

"What? McKinley? That's disgraceful!" I clicked my tongue in disgust. "What is this world coming to? Pretty soon it won't be safe for a person to walk down the street!"

At the depot we were delighted to find Gladys's September shipment of books and magazines waiting for us. Before the train pulled out of the station, James opened the crate. "Give us something to do on the ride home," he explained.

Recently I'd come to believe he appreciated Gladys's gift more than I. Jamie pawed through the books. One look at the copy of *The Adventures of Huckleberry Finn* by Mark Twain, and the boy headed off to a quiet seat by himself.

James chose a copy of *McClure's Magazine* for himself. "Would you like something to read too?"

I shook my head. The thought of reading while the train snaked through the narrow canyons made my stomach heave.

James held up a thick catalog. "Here's Sears Roebuck's wishbook."

I glanced down at CeeCee asleep in the basket on the floor beside me. "Well, maybe it won't bother me to look at pictures."

He handed me the catalog and we both settled down for the ride home. *Hmm, styles haven't changed much since last winter. Skirts a little shorter, less trim. The bustle is finally on its way out.* I caught sight of my gently protruding tummy. *Can't hide that with gathers and pleats,* I thought. *Looks like it's back to the whale-bone stays for me.*

"Chloe," James interrupted, "what was the name of that missionary couple you always talk about? The army evacuated all sick and wounded U.S. citizens from Tientsin on August four. The names are listed here."

"Um." I thought for a moment, surprised that I couldn't remember instantly. "The Van Dorns, Annabelle and, uh— I can't remember his name."

"Could it be Victor?"

I snapped my fingers. "Yeah, that's it." I peered over his shoulder at the names.

"They are scheduled to arrive in San Francisco some-time this month. Col. Liscain of the Ninth Infantry says that China is now shut to all westerners."

I shook my head, feeling nothing more than a twinge of regret. *Oh, well, looks like it was best I didn't go, after all.*

Lost in my own thoughts, I failed to notice that James had grown strangely quiet. I glanced toward him. The magazine lay folded on his lap.

I rested my hand on his knee. "Tired of reading, honey?"

"There was a letter from Ian too." I knew by his quiet, even tone that something was wrong.

"What is it? What's happened? Is baby Ashley all right?"

He nodded slowly, his face pale.

"Then tell me, what is wrong?"

He took a deep breath. "There's been an accident." He paused. I wanted to shout, to shake him, to demand that he tell me what had happened. "A twister touched down at our place." He shook his head. "The barn and the tack house are still standing."

I gasped. "And the house? Our home?"

He pinched the bridge of his nose and squeezed his eyes shut. A tear fell on the magazine cover. "It's all gone," he whispered. "The twister destroyed Pagets' barn as well as the Evans's place—all turned to rubble. A few smaller pieces of furniture survived without a scratch. They found the silver tea set, your metal trunk with your wedding gown and my grandma's watch intact, as well as a few of Jamie's lead Civil War soldiers." He sighed again. "Our wedding photo and your dresser set were destroyed. They did come across Jamie's confederate button. Aunt Bea is storing everything at her place until we decide what we're going to do."

I squeezed his knee encouragingly. "Things don't matter. Was anyone hurt?"

"Minna sprained her ankle climbing across the rubble to

rescue Muffin. Drucilla lost the baby she was carrying." He cleared his throat. I leaned against his shoulder. My silent tears moistened his scratchy wool jacket.

"Oh, James, I'm so sorry."

"It's gone, Chloe, all gone. How many times do we have to go through this? It's like our lives are cursed."

"Don't say that. We've been so blessed; you know we have. What about Drucilla and Ian?"

"Dru may be the biggest tragedy of all." He shrugged. "She's demanding he take her and Ashley back to Boston. He says after the tornado, it was like something snapped in her mind. Nightmares, days when she refuses to speak to anyone or even get out of bed, bouts of crying, unprovoked fits of hysteria—no one can get through to her."

I massaged my forehead. My mind couldn't absorb it all. "What about Sam and the men?"

"There are still crops to harvest and animals to tend. Ian says Sam will oversee the place until we decide what we want to do. As for Ian and Dru and little Ashley, they're returning to Boston."

"And what about us? What are we going to do now?"

"I don't know yet. We're so close to the mother lode—"

"The mother lode! I'm so tired of hearing about this elusive mother lode." I folded my arms and turned my face to the window. "Do you want to spend the rest of your life digging in some hole in a mountain?"

I could see James's reflection in the window. The worry lines that had developed over the past year deepened. "Honey, I can't abandon the project now, especially after the enormous financial loss at the ranch. If we ever expect to rebuild the farmhouse, we'll need cash, cash from the mother lode."

"Fine, go find your mother lode, I don't care. . . ."

He shook his head and rose to his feet. He stretched, then crossed to the empty seat on the other side of the aisle. Guilt washed over me. My inner voice said, *Go to him. You need him, and he needs you.* My heart cried out, *James, please don't walk away. Let's talk about this together. Please . . .*

I knew if I spoke the words aloud, he'd return. But the taste of pride welled up inside my throat. We sat like stone statues in the park the rest of the way to Hahn's Peak. CeeCee was wet and hungry by the time James returned from the stables with the horse and wagon. Jamie looked at us questioningly as we climbed aboard and started for the mine. James concentrated on driving us home while I nursed the baby.

At home, I deposited the satisfied infant in her cradle and started fixing supper. James called his son down from the loft and told him about the tornado. Once he was assured that Cookie and the other animals were safe, Jamie took the tragedy well. "Will we be staying here, Dad?"

James glanced over at me. I stirred the biscuit batter with the same vengeance Ma applied to her knitting needles at such times. "For a time, son."

Jamie nodded and went back to his book. He hadn't asked about any of his possessions. As for James and me, the icy barrier between us thickened over the coming days. On Jamie's birthday, a letter arrived from James's father, inviting James to send the child back to Boston to a renowned prep school. After Jamie went to bed for the night, James read the letter aloud.

"Your son needs a better education than he can get in Columbine if he ever wants to succeed at Harvard. You owe it to him to give him the advantage . . ."

James lowered the piece of parchment. "He's right, you know. If Jamie wants to pass the entrance exams for Harvard, he must attend a rigorous preparatory school. And to qualify for a decent prep school, he'll need a number of years at a boarding school for boys."

I couldn't believe what I was hearing. *You'll send your eight-year-old son two thousand miles across the continent alone so he can prepare, to prepare, to attend your alma mater?* I knew that for the McCall family, Harvard was everything, but this was more than I could handle. "James, are you serious? He's a little boy who needs to be at home with his parents, not in a cold, forbidding dormitory thousands of miles from us."

"He is a little young to be so far away. Maybe next year when he's nine . . ."

Nine! Of all the stupid . . . I exhaled sharply.

"Chloe." James walked up behind me and slipped his arms around my waist. "I know this is hard for you to understand, coming from a little town in western Pennsylvania, but for Jamie to get ahead in the world, he will need a degree from Harvard behind his name. He's my son, and I have to do what I believe is best for him."

I sizzled. *Hard to understand. A little town in Pennsylvania. My son.* Since the day we married, James and I never referred to Jamie as my son or your son, but as our son. I considered myself as much a mother to him as I was to CeeCee. Now, suddenly . . .

I removed James's arms from my waist. When I opened my mouth, Pa's southern brogue came out.

"Is that all y'all be needin' me fo' t'night, cap'n? It's 'bout t'am I went out yonda and slopped de hogs."

"Chloe . . ." James sighed. "Chloe, I didn't mean to cast aspersions on your heritage."

"M'ghty gen'rous of ya, cap'n," I simpered, slipping away from his grasp.

He followed me into the bedroom. "Cut it out! You're acting like a child."

I picked up the whimpering CeeCee and sarcastically added. "A chal'? A stepchal', ya mean."

"I didn't say that. I didn't even imply—Oh, forget it!" My

husband whirled about and stormed from the cabin. I sat granite still on the edge of the bed as the cabin door slammed behind him. Rags sidled up to my legs and whimpered. Above my head I could hear Jamie shuffling about in the loft. He'd heard it all. *Oh, Jamie, I'm sorry. It wasn't your fault, you know.*

We'd had so many squabbles lately, some my fault, others James's. But all with the same results—him storming from the cabin. *Why do I always feel like a whipped puppy instead of a celebrating hero?*

I knew I should climb the ladder and talk with the child, but I didn't know what I could say that he hadn't already heard. Stiffly, I changed into my nightdress and lay on the bed beside the baby. Tears moistened my pillow as I caressed our daughter's red halo of hair and peachy cheek. "Sorry, little one. Your daddy and I do love each other, you know."

I understood my husband's concern regarding Jamie, even if I was from the hills of Pennsylvania instead of Boston. And I was acting like a child. *It's not as if Jamie's leaving for Boston tomorrow. And there are other ways of winning a disagreement without becoming disagreeable.*

When CeeCee fell asleep, I placed her in her cradle and tiptoed into the living room. At the bottom of the ladder, I called gently, "Jamie? Jamie, are you still awake?"

No one answered. I climbed the rungs until I could peer over the edge. "Jamie?" I whispered, scrambling into the loft on my hands and knees. I stood up and tiptoed over to his cot under the eaves. Even as the boy slept, tears stained his face. I brushed a lock of hair away from his forehead, bent down, and kissed him.

He stirred. His red and swollen eyes opened to narrow slits. "Mama?"

"I just came to say I'm sorry your daddy and I argued tonight."

He nodded, his eyes hazy with sleep.

"We do love each other, you know, very much." I hugged him gently. "And we love you very much also, you and CeeCee."

"I know."

I adjusted the quilts about his shoulders. "Never, ever forget that."

He smiled, then closed his eyes once again. For some time, I stared down at his face, half hidden in the shadows. *Can you ever possibly know how much I love you, cowboy? And your daddy, he wants only what's best for you. I know that. I hope you do too.*

I picked up a folded quilt lying on the foot of his bed and sat down on the floor beside him. Drawing my knees up to my chest, I watched the shadows and the light from the fireplace dance on the open-beam ceiling and rough-hewn walls. For the first time, I understood why Jamie enjoyed his attic hideaway.

Memories welled up inside me—poignant, painful, tender memories. I leaned my head against the cot and inhaled the aroma of drying oregano and parsley. I could almost see Pa's giant shadow looming over his wooden bench, measuring out the ingredients for a burn ointment or a stomachache elixir. His bass voice filled my senses. "Yep, that railway strike will cripple the nation, mark my words. President McKinley is doin' the only thing . . ."

Below I heard the barn door open and footsteps cross the wooden floor. *It must be Joe, looking for Pa.*

The herbs, Pa, and Pa's bench disappeared in the bright lantern light shining in my face. "Chloe," James whispered. "There you are. I've been looking all over for you. Don't you want to come to bed?"

I lifted my head and gazed about the loft. A moment of sadness clutched my heart. I was no longer in Pennsylvania, and I was no longer a child. I was in my own home in

Colorado. I extended my hand, and James helped me to my feet. He led the way down the ladder.

As I stepped off the lowest rung, I turned. "I'm sor—"

"I'm sorry too," James whispered. "I thought you were gone."

"Where would I go in the middle of the night, in the Colorado Rockies?" Tenderly, I caressed the side of his face. "And even if I wanted to, I couldn't walk out on you and the children."

"I'm sorry I ran out on you tonight. Running away has been a pattern of mine since I was a kid." He drew me into his arms. "I ran out on Mary when she needed me. I should have been there for her."

"No, James . . ." I wanted to erase the pain I saw in his face.

"Yes." He took my hand and led me to the sofa. "I never told you, but Mary and I had been having trouble for some time before I left with Ian for Kansas. She'd hoped getting pregnant with Agatha would keep me in Boston and heal our marriage. I felt trapped by the prospect, like I'd never escape the oppressive atmosphere of living near our parents."

I didn't know what to say. Neither he nor Mary had ever hinted at a rift in their relationship. I stared into the dying embers of the fireplace.

James placed his elbows on his knees and cupped his chin in his hands. "From the nursery, Jamie overheard us argue many times, followed by Mary sobbing and me storming from the house. One night he heard me say I was leaving and never coming back . . ."

I touched his arm. "You don't have to tell me this."

"Yes, I do." He gazed into my eyes for a few seconds before continuing. "Mary grabbed my arm and started screaming, 'I hate you!' In my attempt to shake free of her, she lost her balance and fell against a marble-topped table. When she cried out, I turned back to catch her and saw Jamie watching from his bedroom doorway."

"Oh, the poor little . . ." The lines on James's face deepened as I spoke.

"The next day when Ian and I made arrangements to leave Boston, Mary took medication that was supposed to end her pregnancy. When it didn't, I stubbornly proceeded with my plans to leave."

"Is that about the time Jamie stopped talking?"

James nodded. "Yes. By the time I left, I didn't really want to go. However, it had become a matter of pride with us both, and no one was willing to give in."

I recalled Mary's stubborn determination to continue her trip to Kansas in spite of her illness. Now I understood why.

He turned to face me, desperately grasping my arms. "I don't want that to happen to us, Chloe."

"Neither do I." I choked back a wave of tears. "We've both been behaving like children. I've been running away from you also. Not physically, but mentally and emotionally."

His eyes never leaving my face, James asked, "What can we do about it?"

"I know how difficult it was for you to tell me tonight about you and Mary. But I've never felt so close to you as I do now." I smiled and chuckled. "Isn't it ironic that two runners would fall in love and marry?"

"I do love you—very, very much. And if it's possible, this runner has sprinted his last mile." He lifted my chin toward him.

"Me too. You know, together, I think we can work this out."

As he pressed his lips to mine, his kiss held the promise of exciting new beginnings.

Dueling With Death

The fire crackled in the fireplace, casting a warm glow over the kitchen and parlor. A jumble of cookie cutters lay strewn about the flour-coated tabletop. "Would you like to roll the dough this time, Jamie?" I handed him the rolling pin.

He grinned and nodded. He took a handful of cookie dough from the pottery mixing bowl and formed it into a neat and compact ball. *It doesn't have to be precisely round. You're only going to flatten it, kiddo.* I bit my tongue and walked to the cupboard to locate the tin of raisins for the snowmen's eyes.

Carefully he lined up the two half-inch strips of wood I used so that I wouldn't roll the dough out too thin. By the time I returned, he was ready to press the tin forms into the smooth, flat dough.

"Think we need more snowmen?" I asked.

"No, we need stars. See, there are fifteen bells and seventeen snowmen, thirteen trees, and only eight stars. Definitely we need more stars."

I'd never seen a kid be so precise about everything he did. Long ago, I learned he would measure out the ingredients for my herbal recipes more accurately than I. While his nature demanded accuracy, mine wanted to get the job done and move on to the next project. His patience was evident in all he did. If an inkblot fell on his arithmetic assignment in long division, he would recopy the entire page rather than hand in a blotched page.

After he carefully transferred the cut cookies from the table to the cookie sheet, I scraped the excess dough together and rolled out another batch before he could ask to do it. Then I suggested he put the eyes on the snowmen.

Leaning over the cookie sheet, he meticulously pressed each raisin in place, then added the mouth and buttons. Joking, I said, "Looks good, Dr. McCall. Even the belly buttons are in the right spots."

He grinned at my praise. "I think it would be fun to become a doctor when I grow up."

My breath caught in my throat. My eyes swam with tears. "Jamie, when did you decide this?"

He shrugged and dropped another raisin in place. "I don't know. I've watched you take care of the sick and, well, I think I'd like to do that too."

I picked up a sheet of cookies and placed them in the oven so he wouldn't see my tears. *Pa, the legacy lives on. If only you and Jamie could know one another.*

The two and a half months since Jamie's eighth birthday had been special for all four of us. CeeCee had cut her first tooth. I had learned how to better deal with Jamie. And when there were problems, his father and I were turning toward one another instead of away. All in all, I felt content with the way things were going.

The cold season in Columbine had begun earlier than usual. I'd been called out a number of times to help ease chest colds. So often that Mrs. Jones suggested I conduct regular office hours a couple days a week at the jail. That way she could care for CeeCee while I treated my patients. When people learned I was available to help them during the day, their night treks out to the mine dwindled.

Now that I knew Jamie was genuinely interested in

medicine, I started teaching him about herbs and their uses. One afternoon, when we were grinding dried roots for a spring tonic, he said, "Wouldn't it be great to know every cure for every disease? No one would ever have to die, would they?"

When I didn't reply right away, he asked, "Well, would they? Could any doctor become that good?"

"A doctor can only diagnose the problem. He can't cure. He can prescribe medicines, herbs, even time, but he himself can only hope and pray his patient will get better." I drew my lips into a tight, helpless grin. "It seems that when a cure is found for one disease, another disease pops up to take its place."

Wondering whether I was overwhelming the child, I continued. "My pa says a doctor's greatest skill lies in his ability to love, listen to, and care about his patient. And if that's true, Jamie, you're going to make a terrific physician."

Jamie grinned up at me. "Do you think I can help deliver Mrs. Overton's baby when it comes?"

I cleared my throat, trying to bury my smile. *An eight-year-old male midwife—that would take some getting used to.* "I think you'll have to wait a while before you do that, son. But don't worry, if you want to do it badly enough, your turn will come."

While we'd been talking, CeeCee had crawled over to the sofa and dumped the contents of my knitting basket all over the floor. I didn't notice until both she and Hector were decorated like a Christmas tree with yarn of red, green, and blue.

Christmas came and went. Packages arrived from the Putnams and from my family, as well as a bond for Jamie from James's parents.

As the mountain passes filled with snow, the world

outside Columbine faded into insignificance. Noah had an attack of gout. Sheriff Jones complained of bursitis in his knee. The Walsh boy had an ingrown toenail. James and Pete spent evenings at the kitchen table, pouring over diagrams and sketches of the mountain, deciding which direction would lead them to the mother lode. Jamie, his hunger for knowledge apparently insatiable, read every book he could find.

And for me, the biggest change was inside. I started studying the Bible again, for myself. I had come across a text that said something like, "Give thanks in all things." When I tried to find it later, I couldn't. But I did decide to give it a try. The experiment worked until the end of January, when I thought I might be pregnant again. Fortunately, it proved to be a false alarm, so I didn't have to put the text to the ultimate test.

At the end of January, James sent Pete to the assayer's office in Steamboat Springs with an ore sample. He returned with Gladys's January supply of books and magazines, and letters from Pennsylvania, from Joe in California, from Aunt Bea in Kansas, and from Ian in Boston. I devoured the news like a half-starved kitten.

I was nursing CeeCee when I read Aunt Bea's letter. She told about an outbreak of smallpox in Hays. "The disease has swept the county. One out of every four or five stricken has died, children mainly. I've heard rumor that the outbreaks have been far worse in the East and far West, especially the cities."

My hungry baby wrapped her tiny fingers around my finger. I smiled and studied her healthy, glowing eyes. *For once, I feel grateful for the mountains that protect and separate us from the rest of the world.*

Two weeks later, I'd just put CeeCee down for her afternoon nap and taken the bread from the oven to cool when I heard a knock at the door.

One of the Chinese mule skinners stood at the door wringing his hands and bowing. "Must come. Indian Pete very, very sick at his cabin. Very high fever."

"Of course." I glanced about the room. I couldn't leave CeeCee unattended. "Can you go up to the mine and get my husband while I change clothes?"

The man nodded and hurried toward the mining office. *Influenza? Pneumonia?* All terrifying words when applied to a friend. I'd just slipped into my heavy linsey-woolsey dress when James burst into the cabin. "Ho Soong says Pete's sick and you need me. Is that right?"

Distracted, I rushed about, collecting everything I might need to help our friend. "Yes. I couldn't leave CeeCee here alone. Perhaps, if you're too busy at the office, you can take her to stay with Mrs. Jones or Ula while I'm gone."

He nodded. "I'll have Ho take you to Pete's cabin while I stay home with the baby. I can work here as well as at the office this afternoon. I wondered why Pete didn't show up at the mine this morning."

When I arrived at Pete's one-room cabin, I hopped down from the wagon and instructed Ho to wait for me. Running up to the door, I pounded with my fist on the heavy alder door. "Pete, it's me. Chloe. I heard you're sick. Open up."

I heard him shuffle to the door and open it a crack. One bloodshot eye appeared. "Go away, Chloe. I don't want to expose you. I think I have influenza."

"Nonsense." I pushed the door open wide. "You need my help, and you're going to get it. Now get back in bed where you belong, and let me figure out what's wrong."

The fire had died in the fireplace. I shuddered in the heavy chill of the room. The only available light came through a small window next to the door. I asked Pete about his symptoms as I hustled him back to his cot—headaches, fever, and backaches. "When did you start feeling sick?" I asked, pressing my wrist against his fore-head.

"On Friday." He sat up, leaning on one elbow. "What's today?"

"It's Monday, Pete."

"I've got to go to work. James is expecting me." He bolted upright and tried to stand.

I forced him back down on the cot. "Oh, no, you don't! You stay right where you are."

The first thing I had to do was break his fever. After locating a metal tub, I called to Ho and asked him to fill it with snow. I started a fire in the fireplace while I waited. Then I prepared a pot of sage tea to help break the fever.

Getting Pete to remove his undershirt took the skills of a diplomat. Finally, I tossed the shirt, saturated with sweat, to the floor. That's when I saw them—angry red lesions on his arms and chest. I took a deep breath. *This is hardly a case of influenza. I think I may be looking at my first case of smallpox.* The voice inside me emphasized "first case," for if Pete had been exposed, there was a good chance others in Columbine had been too, including Ho and me.

A thump at the door drew me back to my first concern, getting Pete's fever down. I ran to the door and opened it so Ho could carry in the tub of snow. "Ho, there's a canvas tarp in the back of the wagon. Bring it in, please. We're going to need to lay Pete on the tarp, then surround his body with snow to bring his fever down. Do you understand?"

The man nodded and went for the tarp. Pete had over-heard my instructions. As I approached his cot, he shook his head. "No, no."

One glance at his face, and I started to laugh. "Pete, relax. If you promise to cooperate, I will step outside the cabin while Ho wraps you in the canvas. Then once the fever has broken, I'll go back outside while Ho gets you back into bed."

Pete's face, already suffused with color from the fever, flushed to scarlet. I sighed and shook my head. "Is that satisfactory?"

He nodded.

Once the fever broke and I had forced three cups of sage tea into him, Pete fell asleep. I turned toward Ho. "I hate to tell you this, but you and I have been exposed to what I think is smallpox, which means we need to be quarantined."

The Chinese man's eyes widened in fright. He turned to charge from the cabin. I intercepted him at the door. "No, you can't go. You'll expose other people if you do. All we can do now is wait until James comes up here to find out what's wrong."

Ho slunk over to the corner by the hearth and sat down. I sat in a straight-back chair, the only chair in the cabin, and rested my head in my hands. I remembered my father talking about a smallpox epidemic in '85. Twenty percent of those contracting the disease, mostly children, died. *If I'm right, I can't risk exposing Jamie and CeeCee to the disease.* While I could remember the symptoms from one of Pa's medical books, I couldn't recall what he used for treatment.

I can't go wrong if I make a paste of Epsom salts and cream of tartar to ease the rash. Ho eyed me suspiciously as I stood up from the table and walked over to the cupboard where Pete kept his belongings. I tried to explain. "I'm looking for a piece of paper, a pen, and ink. I need to make a list of things we'll need during the next few days." I didn't tell Ho that it might be weeks before we were free to leave the building.

I found what I'd been looking for on a shelf next to three massive law books. Returning to the table, I compiled my list: Epsom salts, cream of tartar, oatmeal, milk, a change of clothing a day.

When I heard a horse whinny, I ran to the door and forced myself to give James the dreadful news. I sensed Ho standing close behind me, listening to every word.

"Don't come any closer, James. There's an excellent chance that Pete has smallpox. I've made a list of things I'll need—"

My husband stopped fifteen feet from the door. "I already know about the smallpox. Half the town of Hahn's Peak is down with it. The doctor in Steamboat Springs can't come to help because so many are sick there."

"What? How in the world did it reach Hahn's Peak so fast?"

James shrugged. "The miners brought it back after the holidays. Anyway, the sheriff of Hahn's Peak came out personally to the mine to fetch you since you're the only medical person for miles around. He's set up a hospital in Whitey's Bar. It's the largest in town."

Before I could say a word, James added, "Of course, I don't want you within ten miles of this epidemic."

"It's too late for that. Ho and I have already been exposed. Besides, someone has to take care of these people, including our friend Pete."

"Pete? How's he doing?"

"Sleeping now. His fever broke."

"Good." James paced back and forth in the snow. "What about the children? Ula is with them right now. I sent Paddy, the foreman, after her."

"Good. I think it would be best if Ho and I take Pete to Whitey's Bar to be cared for with the rest of the smallpox victims. I'll need you to be my outside connection for supplies each day and for—" I had difficulty saying it. "Disposal of the bodies." I was talking about friends, people I knew, possibly even Pete. "If the healthy men in town will dig the graves, Ho and I will drag the bodies to the grave and cover them. We'll use our own shovel."

My calm, matter-of-fact voice steadied my husband's nerves. I ached to hold him in my arms and kiss away the furrows in his brow. *CeeCee.* I pressed my hand on the bodice of my dress. *She's still nursing.*

"James? How will I nurse CeeCee?"

He lifted his hat with one hand and ran the other through his hair. "Ula was coaxing her to drink from a bottle when I left."

"Oh." Suddenly the realization that I might not survive washed over me, and tears filled my eyes. *I may never see my baby again. I may never hold James in my arms or kiss Jamie on the forehead as he sleeps or . . .*

"Hey," James encouraged, "none of that. We're going to get through this together, you hear?"

I nodded.

"Now give me a list of the things you'll be needing. I'll bring them down to the bar this evening."

I watched until James disappeared around the bend of the road. Reluctantly, I stepped back inside the cabin, leaned against the door, and closed my eyes.

"We're ready to go now," Ho announced. I opened my eyes to find Ho standing in front of me, supporting the fully dressed Pete.

"But, I . . ." I glanced around the cabin. Ho had collected my medical supplies and placed them back in the case. There was nothing left to do but ride to Hahn's Peak before the sun set.

Ho placed Pete's cot in the wagon bed, spread out a blanket on the floor of the wagon, then helped Pete aboard. Once I was certain Pete was as comfortable as possible, I climbed up on the seat next to Ho, and we headed for Hahn's Peak.

As we passed the mine and our cabin, I saw Jamie's tear-stained face pressed to the kitchen window. I waved and forced a smile. Jamie returned my wave. The drive through Columbine was equally depressing. My friends stood in their doorways and shouted encouragement to us. Noah came out of his cabin and flagged us down. He carried his tattered Bible in one hand and a small valise in the other.

"I'm going with you," the old man said.

"No, Noah. I can't let you do that." I waved him back.

He strode up to the side of the wagon. "Either take me in the wagon with you, or I'll walk to town on my own."

I sighed and made room on the seat beside me.

Noah introduced himself to Ho. "The best thing we can do is to get organized. Mrs. McCall, you will give the orders while Ho and I carry them out. We'll have three shifts round the clock, two on duty at a time, while one sleeps."

I stared in amazement at the usually mild-mannered, soft-spoken man. He chuckled. "Sorry. I was a lieutenant in the Union army during the war. I got used to giving orders."

"No, that's perfectly fine. I appreciate it. I just never imagined . . ."

He winked at me. "Ula has to keep me in line every now and then."

Ho nodded and smiled. I could tell he felt better about the situation having a man in charge instead of a nineteen-year-old woman. *I feel the same way!*

The situation at the bar was worse than I imagined. The stench of sweat-and-urine-soaked sheets filled the room. Twelve cots lined the east wall; thirteen, once Ho brought in Pete's. The sick ranged in age from a two-year-old boy to a fifty-seven-year-old miner. On the other side of the room an area had been partitioned off for the three female patients—an eight year old, a crib girl of perhaps fourteen, and a thirty-seven-year-old mother of five.

My gaze rose to the wall over the bar. Someone had

turned the massive gilt-framed painting to face the wall. I could only imagine the subject of the painting. I planted my hands on my hips and announced, "First, we need to clean this place up. Ho, boil water, lots of it. Open the doors and windows to air out the place; then go through everything for some clean bedding." I shook my head in disgust. "Noah, I need you to bathe and dress the male patients in clean clothes after I examine them. I'll care for the women myself. When my husband arrives with the supplies I requested, we can begin actually treating them."

During the next two weeks the number of patients grew in spite of the deaths. The three of us worked endlessly as maid, cook, doctor, water boy, pastor, and undertaker. Ho's good humor never faded, even when performing the most gruesome tasks. He had a Chinese saying for every situation, and his legends and folk tales entertained us for hours.

Noah was my steadying rock of strength. Whenever I pulled night duty with him, I listened from the women's side of the room while he read the Word of God aloud to the grateful patients. One night, as I handed him a cup of mint tea, I mused aloud, "Isn't it interesting that their favorite scripture seems to be the story of Job—outside of Psalm 23, of course. They must feel akin to him, don't you think?"

Noah nodded and sighed. "Don't we all, especially when a disaster like this occurs?"

"I suppose so." I sipped the hot liquid. "You know, I never told you how much you helped me put God into a proper perspective last year."

The old man smiled, his eyes misting with emotion. "I'm glad. God has a special purpose for your life, young lady. Maybe not China, but it is still special indeed."

I started in surprise. "How did you know about China?"

He laughed. "Ula, of course."

The next morning, Abby, the crib girl, died, along with

the two-year-old boy. By midafternoon, a grieving man arrived carrying his son, a boy around Jamie's age. The boy's mother had died two days earlier.

"I can't take care of him," the man wailed. "I already killed his mother. I don't want to kill Lucas too."

Noah tried to comfort the man, but he was inconsolable. The man explained that there were three younger children still at home who hadn't come down with the disease.

That was the day Pete took a turn for the better. Within days, he was up and around, relieving the rest of us of some of our duties. Whenever he was off duty, I knew I could find him either sleeping or sitting by Lucas, telling him tales about his days of fur trapping in the Northwest.

One night soon after Lucas's arrival at the emergency hospital, the child's fever soared. Though I did everything I could to keep the child comfortable and dry, sleep was impossible for the miserable boy.

After I had settled the patients down for the night, I wrapped myself in my quilt and pulled up a chair near Lucas's cot and listened while Pete diverted the boy by instructing him on the precise art of killing and cleaning a deer carcass. I shuddered with revulsion at the thought of anyone killing the beautiful animals. I'd often seen them feeding in the meadows near Columbine.

Observing my disgust, Pete arched a knowing eyebrow. "When it's a matter of survival, you would be surprised at what a body is willing to do."

I looked forward each morning and evening to James's arrival with supplies. Shouting back and forth across the street was frustrating—but better than no communication at all. His visits relieved my anxiety over Jamie's and CeeCee's health.

"It's lonely at the cabin without you," James admitted. "Jamie's been worried about you. He begged to come with me to help."

My little doctor-to-be. How many times did I do the same thing with Pa only to hear the same answer?

"And CeeCee?"

"She's doing beautifully. The child adores Ula."

My smile faded—that wasn't what I wanted to hear. I scraped my fingernail at a loose chip of paint on the doorjamb. I missed her terribly. Though I didn't want her wailing night and day for me, I did want her to miss me— at least a little.

Our number of patients dwindled during the first week of March. By the second week of the month, the four of us made plans to return to our homes. We disinfected the premises and ourselves thoroughly, then took one last look around the empty barroom that had been our home for almost a month.

During that time we'd performed tasks so repulsive I paled at the remembrance. We ate enough oatmeal for each of us to swear off the cereal for the rest of our lives. We prayed our way through never-ending, bone-weary nights. We scrubbed our knuckles bare, trying to keep ahead of the germs. And we wept when our efforts failed. As eager as I was to leave, I knew that once I walked out the door to meet James and the children, nothing would be the same between Ho, Pete, Noah, and myself. The ugly cultural barriers would divide us, no matter how hard we tried to prevent it.

I could tell the others, too, were reluctant to leave. The evening before, Ho had mentioned that he planned to return to his father's house in Hong Kong. "Family is more important to me now than it was when I ran away to make my fortune," he admitted. Each of us knew that when we left the building, we would never all be together again.

Noah knew how to handle the farewell. He opened his Bible to Proverbs 18. "There is a friend that sticketh closer than a brother." Noah nodded toward me. "And a sister.

With the help of the good Lord, we lost some battles, but we won many more."

Ho, a lifelong Buddhist, said, "Can we pray together one more time?"

We joined hands. Noah's gnarled fingers grasped my red, chapped hand. I took hold of one of Ho's hands, rough with callouses and scars. Pete's large, strong hands completed the circle.

Formally, Ho bowed in front of me. "Goodbye, dear sister. You are a diamond in your husband's crown, a truly remarkable woman." Coming from a mule skinner who until a few weeks before had viewed the female sex as little better than the mules in his team, his compliment brought tears to my eyes.

I bowed graciously. "Farewell, dear brother, I will treasure the memory of you in my heart."

He turned to Pete. "Dear brother, your heart is made of a purer gold than you'll ever find in the side of a mountain."

Uncomfortable with the praise, Pete bowed awkwardly. "Thank you, Ho. I'll never forget you. You truly are my brother and one unbelievable storyteller."

Last, Ho bowed to Noah. "Dear spiritual father, may your home be filled with peace and prosperity. You have made your God, my God. I will take Him with me, always."

Noah bowed properly, then cast aside all Oriental formality by throwing his arms around the startled young man. "Son, I'm gonna miss you, but it's good you're going home to make peace with your father. Here." He placed the Bible in Ho's hands. "Let this guide you the rest of the way home to your heavenly Father."

Going home. Making peace with my father. Noah had spoken to my heart. I glanced away and dabbed a linen handkerchief at my tears. *Will I ever go home, Lord? Will Pa ever accept me back in his heart again?*

Goodwill
Comes in All Sizes

"Mommy! Over here. We're over here." Jamie hopped up and down in the back of the wagon when I stepped out of the bar into the sunlight. It looked like the entire population of the town had assembled to welcome Ho, Noah, Pete, and me out of quarantine. Their faces and greetings were a blur, for my attention was on the faces of my family. James pushed his way through the crowd, swept me into his arms, and twirled me in a circle.

"James," I laughed, "put me down. Everyone's watching."

"Who cares?" He nuzzled my neck. "It feels so good to have you in my arms again. You've lost weight. Are you feeling all right?"

"I'm feeling fabulous. You'd lose weight too if you had to dine on oatmeal, oatmeal, and more oatmeal. Now put me down."

"I don't want to let you go—ever!"

"But the children," I argued, pointing toward the wagon.

He set me down, grabbed my hand, and pulled me through the grateful crowd of people.

"Mommy!" Jamie leaped from the wagon into my arms. I staggered under the impact.

I hugged him, then lowered him to the ground.

Jamie glared at his father. "I wanted to come help you,

but Daddy wouldn't let me."

"Oh, sweetheart." I knelt down to his height. "I missed you terribly too, and I'm sure you would have been a big help, but I needed you even more at home to help Mrs. VanArsdale with CeeCee."

I turned toward my precious daughter. She'd grown so much in the time I was gone. With eager arms, I reached for her. "Here, doll baby, come to Mommy."

My carrot-topped daughter took one look at me, screwed up her face, and wailed into Ula's shoulder. Frantic, I turned toward my husband, then back toward Ula. I had yearned for this moment every night I'd been away, and now she was rejecting me.

"There, there, CeeCee. It's all right. It's your mommy, remember?" Ula patted CeeCee's bottom, then eased the child's face from her shoulder. CeeCee eyed me suspiciously. "Give her time, Chloe. She's at that age, you know. Don't worry, she'll remember."

Silently, I asked, *But what if you're wrong?* Before we'd dropped Ula and Noah off at their cabin, I held a contented CeeCee in my arms.

Beside me, Ula coaxed CeeCee to show me her two new teeth. "Come on, sweetheart, open your mouth for Grandma Ula."

As Ula disembarked from the wagon, she turned. " 'Bye 'bye, CeeCee. Be good for your mommy, won't you?"

My chubby-faced baby stared in horror, first at me, then at the departing Ula. "Mama!" The resulting wail echoed across the valley. Tears streamed down my face as I clutched her wriggling body. It was the first time she said "mama"—and she said it to another woman.

James came to my rescue. "Here, CeeCee, here. Come to Daddy. Say 'bye 'bye like a good girl to Grandma Ula." He shouted to me over her screams. "Drive the wagon, Chloe. I'll hold her. You just drive the wagon."

I shook the reins over the horse's back. The wagon lurched forward. My hands controlled the horse's reins better than my brain managed to rein in my emotions. *This is not how I imagined my homecoming! I sacrifice my home and my family, risking my very life, and what happens, Lord? It isn't fair. My daughter, my only daughter, calls another woman "mama."*

Long before my emotions quieted, CeeCee settled down in her father's lap, contented to play with the buttons on his wool jacket. I stopped the wagon in front of the cabin. James handed the baby to Jamie, hopped down, then helped me from the wagon. Taking CeeCee from Jamie's hands, James led us into the cabin. Rags bounded around the corner of the house, leaping and barking his welcome. I reached down and patted him. *At least you remember me, old friend.*

Pausing in the doorway, I took in the sight and smell of home. I loved my little cabin, cramped and homely as it might be, but I hadn't realized how much until that moment. James set CeeCee down on the rag rug in front of the sofa and handed her a rattle. Rags skidded to a stop in front of the baby, licking her face, from chin to hair line. When I started to protest, James turned and smiled.

"Welcome home, darling. I almost feel like I should carry you across the threshold or something."

I laughed. "It's a little late for that."

"Jamie, watch the baby for a few minutes while Mama and I talk in the bedroom." To me, he added, "You've got to watch the little scamp every minute now that she's begun crawling. I had the blacksmith make that screen to keep her away from the fire in the fireplace."

I glanced at the screen and at CeeCee. *She's crawling too?*

"Ula says she'll be walking before her birthday the rate she's going."

I sniffed back a fresh supply of tears. "If I'm lucky, I may get to see her take her first steps, maybe even be around to see her walk down the aisle as a bride!"

James threw back his head and laughed. "Chloe Mae, aren't you being a little dramatic?"

"Imagine how I feel, hearing my daughter utter 'mama' for the first time, but having her say it to another woman."

He cleared his throat. "Er, she's been saying 'mama' and 'dada' for a couple of weeks now. Babies develop quickly, you know."

"A couple of weeks?" I sank onto the edge of the bed, staring at the window on the other side of the room. "A couple of weeks!"

Certain I'd been delivered life's cruelest blow, I wrapped my arms about me and rocked back and forth in agony. James sat down, engulfing me in his arms. "Come on, Chloe. Sure, you missed a small part of your child's life, but it isn't as bad as all that. I feel so blessed that our family survived the epidemic unscathed. Considering all that could have happened, I'd say we're very fortunate indeed."

I knew he was right. Of course he was right. But my perverse nature refused to acknowledge the fact aloud. I wanted to punish someone for my pain, and since he was closest—

By evening, CeeCee accepted me almost as naturally as she had before I left. However, James and I took longer to adjust to my return. We'd both grown accustomed to thinking independently of the other and would snap at each other over the most trivial of things.

Late one afternoon, Jamie and I packed CeeCee in a wheelbarrow and headed down the road toward town, hoping to find some herbs to replenish my stock. Both Jamie and I treasured our herb searches. Patches of snow still dotted the woods, but tiny alpine flowers blanketed sunny open places.

At one spot, we left the wheelbarrow beside the road. I set CeeCee in an over-the-shoulder sling that rested on my hip, and we set out through the woods in search of what remedies the forest had to offer.

"Mama," Jamie said. "I'm glad you're home again. I missed you lots. So did Daddy."

I glanced up from the root I'd been digging. "I missed you too, son."

"Daddy does love you, you know. He won't go away again. He promised, remember?"

I dropped my trowel and turned toward my son. The haunted look in his eyes had returned. "Oh, Jamie, your dad and I love each other very much. No one is going away. And I'm sorry. It's my fault too, you know, if we've been fighting too much."

He dropped his gaze to the ground.

I tilted his face up toward mine. "Remember, it takes two to make an argument."

That night, in the living room, James and I talked about our son's observation, then prayed together. As we got up from our knees, James took me into his arms. "He's quite the kid, you know, that boy of ours."

"You can say that again." I ran my fingers through the mat of dark curls peeking out above his open-neck shirt. "I do love you, totally and unconditionally. And I know you love me. Now all we have to do is convince our son of that."

"Well, you can start by kissing me."

"Oh, James," I cooed softly.

He tipped his face toward mine. "Don't look now, but our son is spying on us from the loft," he whispered. His eyes sparkled as he captured my face with his hands and kissed me soundly. As our lips parted, he hissed, "We should consider adding on a couple of rooms for the children this summer, for our privacy, not theirs!"

I looked at my husband through misty eyes. The thought that we would be staying in Colorado throughout the summer didn't register.

As the incredible Rocky Mountain springtime performed her pageant of beauty beyond my front door, the idea bothered me less and less. Beside the house, I planted the vegetable seeds I'd saved all winter. I didn't know if they'd actually grow, but I was going to try anyway.

About the third week in May I was putting CeeCee down for her afternoon nap when the mine whistle sounded four times. Panic filled me as I rushed toward the door. Before I could open it, James burst into the cabin, lifted me off my feet, and whirled me about. "It's happened! It's happened! We did it!" He set me down and planted a kiss on my lips. "We tapped into the motherlode this morning! It's true, I need to have the sample assayed, but I'm sure we hit it. So, pack your bags, lady, I'm taking you and the kids to Denver!"

"Denver?"

"That's right. Pete is running the sample to Steamboat Springs even as we speak. He'll be back by morning with the results. Then, we're off to Denver." James explained how he would build a steam-powered plant for processing the ore on site. "If we prove right about the ore, Pete will send word to Phineas to set up a meeting with a mining architect. Now I can build you a grand house in Columbine, instead of a small addition on this place. I'll even have them install a bathroom with hot and cold running water, like the one at the ranch!"

His joy spilled over onto me. "Wonderful about the motherlode, but I'm not sure I want to move into town. I like being closer to you and to the action at the mine."

"Are you sure?"

I nodded.

"All right, if you're sure." He gazed about the room. "All

right, but we'll add two rooms and a bath. With the coal I'll need to ship in for operating the processing plant, we can heat the water for our kitchen and bathroom."

"No more baths in a washtub in the middle of the bedroom floor!" I squealed.

The next morning the assayer's report confirmed James's prediction. And later that day we were on the train heading toward Steamboat Springs and Denver. We had a pack of mail waiting for us at Steamboat Springs. In it was a terse letter from my brother Joe, telling me his fiancée Cathy had taken sick and died of influenza.

"I know you or Dad could have saved her," he wrote accusingly. "I feel like I can't go on, Chloe. It's like someone turned out the light inside me, leaving a dark cavern."

My heart reached out to him, but what could I do? I was a thousand miles away. I vowed to write to him as soon as I reached Denver.

The news of the gold strike preceded us. The matrons who earlier had cast disdainful glances toward us now insisted on dropping by Gladys's home to chat over afternoon tea.

There was no other way to describe it; Gladys fell madly in love with CeeCee. CeeCee rewarded Grandma Gladys by taking her first steps in the Putnam atrium.

While James and Phineas drew the plans for the ore processing plant, I luxuriated in civilization—shopping, bathing in a real bathtub, wearing dresses not made of cotton or linsey-woolsey. Jamie spent his days down at the stables. We celebrated CeeCee's first birthday with the Putnams. When it came time for us to leave for Columbine, we all felt the pain.

"Come back for Jamie's birthday or perhaps the Christmas holidays," Gladys suggested as I took CeeCee from her arms. The longing in her eyes brought tears to mine.

James kissed the woman's cheek. "We'll see how far

along the construction is by then."

From that time until Jamie's birthday in October, we talked, ate, and slept construction. My husband hired two contractors, one for the processing mill and the other for the cabin. Crews under both were hammering and sawing every daylight hour possible.

Much to our surprise, Jamie chose to stay in the loft, so James had it enclosed for privacy—ours. The room he'd intended for his son he turned into a small library. Along the way, the carpenters constructed more shelves and cabinets in my kitchen.

With Jamie's birthday came the customary letter from Jamie's father in Boston, begging us to send Jamie to school in the East. James appeased us both by writing back and saying, "Perhaps next year."

On the first day of November, the plant processed the first carload of gold ore. James escorted me through the six levels of the mill.

"The entire process depends on gravity and steam from the boilers at the foot of the hill," he said. "The ore comes from the mine to the crushers, to the stamps—"

I held up my hand. "The crushers I understand, but, please, explain about the stamps."

He pointed to the cages holding the fist-size chunks of rough ore that fell down from the crushers. "The ore drops into the water and is smashed beneath half-ton stamps; then the mixture passes through fine screens." He pointed to the massive pieces of equipment.

"Let's go down to the vanners next." We walked down a long flight of stairs at the far end of the building and entered the third level. I waved and smiled at one of the workers whom I had treated for a barroom injury. Speaking to him would have been impossible over the ear-shattering machine racket.

The vanners were six-foot-wide oscillating belts that winnowed out the lead and some silver. "What remains goes into amalgamated pans to be cooked with mercury and other chemicals for eight hours."

"Like a stew," I shouted and smiled devilishly at my husband.

He snorted. "A stew! Be serious. From here it goes to the settling tanks—out of which the tailings are flushed."

"Tailings?"

He eyed me suspiciously, wondering if I were joking once more. When he decided I must be serious, he answered my question. "That's the worthless slime left over after the ore has been processed. And last, we have the boilers."

We walked outside into the late-autumn sunlight, where I shook my head to clear the worst of the roar from my brain. James slid his arm comfortably around my waist as we strolled to the mining office. "When the plant's in full swing, we expect to process one hundred seventy tons of ore a day."

I turned to study the ugly monster that had come to absorb my husband's every waking thought. I remembered the words my father said every time one of us children envied the Chamberlains' luxury. *If you have food on your table and clothes on your back, and if the boots on your feet aren't full of holes, how much more do you need?*

Operating the mill demanded more and more from my husband. When I mentioned the possibility of going to Denver for the holidays, James shook his head. "I can't possibly go now. We've had a number of breakdowns lately. I don't know what's wrong." I sighed and petted Hector behind the ears. James sighed. "Wildcat strikes have been popping up all over the West. We can't afford to lose even a day. But, of course, you and the children can go if you wish."

I shook my head. "Be away from you at Christmas?

Nonsense! A family belongs together for the holidays. I'll leave CeeCee with Ula and do my shopping in Steamboat Springs."

"If you can arrange to go tomorrow morning, you can go with Pete. He has business at the assayers' office anyway."

I thought about it for a moment. "Hmm, I'd like that. Maybe you and I and the children can go together during the week before Christmas as a special treat."

With the month of December unseasonably warm, the train ride to Steamboat Springs proved delightful, and Pete proved to be a charming escort. It was nice to be around a male who chose to talk about things other than the mill and the mother lode. When we reached Steamboat Springs, Pete took care of his business while I went shopping. We had agreed to meet at the restaurant at noon for lunch.

I sauntered through the shops at my leisure. The purse, swinging from a chain about my wrist, was stuffed with cash. I was a married woman, a matron, an adult allowed to go where I wanted and buy what I liked. I noticed how the shop girls treated me with a new respect. I straightened my back and lifted my chin.

At the hardware store I bought a marble mortar and pestle for Jamie, for grinding up his own herbs. On a nearby shelf, I spotted a set of marble bookends carved in the shape of horses' heads. *James would love those for his office.* He'd complained how his stack of mining books were always tumbling off the edge of his desk onto the floor.

At the men's shop, I bought a new cowboy hat for Jamie, complete with a snakeskin band and red feather, and for James four plaid wool shirts and a pair of dungarees.

I was halfway down my gift list when I heard a whistle blow, announcing the noon break. Gathering up my packages, I hurried toward the restaurant. I breezed through the door into a maelstrom of violence. I could see Pete's sleek dark hair over the heads of the shouting, screaming mob. Cries of "dirty Injun," "string 'im up," and "the only good Injun is a dead Injun" filled the room.

Horrified, I pushed through the crowd. When I reached Pete's side, the restaurant owner turned toward me and snarled, "Are you this Injun's squaw?"

My eyes snapped with fury. "I beg your pardon?"

"Lady, if ya ain't his squaw, you'd better keep that purty lil' nose out of business that don't concern you." The grizzled man stared threateningly, inches from my face. "And if ya are, ya ain't no lady anaways!"

Determined not to flinch, I glared into the angry man's eyes. Without looking away, I let go of my packages. The bags crashed to the floor.

"Yeow!" Both the restaurant owner and I turned to see two men, one on each side of me, dancing in circles and swearing. I smiled to myself—the bookends and the mortar had obviously hit a couple tender toes. The surrounding miners and cowboys broke into laughter at the hapless victims.

Seizing the moment, I turned back to face the restaurant owner. I arched one eyebrow disdainfully, "Would you be so kind as to tell me why my friend is being hassled. We came here intending to eat."

"No Injun eats in my establishment! And no squaws either, red haired or bald." The owner growled. The crowd laughed at his humor.

Pete picked up my packages and growled, "Let's get out of here, Chloe."

A tall, shabbily dressed cowboy shouted, "Someone go git the sheriff. Let these two cool their heels in the slammer for a few hours."

One of the miners in the crowd yelled, "You gonna eat with a dirty Injun? Aren't you afraid of getting lice or something?"

Whirling about to face the source of the remark, I sent him a withering stare, and snarled, "Before you cast aspersions on my friend's hygiene, tell me, when did you last bathe?"

A rumble passed through the crowd. "What'd she say? What in tarnation is hygiene?"

A voice from the doorway called, "She's telling you you're the one who's dirty." The stranger, dressed in an Eastern business suit, wearing a diamond stick pin, and carrying an ivory-headed cane, sniffed the air. "And by the smell of things, she's probably right."

He tapped one of the men on the upper arm. "Now, if you will excuse me, my friends and I intended to dine in this—" He paused and looked about the shabby room. "Charming establishment."

The awed miners parted. The stranger strolled over to me, bowed and tipped his bowler hat. "Sir Godfrey Hansel Harcourt, recently of St. Edmonds, England, at your service, madam."

When I extended my hand to thank him, he took my hand and kissed my fingertips. Flustered with the unusual treatment, I introduced myself, then introduced Pete. After shaking Pete's hand, Sir Harcourt led us to a window table.

Before we sat down, he tossed a small chunk of gold ore to the startled restaurant owner. "Would you be so kind, dear sir, as to wash this tabletop?"

The owner bobbed his head up and down, bowing and backing away. Uncertain after the sudden turn of events, the cowardly mob faded away also. By the time the sheriff burst through the door, waving his gun and shouting for order, we had ordered our meals and were waiting for them to be delivered to the table.

The sheriff strutted arrogantly toward Pete. "So you're the Injun causing this hullabaloo?"

Before the three of us could reply, the owner rushed from the back room, waving his hands nervously in the air. "Sorry, sheriff, just a simple misunderstanding. Everything's under control now."

Sir Harcourt turned toward me and snorted, "Surprising what a little gold can do to a man's scruples, isn't it?"

I nodded. "We really appreciate your coming to our rescue. I hate to think what might have happened in another minute or two."

Pete turned to me. "What were you thinking, charging in here to rescue me like that? You could have been seriously hurt, you know."

"You're my friend. And besides, I didn't think they'd turn on a woman."

Pete shook his head. "While I admit being a woman elevates you a step or two above an Indian on the social ladder, those men still considered you beneath them—and thus fair game."

The owner arrived with our dinners. When I reached for my purse to pay, the stranger waved my money aside. "This is my treat. Seldom in my travels do I manage to dine with a beautiful and intelligent woman as well as a brother."

Pete stared at Sir Harcourt for a moment. The Englishman smiled. "My mother was Nez Percé Indian. My father met her on a hunting expedition to your fair country. He brought her back to England with him, a sad mistake." He cleared his throat. "The snubs and the derision killed her."

As we ate, the men discussed the Renegade Mine and the big strike. After finishing my apple pie, I excused myself. "I have more holiday shopping to do."

The men rose to their feet, and Sir Harcourt pulled back my chair. "Thank you again for coming to our aid. What they say about British gentlemen is true."

When I reached for the packages, Pete told me he'd carry them and that I should meet him back at the station by three. "It's the least I can do after you used them as a lethal weapon. Whatever do you have in there?"

I smiled coyly. "Would you believe a cowboy hat—as well as marble bookends?"

The restaurant owner hurried to the door and opened it for me. I merely nodded and stepped out onto the wooden sidewalk. I finished my shopping in plenty of time to make it to the station before three. With undue haste, I hurried along the row of shops, my earlier innocence replaced with a wariness I'd never before felt.

When I entered the depot, a cold chill skittered along my spine. A pair of cold, hateful eyes stared at me from across the room. *No, it can't be. I must be mistaken. He's long since gone from these parts—hasn't he?* I craned my neck to see past the crowd of travelers waiting to board the afternoon trains. A short, stocky businessman now leaned up against the wall where the bearded man had been standing. I scanned the crowd again, hoping to catch one last glimpse, to assure myself I wasn't becoming paranoid after the day's events. Instead, I spotted Pete walking toward me.

We boarded the little mine train for Hahn's Peak and seated ourselves in the back of the passenger car.

"Do you suffer that kind of indignity often?" I asked.

"Occasionally. I should have known better today—I apologize for that."

"Nonsense! You can't blame yourself for the ill manners of others." I adjusted my woolen scarf about my neck, then settled back against the seat. To change the subject, I asked, "So whatever was Sir Harcourt doing in Steamboat Springs, Colorado?"

Pete took out a business card and handed it to me. "He's hoping to buy a few established mines. He told me to have James contact him if you folks decide to sell any time in the near future."

I handed the card back to Pete. "You'd better tell James

yourself. If I do, he'll interpret it as henpecking."

Pete laughed and tucked the card in his jacket pocket.

As promised, a week before Christmas, James took me and the children to Steamboat Springs so Jamie could do his Christmas shopping. Jamie taught CeeCee "Jingle Bells" during the train ride. For the rest of the day, the little girl sang the words "jingle bells" to her own singsong melody.

Before it was time to head back home, we dropped off our packages at the train station. That's when James suggested we walk to the restaurant to eat. I knew which restaurant he had in mind, and I knew the children were hungry—but the thought of returning to the place where Pete and I were accosted made me almost physically ill. On the boardwalk outside the restaurant, I fought back the urge to turn and run. I might have run if James hadn't trapped my hand on his arm.

"You can do it, Chloe girl. Never let the bullies of life win! Or you'll live out your days in a shadow of fear." James lifted CeeCee in his arms and held the door open for me.

"At which table did you sit?" he whispered.

I averted my eyes from the rough-looking miners glancing our way. "The table by the window."

Without a word, James led us to the table, set CeeCee on one of the chairs, motioned Jamie to another, and then pulled out a third chair for me. Once we were all seated, the owner came to our table. His eyes rested for a moment on my red hair, then drifted down to my face. A look of recognition flashed across his face.

James diverted the man's attention. "Tell me, what is your special today?"

The man glanced nervously toward me, then back at James. "The menu's on the wall. We ain't no fancy Eastern establishment, mister."

James smiled graciously. "Oh, I can see that." After reading the menu, we placed our order. The food arrived fast and hot. The mountain of mashed potatoes and gravy on my platter made me almost forget my discomfort. CeeCee enjoyed the miniature mound of potatoes I placed on a saucer in front of her.

When the owner came to the table with our check, James reached into his pocket, pulled out a ten-dollar bill, and handed it to him. "Keep the change, sir."

I shot a surprised look at my husband. So did the owner, since our total hadn't come to even four dollars.

My husband stood up and shook the stunned man's hand. "I just want to thank you, sir, for coming to the aid of my wife and best friend a few weeks ago. It's a dirty shame good, honest women can't feel safe in our streets today." His heavy baritone voice filled the suddenly quiet restaurant. As he assisted me to my feet, I avoided looking at the other customers. "It falls to you and me, as gentlemen, to maintain that fine line between civilization and savagery, don't you agree?"

The owner bobbed his head up and down, fidgeting the ten-dollar bill between his thumb and forefinger. James put CeeCee on one arm, then patted the man's shoulder with his free hand. "Keep up the good work, sir."

I choked back an overwhelming urge to burst with laughter until we reached the sidewalk. "James, how could you? You gave the poor man heart failure."

Jamie tugged at my sleeve, his eyes dancing with amusement. "Did you see the sick look on his face when he recognized you, Mama?"

We stepped off the boardwalk and minced our way across the muddy street on the irregular pathway of narrow planks. When we reached the other side, I glanced back at the restaurant for a moment.

"I think I dropped the packages on the toes of the bearded

man in the back corner, the one wearing the leather vest and dirty brown felt hat."

"I wish you'd said something while we were in there. I would have—"

Before he could complete his statement, I interrupted coyly, "And why do you think I waited until we were outside the restaurant to tell you?"

In the Chill of Winter

The holidays disappeared amid a flurry of snowflakes. With Jamie back at school and James preoccupied with the mine, I spent time cooking, caring for the house, and enjoying CeeCee. And during CeeCee's afternoon naps, I knitted and woolgathered like I'd seen my mother do so many times during my childhood. Perhaps for the same reason, for I believed I might be pregnant again. This time the thought pleased me.

The evening I planned to tell James of my suspicions, he guessed. CeeCee was in bed for the night, Jamie was at the table making a map of South America for his geography class, and I'd just finished the dinner dishes. As I lifted the apron over my head, James stepped up behind me, turned me gently, and kissed me.

An avalanche of love tumbled over me as I gazed into his sparkling eyes. I caressed his cheek. When I started to speak, he said, "Let's take a walk in the snow."

I nodded eagerly. After putting on his coat, he helped me into mine. Rags whined to go with us, but James told him to stay with Jamie. We stepped out of the cabin into a magical world of silence and starlight. A fresh, clean layer of snow blanketed the ugly man-made scars on the side of the mountain. Even the machinery at the mill had been shut down for repairs. I hugged my coat about me and skipped through the snow, sending showers of powder before me.

James caught up with me, laughing. "You remind me of a filly my father once owned." He wrapped his arm about my shoulders as we strolled in the crisp night air. "I loved watching her cavort across the field, tossing her mane in the wind."

One at a time I removed the hairpins from my hair, allowing it to tumble down around my shoulders. Thanks to the fire, I had discovered that shorter hair was much easier to maintain, and more comfortable, with no heavy braid tugging at the back of my neck.

"You know, the last few days, you've been acting mighty suspicious," James remarked.

"Oh?" I lifted one eyebrow and smiled up at him.

"I've thought and thought about what could bring such a sparkle to your eyes and a glow to your face. I can only think of one thing, Mrs. McCall." He placed his hand on my stomach. "You aren't pregnant again, are you?"

"I-I-I'm not sure. I hope so. Would you be happy if I were?"

He drew me into his arms and buried his face in my hair. "Would I be happy? I'd be delighted. What a question to ask!"

The rough wool texture of his jacket caressed my cheek, and I inhaled the clean aroma of shaving cream and laundry soap. At that moment I realized there was nowhere on earth I'd rather be than standing on the side of a Colorado mountain in the arms of the man I loved.

"So the newest member of the McCall family should arrive sometime in September?" he asked.

"I guess." I tightened my hold on him.

"What would you say if I told you we might be living in Denver by then? Would you like that? I figure by June I can leave the mine in Pete's hands."

"In Denver?" I pulled back and looked up into his face.

"Nothing as elaborate as Gladys and Phineas's home perhaps, but nice—comfortable. Or would you prefer to rebuild the ranch? Or perhaps, move east to Boston so Jamie wouldn't have to be so far away from home?"

My mind reeled. I hadn't thought about leaving Columbine in months. In spite of the ugliness of the mine, in spite of the primitive conditions, in spite of the isolation, out of necessity it had become my home. I couldn't think of a reply.

"Well?"

I turned away from him and walked to a spot that overlooked the valley. "I don't know. Do I have to decide tonight?"

I felt his arms slip around my waist and draw me back against him. He bent and kissed the tip of my right ear. "You don't have to do anything you don't want to do tonight, my love." Our two silhouettes blended into one as we gazed at the distant lights of Hahn's Peak.

Unfortunately, the next morning my joy was turned to disappointment, for I discovered there would be no baby born to us—at least not in September. When I told James the disappointing news, he held me in his arms and kissed away my tears. "Hey, why the tears? There'll be another time." I nodded and buried my face in his shirt.

One icy February day I was making bread at the kitchen table. CeeCee stood on the chair across from me, kneading her little batch of dough, when the mining whistle sounded—one, two, three, four. Four whistles meant trouble down below. The mining engineers James had brought in from Denver had been dynamiting all morning, so I hadn't even glanced up from the dough when a larger boom rattled the dishes in my cupboard.

Again four whistles in rapid succession. I threw on my

coat, wrapped CeeCee in my shawl, and ran out of the cabin. I got only as far as the porch before returning for my medicine bag.

"What's happened?" I shouted at a miner as I neared the mine office.

"Explosion! Main shaft is blown."

"Main . . ." I gulped back my panic. *What was it James told me this morning?* I was only half-listening. Dressing CeeCee had taken all my attention and dexterity. *Didn't he say he'd be working in the main shaft today?*

I held my daughter tighter and ran up the steps into the office. "Pete! Pete! What's happening?"

A sandy-haired young man whom I'd never met jumped up from the desk when I barged into the room. "I'm sorry ma'am, Indian Pete and Mr. McCall are up top."

"Oh." Wobbly with relief, I sank into the nearest chair. "Then Mr. McCall is safe."

"I couldn't say, ma'am. I just arrived from Steamboat Springs with the weekly report."

"But you said . . ." I put CeeCee down on the chair beside me.

The man shrugged. "Well, I just meant they're not here. So where else would they be during an emergency?"

As the whistle again blew four warning blasts, the man strode across the room. "If you'll excuse me, ma'am, I'd better get up top, too, to see what I can do to help."

"No!" I stood to my feet and barred the door with my arm. "You are going to stay right here and take care of my daughter while I go up top." I held up my medicine bag in my hand. "I'm a physician. I will be of much better use than you at this moment."

"But, ma'am—"

"What did you say your name was?" I leveled at him my most threatening glare. "Oh, and did I mention that my name is Mrs. McCall? Mrs. James McCall?"

He blew the air out of his cheeks slowly. "No, ma'am, you didn't. And I'll be glad to watch over your little girl. And my name is Sven, Sven Jorghensen."

"Thank you." I turned toward my daughter. "CeeCee, this is Sven. He's going to stay with you while I go help Daddy. You stay right here in this office and be a good girl, promise?"

CeeCee glanced shyly at the young man, then nodded slowly. I opened the door. "Stay right here with her, Sven, until either James, Indian Pete, or I return. Do you understand?"

"Yes, ma'am. I understand."

I ran from the office and over to the processing mill. Once the mill was built, getting to the mine shaft meant only climbing a dozen flights of stairs—a great improvement over riding up on the old ore tram. The mill stood empty of workers, but the noisy machines continued grinding, hammering, and groaning. When I reached the top, I fought to catch my breath. Pushing my way through the crowd of workers, I spotted Pete's dark hair, head and shoulders above the other men.

"Pete! Pete!" I rushed to his side. "What's happened? Where's James?" I searched the crowd for my husband's face. "Is he working down below with the rescue team? Are there any injuries?"

Pete took my elbow and led me away from the area. I struggled to break free, but he held tight. One look in Pete's eyes, and the old nightmare returned. I knew James was behind the wall of debris.

"Wait. I can't go anywhere. I've got to find James. He needs me." I could hear myself babbling, but I couldn't stop. "Pete, let me find my husband. I must help my husband."

"Chloe, stop. You can't do anything right now. We're doing all we can to reach the men."

"But you will reach them. Like last time, when Otis

kicked the supports, you'll dig them out, right?"

Pete shook his head slowly. "This isn't the same. I'd just gone to check with the mining engineers working on the other side of the clearing when I heard the explosion. I don't know what went wrong." He ran his fingers through his hair in frustration. "They weren't using explosives in the main shaft today. There'd been no gas leaks or any other warning of danger."

I squeezed my eyes shut. "What are you trying to tell me, Pete?"

"I'm telling you that I don't know what happened down there. And I don't know how far away from the explosion James and the other miners were when she blew."

"You are going to work under the assumption that they are safe and alive, aren't you?"

He took a deep breath. "Our problem is, the elevator was destroyed. Men are using the old ore buckets, going down eight at a time. Paddy is down there supervising the rescue team until I can relieve him."

I nodded slowly. My fingernails dug into the palms of my hands. "Go to him, Pete. Find James. Please find James for me."

Pete frowned and pounded a fist in the palm of his other hand. "I'll do everything I can."

"I know you will."

"In the meantime, pray." He sprinted back to the shaft house, disappearing into the crowd of miners.

Pray? What do you think I've been doing from the moment I first heard the whistles blow? I stumbled back down the stairs to the mining office, thanked Sven for caring for CeeCee, then hurried to the mining kitchen. At the very least I could help prepare and serve food to the exhausted miners.

Sometime during the afternoon Jamie, Ula, and Noah arrived to help. When the first men came out of the mine,

I was kept busy cleaning and bandaging their wounds. I tried to shut the bad news from my mind as the men related the condition of the mine shaft.

Noah urged me to take CeeCee home, but I refused. "I want to be right here when James . . ." My words died away into a whisper.

Noah nodded. "Then I'm staying right here with you." Jamie also insisted on staying and helping while Ula took CeeCee back to the cabin.

One old miner shook his head. "I've seen a lot of cave-ins and accidental explosions during my life, but it was as if someone deliberately meant to blow the shaft, to close it up forever."

The miner sitting across the table from him said, "I've never been so glad to get top side before in my life. The walls are so unsteady; I would not be surprised if the whole place gives way."

Jamie, who'd been serving pancakes and hot coffee to the men, sidled over to me. "Dad is all right, isn't he, Mama?"

I bit my lip and closed my eyes. "I hope so, son. I desperately hope so."

"Poor CeeCee," Jamie whispered, "she probably won't remember Daddy at all."

I whirled about, fire darting from my eyes. "James Edward McCall, don't you say that! Your father is going to be all right. He has to be all right."

The room fell silent. The embarrassed miners stared into their cups of coffee. Jamie whimpered, "I'm sorry, Mommy."

Let me out of here! I've got to get out of here! I heard someone moan. I grabbed my coat and fled the building into the gathering darkness. I ran to the spot where James and I had shared the anticipation of the child who would never exist.

Falling against a tree stump, I wailed, my voice echoing across the valley. "No, Lord, no. I can bear anything but this." Hearing steps approaching behind me, I swiped at my tears with my sleeve.

"It's all right to cry, you know."

I recognized Noah's voice. "I'm sorry. I know you expect me to be strong."

" 'God's strength is made perfect in weakness.' You still hold the most powerful tool for James's rescue—prayer and faith."

I wrapped my arms about myself and shivered. "And if God says No?"

Noah stared out over the valley. "One step at a time."

Noah stayed silently beside me as the sky turned from crimson to indigo. Only the lights on the hill behind us disturbed the tranquility of the evening. An hour passed before I could face returning to the camp kitchen and my son, Jamie.

When the second rescue team returned, I hurried back. There'd be injuries to treat. As I entered the room, Jamie ran to me and buried his face in my dress. I knelt down and held him close.

Throughout the night, rescue teams came and went. With each team, the men spoke less and less about the operation. I blamed the silence on their increasing exhaustion. At one point, the pot of hot coffee I was carrying crashed to the floor when I heard a miner mention the name of Otis Roy. But when I hurried over to question him, the man blanched and refused to say more.

I staggered against the table as the memory of Otis's face in the crowd at Steamboat Springs sprang up before me. *No, James, could I have been responsible for this because I didn't tell you? "Oh, I couldn't bear such a thought, Lord."*

At dawn, Pete and Paddy stumbled into the camp kitchen. One look at Pete's face, and I knew. I knew. I filled their cups with hot coffee, then walked to the window and stared up at the dancing lights on top of the hill. *"Though I walk*

*through the valley of the shadow of death, I will fear no evil:
for thou art with me, thy rod and thy staff they comfort me."*

I couldn't pray. I tried, but my thoughts scrambled in disarray. A comforting haze settled in my mind, blocking out everything except my next action, whatever that needed to be.

It was at sunset on the second day when the remaining mine shaft collapsed, ending the rescue attempt.

When I heard they'd given up, sorrow overwhelmed me. I would never see James again. I raced up the stairs to the top of the mine. Crazy spots danced before my eyes as I struggled to breathe. I ran to Pete and grabbed him by his shirt. "Pete, you can't stop now. You promised you wouldn't give up. God won't let him die, I know it."

"I'm sorry. We've done all we can." Pete averted his eyes. I started to protest. "Chloe, there is at least two hundred feet of rock and mud on top of the rescue team. And who knows how much fell in the original cave-in. Last time I was down there, we hadn't made a dent in the wall."

"But what about an air pocket? They could have found an air pocket, couldn't they?"

He shook his head slowly. "If I thought there was any hope at all, even the most remote possibility James was alive, if I had to, I'd dig my way through the mountain with a teaspoon. Your husband was the best friend I've ever had."

"Is, Pete. Is. He is the best friend . . ." The words caught in my throat.

"Come, let me walk you home."

"No, I won't leave. I won't leave James alone in there to die. I c-c-can't." From an indefinable distance came a mournful wail—mine. Echoing off the silent mountain, the mountain that stole James from me, the cry caught me and held me with desperate fingers.

My first thought was to run away. But where? Where

could I run this time? This time it was different. This time I understood what the Bible meant when it said, "They shall be as one flesh." I again struggled to breathe. I was buried in the rubble of the cave-in. I was trapped by tons of rock, gold ore, and debris.

My mind clung to the hope that in spite of everything I'd been told, I'd look up toward the shaft house and see James emerge into the twilight. Suddenly, a wave of cold reality swept through me. *You can't stay up here. Two little children need you. You need to be strong for them.*

I stumbled over to the stairs. A sound of surging water filled my head, drowning out the roar of the machinery, and my knees started to buckle. Pete lifted me into his arms and carried me down the stairs. My head dropped, exhausted, against his shoulder. As we passed the camp kitchen, I lifted my head and struggled to be set down. "Jamie needs me."

Pete kept walking. "Noah took Jamie to the cabin. The women are there too, to help you."

My head fell back once more. "Women?"

"Half the female population of Columbine. The other half will be here tomorrow to help out." He strode up the front walk. Ula met us at the door.

"Be very quiet," she warned. "Jamie and CeeCee are finally sleeping. Noah's staying by Jamie's side all night."

Pete deposited me on the sofa, then dropped to his knee beside me. "Are you going to be all right, Chloe? Would you like me to stay?"

I shook my head, partly to answer his question and partly to clear the fog from my brain. Pete stood up uncertainly.

"She's going to be just fine." Mrs. Jones pushed him toward the kitchen door. "You look like you need someone to take care of you, yourself."

I can't explain what happened next. I seemed to be

falling into a slick, dark pit. I tried to claw my way up the slippery walls but slid back to the bottom each time. I drifted between the pain-filled reality and blessed blackness. Occasionally, I heard my daughter calling to me and felt her wet kisses on my face. Most of the time I heard, saw, and felt nothing. It wasn't until I began seeing Otis Roy's face leering at me in my dreams that I struggled back to consciousness.

Sheriff Jones brought in a Methodist preacher from Steamboat Springs to conduct the memorial service. I stood in the brisk morning air, feeling as if some essential part of me had been severed, the ends flapping in the breeze. I burrowed deeper beneath my upturned coat collar for protection from the biting breeze and from the sympathetic faces surrounding me.

I would have preferred to have Noah officiate. To my satisfaction, he did say a few words. I will always remember the verses he recited from 1 Thessalonians 4:

For the Lord himself shall descend from heaven with a shout, with the voice of the archangel, and with the trump of God: and the dead in Christ shall rise first: then we which are alive and remain shall be caught up together with them in the clouds, to meet the Lord in the air: and so shall we ever be with the Lord. Wherefore comfort one another with these words.

Knowing James and I would one day be together again eased the pain in my heart. As I stood there, gazing up at the gaping hole in the side of the mountain, the mountain that swallowed my husband, I knew that the Lord's return couldn't happen too soon to please me.

After the service, I sent my friends home. I needed to be

alone with my children to inject a few moments of normalcy in their chaotic lives.

Silently, Jamie and I ate the food Ula had prepared for us. As I ate the lentil stew, I could have been eating sawdust in hot water for all the flavor I tasted. Jamie ate his food with similar lack of enthusiasm. Only CeeCee babbled on as if nothing had happened. When we heard a knock at the door, Rags barked and growled while Jamie ran to answer it.

Pete stood in the doorway, his hat clutched in his hands. When Rags recognized the visitor, the dog trotted over to the hearth and lay back down. CeeCee glanced up from her bowl of stew. "Daddy!" she cried.

I gasped at the sudden jab of pain in my chest. "No, honey, that's not Daddy. It's Pete, remember?"

"Sorry to bother you." Pete's face flared with color. "But there are a few things we need to discuss before I leave."

I blanched. "Leave? You're going to leave?"

"Well, with the mine shaft collapsed, I've shut down the entire operation. If you'd like, I can stay until you decide what you are going to do now."

A whimper escaped my throat. "I'd really appreciate it if you could stay a while."

He nodded. "Mind if I sit down?"

"Of course not." Jamie returned to the table. "Would you like a bowl of Ula's lentils?" I asked, hoping I wouldn't have to serve him.

He shook his head. "No, I just came to talk."

I got up from the table. "Let me put CeeCee to bed. Jamie, Pete and I need to discuss mining business—"

"It would be better if the boy stayed."

I glanced at him curiously, then carried CeeCee from the room. Always sweet tempered, CeeCee settled down immediately. I returned to find Pete and Jamie sitting on the sofa. Pete was answering Jamie's questions regarding the accident and the rescue attempts. I didn't want to talk about the tragedy. I wanted to turn and run.

Taking a deep breath, I sat down in my chair and, from habit, picked up my knitting.

Pete worried the arm of the sofa for a moment. "The first thing we need to do is send word to James's family. Also, we need to contact Mr. Putnam in Denver. I figured on riding to Hahn's Peak tomorrow to send the wire."

I hadn't even thought to wire the McCalls of the tragedy. I stared as if Pete were speaking a foreign language. I caught bits and pieces as he tried to explain what had been done in the office and the mill since the accident. For no apparent reason, Otis's face surfaced in my mind. I pushed it aside, but it surfaced again.

"Could it have been sabotage?"

Pete stared at me. "Excuse me?"

"Could the accident possibly have not been an accident?"

"Why do you ask?" He sounded evasive.

I took a deep breath and told him about seeing Otis Roy in Steamboat Springs before Christmas. "James told me Otis wouldn't hang around once he was fired."

"Did you tell James?"

I shook my head no. "I wasn't sure at the time. Then the day of the explosion, I overheard two miners discussing the accident. They mentioned Otis's name." I swallowed hard. "When I asked them about Otis, they refused to talk to me."

Pete stared down at the toe of his boot. Jamie sat tensely watching first me, then Pete. "Is it possible, Mr. Pete? Could my father and all those men have been murdered?"

The question hung in the air, frozen in time. Pete took a long time answering. "There is a possibility of foul play. The head mining engineer told me that a blasting cap was missing from the shed that morning. And yes, I heard the same rumor that Otis had been seen around the mine."

I leaned forward. "Did you tell the sheriff?"

"Yes, but we don't have enough proof to arrest the man. Otis is rumored to be staying at a hotel in Hahn's Peak." Pete jutted his jaw. "Thought I'd stop by and see him tomorrow when I go to town to send the wires."

I shook my head vigorously. "No, please don't. Let's get the proof to have him convicted of murder first."

Pete frowned. "I've been thinking, it might be wise to get you out of the cabin. Isn't there someplace you can go where you'll be safe? How about Denver or the VanArsdales?"

I shook my head again. "This is my home. I feel I should stay here to protect James's interests until I hear from Ian. But I would appreciate it if you went to Denver to speak with Mr. Putnam about the accident." I thought of the kind man who'd befriended us so completely. "You know, he might be able to help us get that conviction. He's a wise old bird, and he's been in on James's investigation from the first."

I held my breath as Pete tapped his fingers on the arm of the sofa. "You may be right. But I would feel a whole lot better if you and the children would come with me." He glanced toward the rifle mounted over the fireplace. "Do you know how to use that rifle?"

I nodded. "After Otis's last threat, James insisted I learn. My aim is lousy, though."

"Then you'd better practice. Are you sure you won't move in with the VanArsdales until I get back?"

I shook my head again. "I will practice, though." Pete left in a few minutes, promising to see Phineas in Denver and return by the end of the week.

The next morning, Jamie stayed home from school another day. I dressed CeeCee in her heavy coat and snow pants while Jamie set up the shooting range over by the clearing. We took turns shooting at tin cans on the stump, teasing each other every time we missed, which was almost every shot.

As I was preparing lunch, I noticed our food supply was low. I hadn't shopped for food in Hahn's Peak since Christmas. With all the meals the women in town had supplied, I hadn't given food much thought. "Tomorrow, we need to drive the wagon to town, Jamie. Do you think you can hitch up the horse?"

Jamie was playing horsie with CeeCee. He whinnied and bucked, causing the little girl to shriek with laughter. He looked toward me. "I think so."

I laughed. "Well, together, we'll figure it out, won't we, cowboy?"

He grinned and crawled around the kitchen table two more times before I called them to eat. Before we finished our meal, the first snowflakes drifted past the kitchen window. By nightfall, the falling snow obliterated the sight of all but the closest fir trees to the cabin.

Memories of another blizzard flooded my mind as I watched Jamie trudge through the snow to the stable. When he returned, I told him, "I have a feeling we won't be going to town tomorrow. But that's all right. We have enough food to last us a week anyway." I rubbed warmth back into my arms. "By then, Pete will be back from Denver."

I stepped back inside and barred the door. *With a storm like this, I'm sure grateful for the indoor plumbing James had installed.* Another rush of memories flooded through me.

Once the children were asleep, I sat down at James's desk and wrote a letter home to my parents. Tears flowed as I relived the horror of the last few weeks. And as I described the events, I grew angry. Angry at God for not rescuing James. Angry at James for going down into the mine. Angry at Pete for not being able to save him. Angry at Otis . . .

I felt a resurgence of hate inside me, the same hate I'd felt for Emmett Sawyer. I'd felt betrayed, abandoned, robbed. I shoved the letter aside and stomped to the kitchen sink, drank a glass of water, then went into my bedroom. As I changed into my nightclothes, my gaze fell on the Bible sitting on the night stand. Picking it up, I turned to 1 Thessalonians to comfort myself with the promise Noah had recited at the service. I found verse 16 and tried to read it aloud. The words blurred before my eyes.

I pushed the book aside and threw myself face down across the bed. I awakened hours later, chilled by the cold air seeping through the tiny chinks in the cabin wall. The fire was low, and the kerosene in my bedside lamp was nearly gone. Weary and discouraged, I checked the children, put a log in the stove, turned off the lamps, and climbed into bed.

The howling storm continued throughout the night and for three days and nights following. I thought of Pete with the Putnams in Denver. Would they treat him with the same courtesy they had James and me? I thought about Ula and Noah and my other friends in Columbine. The snowstorm would have closed down everything on the western slope of the mountain, trapping everyone in their homes.

I thought of James, sleeping beneath tons of debris, no longer cold or hungry or tired or lonely, then pushed the thoughts aside. I had meals to make, a fire to maintain, and children to feed.

A Coward's Curse

The skies cleared for a day. Jamie and I shoveled as far as the stable so that caring for the horse would be easier. The six-foot snowbanks isolated us in a world of silence. Gone was the mill, the office, even the mountain itself. The forest animals who'd been lulled by the mild winter pressed closer to the cabin in search of food. At night I could hear deer gnawing bark on the aspen saplings.

The next day a new storm ripped through the area, dumping two more feet of fresh snow. Two weeks after Pete left for Denver and the first snow had fallen, I went to the cupboard for flour to make the week's supply of bread. As I gazed into the near-empty sack, I thought of the story in the Bible about the woman who fed the prophet. *I haven't seen many prophets roaming around here lately, Lord.*

I opened the bin where I stored the cornmeal. *Pretty low. Maybe by mixing the two we can have a couple meals of johnnycake anyway. By then we should be able to get through to town for supplies.*

We'd used up the last of the fruit preserves two days before, but we still had raisins. I leaned against the cupboard and pressed my forehead against my arm. *And what if, what if you can't get out for help? What if the food runs out, and you have to watch your children die of starvation? Foolish! Stupid! You were too proud to take Pete's advice and go stay with Ula. She would have welcomed you joyfully. Now, see what happened? And it's all Your fault, God!*

I crumpled to the floor in a heap. *No, Lord, I didn't mean that. I know You love me, and You love my children even more than I possibly can.* I wiped my tears on my sleeve. *You promised to feed us, to supply us with bread and water. I trust You, Lord.*

"Mama, is something wrong?" The voice from the loft reminded me I wasn't alone, that I needed to confine my grieving to my bedroom.

"I'm fine, son." I arose stiffly and tossed a log in the fire. Sparks sprayed like a miniature Fourth of July fireworks. I listened until I heard Jamie's door close. *Thank You, Lord, for impressing James to lay in such a large supply of wood for the winter. At least we'll keep warm.*

I remembered the way I'd laughed at him when he and Pete stacked the mountain of logs beside the cabin. "You're going to strip the mountain bare, the rate you're going."

Pete laughed, and James had shaken his head in concern. "You can never have too much firewood."

You were right, darling. You were right about many things. I lifted my eyes from the flames to the mantle. James's favorite books sat at one end—all held securely in place by the marble bookends I had given him for Christmas.

I ran my hand over the carved Swiss clock, my Christmas gift from James. Its brass pendulum swung back and forth, clicking off the seconds. The hand-tied snowshoes Pete had given James filled the other end of the mantle.

I took one down and hefted it. The thought that I could try to snowshoe into town for help crossed my mind. But I'd never worn snowshoes, and I didn't like the thought of leaving the children behind.

As I returned the snowshoe to the mantel, my gaze

rested on the clock, then glided upward to the rifle on the wall. Slowly I lifted the weapon from the wooden pegs that held it in place and cradled it in my arms. I ran my fingers over the smooth barrel and caressed the well-oiled oak stock.

For a moment, a brief, selfish moment, I considered running away again. My exhausted brain longed for the peace my husband now possessed. No more problems, no more pain. At the sound of Jamie's bedsprings squeaking overhead, I snapped back to reality. Horrified at my thoughts, I returned the rifle to its place above the mantle and fled to my room.

Shaken to tears, I sat on the edge of the bed, my head in my hands. *Chloe, what were you thinking? How could you be so selfish? Two innocent children depend on you for their very lives.*

Forgive me, Father, for considering such a heinous crime against You and against my own flesh and blood. Please, tell me what to do. If I ever needed evidence of Your love and protection, I need it now. I'm so alone and so frightened. I need to feel Your loving arms around me. The tears trickled through my fingers.

As the words, "I will never leave thee, nor forsake thee," sprang to mind, I felt a comforting warmth, as if warm arms encircled my shoulders, and a peace replaced my anxiety. I now knew I wasn't alone and had no cause for fear. That's when I heard the scraping in the aspen grove. *The deer. The deer are back.*

I'd never killed one of God's creatures, at least none larger than a mouse or a snake. I was surprised that the thought of my killing one even crossed my mind, but I remembered what Pete had told Jamie about killing for food. And I remembered how my father and brothers would go hunting each fall to bag a buck. My mother, my sisters, and I avoided the workshop until the gruesome mess was cleaned up. Yet, the venison stretched our winter food supply. *Can you actually destroy one of those beautiful creatures? I can if it means saving my children's lives.*

Rushing to the desk, I scribbled out the directions I'd heard Pete give Lucas for killing and cleaning a deer. I studied them, trying to determine if I'd left anything out. I couldn't afford to be wrong.

When I climbed into my cold, lonely bed that night, I wished I were even more tired. Tomorrow would be a stressful day, and I needed rest for what I must do. But I was too agitated at the thought of hunting to sleep. I could still hear the deer in the aspen grove. I closed my eyes. I was torn between praying that God would keep the deer close so I could shoot one and praying He would shoo them away.

The next morning, I arose more tired than I'd been when I went to bed. The storm had blown over and sunlight sparkled on the snow. After baking johnnycake for the children, I dressed in a pair of James's heavy woolen pants, his woolen shirt, and a heavy sweater. Lifting the shirt to my nose, I let James's aroma fill my nostrils. *I can't go through with this. I can't. One step at a time, Chloe. One step at a time.*

Determined, I removed his jacket from the hook behind the door. By the time I had fastened all the jacket buttons, I felt like a walking snowman. *If I fall, I won't be able to get up!*

As I opened James's drawer to look for a pair of his leather work gloves, a little cry escaped my lips as the memories of our days together on the Kansas prairie flooded my mind. I spotted James's sheathed hunting knife next to the gloves. Steeling myself against my weakening resolve, I picked up the gloves and the knife, then slammed the drawer shut.

I found the bullets on the top shelf in our bedroom. Jamie

watched wide eyed as I dropped a handful of them into the pants pocket.

Tying a knitted scarf around my head, I wrapped the ends about my neck. "Son, I need you to watch CeeCee while I try to find us something to eat." I took the snowshoes and rifle to the porch, where I strapped on the snowshoes. Leaving the rifle by the house, I practiced walking until I found a stride and balance that worked for me.

Finally I felt secure enough to sling the rifle strap over my shoulder and head south toward town in search of fresh animal tracks. The best I might do would be to make it to town for food. The worst, I might actually find some animal to kill.

I'd gone less than half a mile from the cabin when I spotted two bucks pawing through the snow at the base of an aspen. I stopped, loaded the rifle, and aimed. The second before my finger squeezed the trigger, one of the bucks looked straight at me, melting my resolve. My arm jerked an instant before the gun exploded, sending the bullet high into the air and my two targets deep into the woods.

By now all the animals between me and town had headed for cover, so I decided to walk in the opposite direction, past the mill to the area where the engineers had been dynamiting. Weary after walking that distance on snowshoes, I sat down on a log to rest and survey the edges of the clearing.

It came into my sights as silently as the softly falling snow. I had dozed for a few minutes and when I opened my eyes, I could hardly believe what I saw. Standing seventy-five or eighty feet from me, was a huge buck elk. I squeezed my eyes shut, certain I was dreaming, but when I opened them again, he was still there. *He's beautiful, absolutely beautiful.* Another part of my brain responded, *This animal means survival. You have to shoot him. Shoot him now!*

Slowly I raised the rifle, aiming for the spot just behind

the shoulder, as Pete had described. My heart pounded so wildly that I was sure the elk would hear it and bound away into the forest, but it stood gazing into the trees. Holding my breath, I squeezed the trigger.

The rifle kick toppled me off the log, though I did see the animal stagger, run several yards, and fall. I scrambled to my feet and plodded over to the elk, fighting back both tears and nausea.

I felt old, very old. My job was to heal, not to destroy. I laid the rifle in the snow beside me and tried to prepare myself for the dreaded job of skinning and dressing the dead elk. Sheer grit carried me through the gory process. With each slash of the knife I vowed I'd never again purposely take the life of one of God's creatures.

It wasn't until I finished that I realized I had no way to transport the meat back to the cabin. If I carried back only part of the meat, hungry predators would devour the remainder before I could return. *There must be something. There has to be something!*

All traces of mining activity were covered by a heavy snowpack. Only the trees, the mountain, the sky, and my bloody kill were visible. Then I noticed the blood stains on the front of the jacket. I felt sick. *The blood stains will never come out of the suede. It's ruined.*

That's what decided it. Taking off the jacket, I tore out the lining and spread both the jacket and the lining on the snow. I piled both pieces of fabric high with the meat, spread the skin over the top as a covering, and pulled with all the strength I had left. My handmade sled didn't move. *This isn't going to work.*

The sun hung dangerously near the horizon. I'd hardly been aware of the passing hours. My shoulders and back muscles ached from butchering the elk. Yet somehow, I had to overcome the pain and weariness and get the load home before dark.

There was only one thing to do—pull one load ten feet, then go back for the other, alternating until I got them both home. When I finally rounded the bend beyond the office, I loaded the gun and fired it into the air, hoping to summon Jamie. The sun had already set, and I heard the distant howl of a wolf. I needed to get the meat inside the cabin before dark.

As I hoped, Jamie rushed out of the cabin. "Mama?" he shouted.

"I'm over here. I need your help." My voice carried clearly in the icy air.

He bounded through the snow as best he could without snowshoes.

"Quick!" I shouted. "Help me pull this."

We tugged and struggled until we hauled both loads of meat inside the cabin.

The morning after the hunt, I lifted the skins from meat packs and stared at the mounds of meat. *Now that you've got it, what do you plan to do with it?*

During the next two days, I remembered all the ways my mother had preserved venison. On the third day, Jamie and I dug a tunnel into the snowbank beside the house and buried what was left. I marked the spot with a red scarf tied to the top of a broomstick. As long as we didn't get a blizzard that buried my marker, we'd have elk meat for weeks to come.

One night a week later, I'd fallen asleep on the sofa when Rags leapt to his feet, his hair standing rigid on his back and tail. He growled, listened, then barked and lunged at the door. *Otis! Otis Roy. He's come to finish the job!*

Before I could reach for the rifle, someone pounded on the door. "Chloe. Chloe McCall," a muffled voice called.

Laughing and crying I ran to the door, threw back the bar, and let Sheriff Jones and Pete into the cabin.

The men shed their snowshoes and hats. "Mrs. McCall,

I was afraid we'd find you and the children dead. We didn't know you were out here alone until Indian Pete got back to town today. When you didn't come to stay with Ula, we assumed you went with him to Denver."

Pete hastily explained, "The return train from Denver was delayed by an avalanche, or I would have been here sooner."

Jamie stood in the doorway of his loft bedroom. "Mr. Pete, you're back. Did Mama tell you what she did? She shot and killed an elk."

The two men turned toward me, their mouths open, their eyes wide.

"She bagged a big one, a twelve pointer." Jamie clambered down the ladder. "But I'm sure glad you're here. I'm mighty sick of elk meat."

They looked at Jamie, then back at me. Pete was the first to speak. "You shot, killed, skinned, and butchered a buck elk all by yourself?"

I laughed self-consciously. "Thanks to you. I listened when you told little Lucas how to do it." I couldn't contain my delight at their surprise. I grinned a sheepish grin. "Your directions were excellent."

Jamie dragged Pete by the arm to the library. "Come see the hide she skinned. I went out the next day and got the antlers. See?"

Sheriff Jones followed. Pete inspected the pelt. "Fine job she did too."

"It was either hunt or watch my children starve. I can tell you, you two are a welcome sight to us. Why don't we go out to the kitchen; I have a couple elk steaks I can throw on the stove."

They laughed and followed me to the kitchen. Pete told about his meeting with Phineas.

"A week or so before the accident, Phineas uncovered some interesting information about Otis Roy. It seems Mr.

Roy once owned half of the Renegade Mine. Because Otis couldn't read, his partner was able to swindle him out of his share and then sell the mine to Ian and James. That's why Otis is so angry."

Everything was fitting together, making sense. "Would that be enough to drive him to kill seventeen men?"

Pete shook his head. "It might be. I saw him in Hahn's Peak when I came through today, sheriff. He was gambling away a fistful of money in Bristow's Saloon."

"There, see. It wouldn't be so hard to find him."

We looked toward the sheriff for a response.

"Can't you arrest him?" Impatience edged my voice.

"Now, lookee here . . ." The sheriff leaned back in his chair. "All you have is speculation and circumstantial evidence. There's not a court in the land that will convict him on such flimsy evidence."

"Especially," I sneered, "if the charges were made by a hysterical woman and a half-Indian, right?"

The sheriff scratched his beard. "I didn't say that, ma'am."

"You didn't have to. I could see it in your eyes."

Jamie hadn't said a word. I'd almost forgotten he was sitting beside me. "Then Mr. Roy gets away with killing my father?"

The sheriff eyed the boy thoughtfully. "Unless Indian Pete here can either link him to the theft of the explosives or make him confess, there isn't much the law can do."

Jamie's lower jaw protruded in the familiar McCall pout. "That's not fair."

"Life isn't fair, son." Sheriff Jones sighed. Turning to me, he added, "The best thing you can do now, ma'am, is put it all behind you and get on with your life."

"Put it behind me?" I stood and pushed my chair back from the table. "You tell me that there's a good chance Otis Roy killed my husband, along with sixteen other men, and I'm supposed to put it behind me!" I pounded my fist on the table. "How I hate that man for destroying our lives!"

Sheriff Jones stood and put his arm about my shoulders. "Hate won't bring your husband back. It will only destroy you, no one else—and least of all a weasel like Otis Roy."

I took a deep breath. If the law couldn't do anything, maybe I could. *Will a judge hang the mother of two children for avenging the death of her husband?*

The sheriff must have seen the murderous glint in my eye. "Now don't go getting any ideas, Mrs. McCall. Killing an elk is in a different category than killing a man."

I laughed nervously. "Oh, sheriff, how could you even think a thought like that?"

"Oh, by the way, Mrs. Putnam insists I put you and the children on the next train for Denver." Pete smiled. "She is a mighty determined lady. If I didn't know better, I'd say she's blood sister to my mother."

I remembered James's description of the blue blood coursing through Gladys's veins and laughed. "Only if your ancestors were there to meet the *Mayflower*."

The sheriff glanced about the cabin. "If we could stay for the night, ma'am, we'll pile you and the children on the travois we rigged up and take you into town tomorrow morning."

"You can put the children on the sled, but there's no reason I can't walk. I've gotten pretty good on snowshoes, if I say so myself." My change of attitude eased the tension. The men smiled.

Jamie asked anxiously, "What about Rags and Hector, and the horse?"

The men looked at one another. "The cat and the dog can go with us. But the horse? Well, we'll have to come back for him later."

The boy started to protest when Pete bent down. "Jamie, we'll water and feed him in the morning. If I have to, I'll snowshoe out here every day until the snow melts. I promise."

"Son, if you sleep in my bed, Pete and the sheriff can have your room." I turned to the sheriff. "One of you can sleep on the cot and the other on the floor. I have plenty of quilts."

Once the arrangements were made, Jamie and I went into my bedroom and shut the door. Seconds after his head hit the pillow, the child was asleep. For me, it wasn't that simple. A fiery hate, stronger than any I'd ever experienced, flared inside me, searing my mind and singeing the edges of my soul.

I flipped through the pages of my Bible, searching the Psalms for the verses I'd read about hate and anger. Surely if King David, a man after God's own heart, could express such violent hatred toward his enemies, God would understand me.

"Break their teeth, O God, in their mouths . . ." I liked that. I laughed aloud at the sight of Otis Roy toothless.

"As a snail which melteth, let every one of them pass away." *The man is, indeed, a snail. No, he's lower than a snail, perhaps a slug!* I flipped over a few more pages to Psalm 94 and read the following words aloud. "O Lord God, to whom vengeance belongeth." *Oops, I don't like the sound of this one.*

"O God, to whom vengeance belongeth, shew thyself. Lift up thyself, thou judge of the earth. . . . Lord, how long shall the wicked, how long shall the wicked triumph? How long shall they utter and speak hard things?" *Vengeance belongs to God? Surely I have a right to avenge the blood of my husband, the father of my children! The law won't help me.* "Surely, Lord, You don't expect me to sit back and let this wicked man get away with murder! Didn't You say, 'God helps those who help themselves'?"

I thought of the rifle over the fireplace. *This man killed my husband! He robbed my children of a father. I have a right, an obligation, to avenge his death. What can I do, Lord? I'm only a woman. More than that, I'm a coward. I could no more shoot one of Your children than I could destroy one of my own.*

My eyes blurred with tears. *I feel so weak and so helpless.* This time, as I turned back a few pages in my Bible, I had a destination—Psalm 84, one of my favorites. I read the words aloud. "Blessed is the [woman] whose strength is in thee." *My strength is in You, Father, not in the rifle or even in frontier justice, but in You. Help me to remember that.*

I admitted that Sheriff Jones was right. Confronting and killing Otis would prove nothing. It would only rob my children of their only other parent for a time and maybe forever. *Like Pa always said, "Chloe's a bulldog. She gets a bone to chew, she won't ever let go." So I'm too cowardly or too sensible to shoot the varmint. Tricking him into confessing is another matter.* I drifted off to sleep, my subconscious still formulating my plan.

The Sword Against the Snake

The next morning, while the men and children ate a hot breakfast of elk stew, I packed the family treasures into our trunks, then locked them and slipped the keys in my pants pocket. By the way the men averted their eyes, I could tell they were uncomfortable with my wearing James's trousers instead of skirts. As it was, I had to cut six inches or more off the legs to stuff them into my boots. But if I planned on walking to town, skirts were out of the question.

After washing the dishes and straightening the pillows on the sofa one last time, I took a final walk through the little cabin that had been James's and my home, knowing I would not be returning. We bundled the children, the pets, and extra clothing onto the travois and headed toward town. Along with the clothing, I packed the weapon vital to my future—the Bible from James.

Exhausted and hungry from the effort of snowshoeing, we arrived at Sheriff Jones's house around noon. After his wife fed us a hearty lunch, I asked her if she'd watch CeeCee and Jamie for a few hours.

"I'd like to wrap up some business before dark."

When she agreed, I went out to the stable to find Pete. Earlier he mentioned that horses could get through to Hahn's Peak. "Why do you want to go to Hahn's Peak?" he asked.

I chose my words carefully. "James often dealt with a lawyer there. I thought I should meet with him before I left for Denver." I was lying, and Pete knew I was lying.

"You want to confront Otis, don't you? Did you bring the rifle, by any chance?"

I shook my head. "No, to the second question; yes, to the first."

His eyes narrowed. "What do you expect to accomplish?"

I took a deep breath. "James once told me, 'Never let the bullies win, or you'll spend your life living in a shadow of fear.' Otis is a bully and a coward. I want to call him that to his face."

A muscle flexed in his jaw. "And have him shoot you down like a dog?"

"You mean, like he shot Rags?"

"You don't know—"

"Come on, Pete! Who's kidding whom? You know as well as I do that the man did everything possible to destroy my family, from shooting Rags to burning down our home to rigging accidents at the mine to finally blowing the shaft and my husband to kingdom come. If anyone has more right to confront him than I do, I'd like to meet 'em." My voice rose to a dangerously high pitch.

Pete kept his voice even and low. "You won't be toting a gun, will you?"

I chuckled. "I considered it, but no, I plan instead, to wield a two-edged sword."

Shock swept across his face. "You can't—"

This time I laughed out loud. "The truth is my two-edged sword, Pete. God is my strength, and the truth is my weapon."

The man sighed, visibly relieved. "I think you're terribly naive. It will still be the word of a hysterical female against his."

"Hysterical? We'll see about that. Will you help me, at

least?" I strolled over to the hitching post and cleared my throat. "What if you came along and say, hid in the next room where you could listen and come to my defense if I needed it?"

"Hmm, I know I'm going to be sorry for this, but the guy is a braggart. He's more than likely to admit to his exploits just for the notoriety." When the muscle in Pete's cheek flexed again, I knew there was hope. "It might work at that."

"Let me get changed into a dress, then we can be on our way. I knew I could count on you."

Pete eyed me suspiciously. "You planned this, right down to my coming with you, didn't you?"

I blushed. "Er, well . . ."

He grinned. "Go on, get changed while I saddle up the horses. But dress warmly. It will still be a cold ride."

The moment I burst into Bristow's Saloon, a mingling of surprise, fear, and hate sprang into Otis Roy's eyes, and the fear and hate froze there. I pasted a hard smile on my lips, though my insides quivered and my hands shook. Clutching my Bible, I strode slowly toward the back table where Otis sat drinking with two buddies. The piano player quit playing in the middle of "Yankee Doodle" at the same instant the shouts and laughter died.

Then as suddenly as the room had quieted, pandemonium broke out around me. Shouts of, "Hey, lady, this is no place for a lady," "Whoa! You don't belong in here," and, "Isn't that the smallpox lady?" erupted from every corner of the room. Chairs skidded away from tables, and boots clomped toward the door. Without taking my eyes off Otis, I shouted, "Sit down, gentlemen. Stay right where you are, if you please. I will need you as witnesses." I sighed with relief when the men returned to their chairs.

In the same instant Otis leapt from the table and reached for his gun, I held out the Bible. "That won't be necessary, Mr. Roy. There has been more than enough violence. Don't you agree?" I set the Bible down firmly on the scarred oak tabletop, splashing amber-colored liquid out of the three glasses. I leaned forward. "I didn't hear your answer, sir. Don't you agree?"

The two men sitting at the table with Otis scrambled away, upturning chairs in their haste to escape. Otis narrowed his eyes. "I ain't sayin' nothin', ma'am."

"Really?" I continued to stare. "I've heard you've been doing a heap of bragging around here—something about getting even. Is that right, Mr. Roy?"

"I ain't sayin' nothin'."

"Tell me, why did you hate my husband so much that you killed him, along with sixteen other miners?"

"I ain't sayin' nothin'."

In my sweetest voice, I asked, "Do you deny it? Do you deny being at the mine the day of the explosion? Do you deny causing the cave-in for which my husband fired you as manager of the Renegade Mine?"

His lips curled into a sneer, but he remained silent.

I continued. "And do you deny setting fire to our cabin? To shooting our dog?" I focused on his right eye. "What kind of hate is eating away at your insides to make you commit such heinous acts?"

Now Otis leaned forward, murder in his eyes. "Your husband robbed me. The Renegade was mine. Your husband and my dead partner stole it right out from under me. Nobody treats Otis Roy like that and gets away with it!"

"What kind of coward would take out his anger on a puppy?"

The man straightened, jabbing his thumbs in his belt. "I ain't no coward. Nobody calls me a coward, especially a woman."

I raised my voice. "Only a coward prowls around a woman's cabin in the cloak of night, peeking in the windows and scaring little children. Only a coward sneaks into a mine shaft and blows it up, trapping seventeen men in the resulting cave-in."

I turned and gazed around the room at Otis's barroom cronies. Their faces told me I spoke the truth. I turned once again to face my enemy. I saw his hand fidget on the butt of his gun, as if trying to decide whether to draw.

"Only a cow-ard, Mr. Roy." I emphasized the *cow* in *coward*. "Would brag to his friend of his dirty tricks, then hide behind a pistol when confronted by a lady."

Lifting my Bible to within inches of his chin, I narrowed my eyes. "Will you put your hand on this Bible and swear you are not responsible for my husband's death?"

When he blanched and looked away, I wondered what deep-seated memory prevented him from lying outright to me. "Go ahead, Mr. Roy, put your hand on the Bible, if you can—or should I say, if you dare!"

A look of terror filled the man's face. He threw both hands in front of him to ward off the book. "I won't touch that thing! Get it away from me."

I pressed it against his hands. "Why, Mr. Roy? Why should you be afraid of a book if you're innocent?"

His hand flew back to his holster. "I mean it, lady. I don't care if you're female or not. I'll kill ya right here and now if you don't back off!" I knew by the glint in his eye that he meant what he said.

With both hands I held the Bible to my chest. Sarcastically I said, "The man who isn't a coward would shoot an unarmed Christian woman, the mother of two children. Thank you for showing everyone here in this room what a brave and respectable human being you really are."

I turned my back on him to face the mesmerized crowd. "You all heard the man as well as confess to the murder of my husband. I would take it kindly if when Mr. Roy is brought to trial, you would think of me as you would your own mother or your own sister and tell the truth about what you've seen and heard this afternoon." Clutching one side of my skirt, I curtsied slightly. "Thank you so much. I'll leave now so you can get back to whatever it was you were doing."

Squaring my shoulders, I strode to the door. Two miners leapt to open it for me. I thanked them and proceeded out of the building onto the wooden sidewalk. When the door slammed shut behind me, I collapsed on the nearest bench. Over the cacophony of excited voices, I heard the pianist pick up "Yankee Doodle" exactly where he'd left off. A few seconds later the door swung open, and Pete stood in front of me. I looked up surprised—I hadn't seen him enter the saloon behind me.

"You caused quite a stir in there, little lady."

"Oh?" My heart was pounding so hard I had to struggle to catch my breath.

He continued to stare across the frozen street at a hardware store. "Yes."

"Do you think I have enough on Otis to call the sheriff?"

"Yes."

"Do you think it's enough to convict him?"

Pete looked down at me, his eyes filled with sadness. "No."

I sighed and leaned back against the rough brick surface of the wall behind me. "But all those men—they know he killed James."

"Yes. But knowing and testifying in a court of law are often horses of two different colors."

Weary, I stood to my feet. "Yet, if there's a chance, even the slightest chance that he could be convicted, I've got to try."

Pete smiled and pushed his hat back. "Then let's get on down to the sheriff's office, Mrs. McCall."

I can't tell you how delighted I was to see the county

sheriff take Otis Roy away in handcuffs. The prisoner threw me a hateful glare, which I returned with a nod and a smile.

We returned to Columbine in silence. All that needed to be said had been said. As Pete helped me off my horse, I turned and smiled. "Thank you, dear friend, for helping me today. I'm not sure I could have gone through with it without your support."

He stared at me for a minute, a strange, unsettling look in his eyes. "I need to thank you. You've taught me a valuable lesson today. I have a few bullies from the past to confront also."

"I don't understand."

"Let's just say your courage has given me courage to face my enemies." Pete tipped his hat to me. "I have a horse to feed in order to keep my promise to Jamie. You wouldn't mind if I stayed in your cabin for the night, would you?"

"Of course not." I laughed. "Help yourself to the elk meat while you're at it." He grinned and collected the horses' bridles in his gloved hands. As I watched him take the horses to the stable, I tried to remember what James had said about Pete's past, but I couldn't.

Behind me, the door swung open, and Jamie bounded out of the house. "Mama, Mama, guess what?"

I turned and caught him in my arms.

"Grandpa and Uncle Ian are coming. They sent a telegram to you. The telegraph man delivered it to Sheriff Jones." He dropped his gaze. "I hope it's all right, but I opened it and read it. I thought it might be important."

I laughed nervously, my thoughts already shifting to encountering James's brisk, opinionated father. "Of course it's all right. Telegrams are always important. Where is it?"

Jamie tugged at my hand. "It's inside. They'll be here tomorrow. They sent it from Denver."

"Tomorrow?" All I knew about the man I'd learned from

James and from his annual birthday letter to Jamie. My stomach knotted. And though I hadn't eaten for hours, a sour acid rose in my throat. I'd faced down a murderer, but could I do the same with the man who produced such a violent anger in my brave and gentle husband?

My night of worry proved to be for nothing. The tall, carefully groomed man, whom Ian introduced as Mr. James Edward McCall, the first, took my hand and kissed my cheek tenderly. "So we finally meet, dear daughter. And these are my grandchildren?" His brown eyes sparkled as Jamie extended his hand to the man.

"It's good to see you again, grandfather."

"My, let me look at you. What a splendid young man we have here." He shook Jamie's hand. "And it's good to see you again also." Mr. McCall glanced at me. "And where's my new granddaughter?"

I smiled and blushed. "It's time to wake her from her nap. I'll go get her." I hurried from the room. *He's not at all the ogre James described. He looks so much like an older version of James, it's eerie.*

CeeCee was stirring when I slipped into the bedroom the Joneses were letting us use. I rummaged through the valise in which I'd packed her clothing until I found the powder blue-and-white ruffled dress Gladys had insisted on buying for her during our last visit to Denver. As I slipped the dress over her willing arms, I told her about the grandfather waiting in the parlor. "He's a nice man. You're going to like him. He's your daddy's daddy."

"Daddy?"

"That's right, honey, your daddy's daddy." I combed her feather-light hair, picked her up, carried her to the parlor and set her down inside the doorway. My daughter tipped her head to one side, batted her eyelashes shyly, and instantly stole her grandfather's heart.

That night, after I had put the children to bed, I reluctantly returned to the parlor to the waiting gentlemen. I knew they were going to ask about my plans for the future, and I didn't know what I was going to tell them. Boston, Shinglehouse, Denver, Columbine, San Francisco—I'd considered them all during the last few hours. Ironically, the only place that was not an option for me was China, my original destination; it was still closed to all "foreign devils." And it was obvious that Dad McCall—he insisted I call him Dad—wanted to take me and the children home with him to Boston.

The men stood as I entered the room. I sat on the sofa beside Ian; Dad McCall chose the wing-back chair beside the fireplace. "James's mother wanted to come with me, of course, but her charity and social calendar is full at this time of year."

I smiled, remembering James's description of his socialite mother.

"Now, my dear, I am sure you are privy to the extent of James's estate."

I stared at him, uncomprehending.

"You are his widow, hence rightfully heir to his fortune. Of course, I would hope that you would place a quarter of the estate in trust for his children."

I frowned.

Dad McCall leaned forward. "You look troubled, my dear."

"I-I'm sorry. This probably sounds silly to you, but so much has happened so fast, I haven't given it a thought."

The old man smiled and drew on his pipe. "If that is true, you are, indeed, the unusual woman my son described in his letters." He glanced toward the silent Ian, then back at me. "My wife is not going to know what to do with you. And I can't wait until she lays eyes on CeeCee."

"She's been spoiling the daylights out of Ashley," Ian interjected.

Disturbed by the thought but not certain why, I glanced down at my hands. Dad McCall pursed his lips. "You are returning with us to Boston, aren't you? I figured we could wrap up the sale of the Renegade in the next two days, then spend the weekend in Denver with the Putnams and be back in Boston before the end of the month."

"The sale of the mine?"

"Of course. You don't expect to reopen it, do you?"

I shook my head, but he didn't notice. "The lawyer in Hahn's Peak has already approached Phineas with a buyer."

I shuddered at the thought of a stranger digging up my husband's body. "Can't they just leave it alone?" My question came out as a whimper.

The older man stared at me with a mixture of disbelief and horror. "He located the mother lode, child!"

Feeling a sudden cold deep within me, I strolled to the fireplace. "Haven't enough lives been destroyed by that hated mine? I don't want to see some other woman's dreams destroyed all for a few nuggets of gold."

Ian rushed to me. Putting his arm around my shoulders, he led me back to the sofa. "The best thing you can do, Chloe, is to get as far away from Columbine as possible. Boston is just that."

I knew they were right. I knew I was acting illogically and not in my children's best interests. Slowly, I sat down. "All right, let's go through the finances step by step. Tell me what I have to sign."

Dad McCall nodded as if saying, "It's about time you came to your senses, woman." Instead he said, "There are a number of ways we can go about this. Ian could make you either a silent or active partner in James's place." The man cleared his throat, then continued. "Do you understand what I mean when I say active or silent partner?"

I bristled at his condescending tone. "I think I follow you."

He reddened and cleared his throat again. "Er, yes, or—"

"Or I can buy out your half of the assets," Ian interrupted. "This would give you a sizable income. You and the children could live quite comfortably in Boston or wherever you might choose." He glanced nervously toward his father. "Remember James's estate includes half of the ranch and half of our three mines, as well as a cottage on Cape Cod. The cottage would be deeded over to you, of course."

A cottage on Cape Cod? I never heard that one before. What other secrets did you forget to share, James dear? I moistened my lips. It wasn't difficult for me to see that this was what the two men preferred. *Maybe I do too.*

I smiled and rose to my feet. The men did also. "Ian, Dad McCall, could I think this over tonight and tell you in the morning?"

Mr. McCall pointed his pipe at me. "There's no rush. You don't have to sign the papers until we sit down with Harvard's best and hammer out the details."

When I glanced away, he added, "You are going with us to Boston, aren't you?"

I tilted my chin a little higher than what I knew he believed a humble woman should. "I will tell you that in the morning also. If you will excuse me, gentlemen. It has been an exhausting day."

The stunned men stared after me as I exited the parlor. My legs quivered as I hurried to the Joneses' guest room and closed the door. Jamie awakened when I lighted the kerosene lamp.

He sat up and rubbed his eyes. "Are we going to Boston, Mommy?"

I adjusted the covers around his shoulders and pushed the stray curls from his forehead. "I don't know, son. I wish I did."

"Grandpa told me that I could go to a special school in Boston to learn how to become a doctor."

"Is that what you'd like?"

The boy nodded. "If you're there too."

I took a deep breath. The thought of being away from Jamie shredded the very fibers of my heart. "And if I'm not, would you still want to go?"

He scowled. "I-I don't know. I'm not sure."

"Well," I kissed his cheek, "nothing needs to be settled tonight. Go to sleep, son; we'll talk more in the morning."

I blew out the lamp and paced to the window. The night scene wrapped itself securely around me, blotting out the realities of stark daylight. The first decision I needed to make was destination. Boston? The thought terrified me. I know I wouldn't fit in with the Back Bay crowd James had described. He'd hated his parents' world enough to leave it behind twice. I knew Ian would never have returned except for Drucilla.

"Dear Father," I prayed softly, "guide me in this most important decision. My children's entire future will be determined by this choice. Place me where You want me to be. Amen."

I climbed into bed and adjusted the covers. I could hear Jamie's slow, steady breathing next to me. I wondered what kind of dreams he might be having. In the cradle beside my bed, CeeCee whimpered. I reached down and patted her back. She stirred, then drifted into a deeper sleep.

I rested my head on the pillow and stared into the darkness. *Shinglehouse? Perhaps, if Pa will accept me back. Denver?* As kind as Gladys and Phineas had been, their world was a miniature Boston. *Columbine?* No. I'd miss my friends, but I couldn't stand living near the mines, hearing the machinery churning out gold ore once more. I'd sacrificed too much already for the mother lode. *Hays? It might be fun living near Aunt Bea and Zerelda once again. The memories of James's and my courtship, of falling in love, of our first kiss, of our wedding day and that silly chivaree—but with the farm gone, what's left?*

And San Francisco? The least likely of all. Other than Joe, Cy, and Phillip, I knew no one. My thoughts drifted back to my wild ride West to Kansas. Familiar faces, each a part of the jumbled pattern in the crazy quilt of my life. *How many times have I headed for California, only to be detoured by my heart?*

When I arose in the morning, I seemed to be no closer to a decision than before I slept. CeeCee kept me occupied at the breakfast table as I tried to convince her to eat her bowl of oatmeal. Even the raisins Mrs. Jones added on top didn't please the little girl. I realized CeeCee's petulance had little to do with oatmeal and a lot to do with the upheaval in her life. I had to make a decision—the sooner, the better.

Ian and his father left immediately for Hahn's Peak to meet with the lawyer. Jamie asked to go to school; it had been weeks since he'd been able to attend. I stayed to help Mrs. Jones with the morning dishes. One look out the window at the blue sky and the bright morning sun, and I decided to take CeeCee to visit Ula and Noah, perhaps for the last time. Besides, the mere thought of the Van Arsdales brought a fresh supply of peace to my mind.

Ula and I sat in their sunny kitchen talking while Noah took the baby out to see the chickens. After I explained my predicament, Ula asked, "If it weren't for anyone else, the children, the grandparents, friends, anyone, which place would interest you the most?"

I laughed. "Oh, that's easy, San Francisco. You should read the letters Joe has sent about the place. It's incredible. Right there on the Pacific Ocean. Why, he describes trees over one hundred fifty feet tall that would take a good thirty men to encircle."

She smiled. "There you have it, child. You say you've prayed about this and received no definite answer. Maybe the Lord is giving you the choice."

"I don't know." I worried a curl that had escaped the tight bun into which I'd drawn my hair. "Probably the wisest move is either Hays or Boston, as much as I hate to admit it. My husband planned to send Jamie to his grandfather this fall to attend the boys' school near Boston."

Ula shook her head tenderly. "I wish I had some words of wisdom for you, but your problem is completely foreign to me."

I laughed. "That's why I'm having such a time—it's foreign to me also." When Noah returned with CeeCee, I asked him to close up the cabin for me.

"I've packed everything that's important to me or to the children in the trunks. I'll write and let you know where you can send them. Everything else is yours to do with as you please." I pressed a few bills in his hand. "If this doesn't cover it, let me know, and I'll reimburse you or telegraph it through to you.

"Oh, no." The man shook his head vigorously and attempted to return the money to me. "I couldn't take anything from you."

"Please?"

He studied my face for a moment. "If you insist."

I stood to leave. Noah picked up CeeCee in his arms. "Before you leave, we need to pray together one more time."

We formed a tight little circle—Noah, Ula, and I. Noah's voice broke as he prayed for the children and my safety and for God's guidance in our lives. After the prayer Ula scurried to the bedroom and returned with handkerchiefs for each of us. We laughed and instantly put them to use blotting our tears.

"I'll never forget you two." I took each of their hands in mine. "You brought James and me to Jesus. We only half knew Him before we met you. You'll always be special for that."

Ula hugged me and wept while Noah blew his nose. When he'd recovered, he shook his finger in my face. "We expect to hear from you, young lady. You will write, won't you?"

I laughed through my tears. "Absolutely. And I'll send pictures of the children on their birthdays and at Christmas and . . ."

"And of you on your wedding day?" Ula interjected.

I looked at her askance. "No, that won't be happening, a wedding, that is. I don't intend ever to marry again."

Ula patted my arm tenderly. "I know you feel that way right now. But don't close the doors God may open." I shook my head the entire time she spoke. She paused and flashed a tiny smile at her husband. "Did you know that it's the second marriage for both of us?"

My mouth dropped open. I stared in shock. "No!"

"Yes. Thirty years." They laughed and hugged each other. Ula explained, "I was married ten years to my first husband and Noah thirteen to his first wife."

"Well, as you said, it's too soon to tell." Agreeing seemed to be the best way to move past the topic. I'd made up my mind, and even my dearest friends in the world wouldn't be able to change it.

As CeeCee and I walked back to the Joneses' house, I passed the Sheriff's office. Sheriff Jones waved to me. I peeked in. "Hi, did you want to see me?"

He grinned and drew us into the overheated office. "I wanted to tell you that the sheriff of Hahn's Peak took Otis Roy to Steamboat Springs today, to stand trial, and—" He paused a moment to scramble the already scrambled stack of papers on his desk. "—to give you this. It came in this morning's mail."

I glanced at the postmark—San Francisco, California.

"Thanks, it's from my brother, Joe."

The sheriff reached across the desk. "Thank you for all the help you've been to this town—the library, the ladies' club, Columbine's very own doc." He grinned broadly.

I chuckled. "You won't be called in to assist with surgery again, will you?"

Blushing, he continued. "Never could handle the sight of blood! My wife says you'll be moving back to Boston with your husband's family. Our prayers go with you and the children."

"Thank you, sheriff. I'll miss everyone here. You've been family to me and mine."

I left the office, eager to read my brother's letter. I hadn't heard from him since he wrote of his fiancée's death. As we unlatched the Joneses' front gate, Mr. McCall stepped out onto the porch and called to CeeCee. She let go of my hand and ran to him.

Tearing open the envelope, I withdrew the letter and read it. My brother's heart-rending cry for help brought unexpected tears to my eyes. I'd never felt so close to him. So many of the feelings he described in the letter I now understood. I looked up from the letter. Mr. McCall had disappeared inside the Joneses' house with CeeCee.

Though my nose tingled from the cold and I was shivering, I sat down on the porch swing and read through the letter a second time. When I had finished, I turned over the envelope and noticed the letter had been posted less than a week before. *How did it get here so fast? San Francisco to Virginia City, to Salt Lake City, to Steamboat Springs, to Hahn's Peak, then to Columbine—in less than a week. It should have taken twice that long, at least.*

Then I knew. I'd asked for direction and received it. My brother needed me. And, maybe, just maybe, I needed him. I thought about his new horse ranch across the bay from the city, the rolling hills, the acres of green grass—and I made my decision. *At least for a while, at least until the children heal, while I heal . . . Maybe in the fall I'll be strong enough to face my mother-in-law and her overbearing friends. Maybe then, maybe then.*

California Bound

To say that James Edward McCall was upset wouldn't fully express his emotion. As I watched his face suffuse with color, I feared he might pop a blood vessel in his forehead. Ian stared down at his boots; he obviously was not used to seeing anyone defy the family patriarch.

The elder McCall stormed from one end of the Joneses' small parlor to the other. "James told me you were a sensible girl, and now you've come up with a harebrained idea like this? There is no way I will allow it."

"I beg your pardon? No way you will allow it?" I arose from the sofa and turned to face the blustering man. "Sir, there is no way you can stop me. I am not a child to be ordered about at your discretion."

"You're wrong. There are ways. I could hold up your inheritance." He glared and chewed on the stem of his pipe.

I arched my eyebrow defiantly. "I have my own money, at least enough to take the children and me to my brother's place outside of San Francisco."

His eyes narrowed; his mouth tightened into a thin line. "And I could take my grandchildren from you like that." He snapped his fingers in my face.

Like a bolt of lightning, intense fear shot through me, followed by disbelief. "You couldn't do that."

"Oh, yes, I could. My lawyers could have you, the grieving widow, declared incompetent in any court in the nation."

"All right, this has gone far enough." Ian planted himself between us. "Threats won't get us anywhere. Let's all sit down and talk this over calmly." He led us to the sofa and then stood, looming over us. "First, Chloe, you need to understand that my father is seldom challenged. His opinions are right, even when they're wrong."

The man rose like a grizzly under attack. "I beg your par—"

"Please sit down, Father. For once in your life, listen to what I have to say." Ian turned to me. "Second, Chloe, I would never allow my father to tie up your inheritance or take your children from you. However, you need to see this from my father's side. Jamie is the only grandson he will ever have."

"You don't know that," I protested. "Drucilla could . . ."

Ian shook his head. "No, when she lost the last baby, the doctor told her she would never be able to get pregnant again. Ashley is our one and only child."

I stared down at my hands on my lap.

"Because Jamie is the only one who will carry on the McCall name and fortune, my father is concerned about his education."

I nodded. James and I had had our most heated arguments over the subject.

"But even more than that, he's a grieving father. And every time he looks at Jamie, he sees his favorite son."

"I never said—" Mr. McCall protested.

Ian lifted his hand. "You didn't have to, Dad. I always knew."

The man beside me fell silent. Ian waited for me to speak.

I searched for the right words to say. "I didn't mean to imply that San Francisco will be my permanent home. I was thinking of staying there a few months, long enough to get over missing James so much. After that, who knows?" I started to cry. Ian handed me a carefully folded handkerchief. I told them about Joe's ranch, the horses, his recent loss.

"I think a few months of solitude at the ranch will be good for the children too. Their lives have been turned upside down too, you know."

Ian turned to his father. "See, it isn't as bad as you thought. It's just for a few months."

The older man shook his head sadly. "No, you'll get out there, meet another man, and you'll want to stay. The children will grow up never knowing me as their grandfather."

When I laughed, the men looked askance at me. "I'm sorry. It's just you're the third person today determined to marry me off." I paused, suddenly recalling a similar conversation I'd had with James a few years back. "Let me assure you, it won't happen. I loved your son with my whole heart. He'd be pretty tough to replace, as you know."

Dad McCall pursed his lips. "What about Jamie's education?"

I nodded slowly, painfully, for I knew I'd have to face the terrible reality of losing him. "James made his wishes clear to me. We agreed that we were going to send him East in September. He would stay with you during the school breaks and return to us in the summers."

The man nodded slowly.

I sighed. I had to force the words from my throat. "I see no reason to change that. As much as I disagreed with James over this issue, I will not go against his wishes."

Ian smiled at me. "My father will agree to arrange for his travel in the fall if you'll take care of his springtime journey across the country."

"I never said I'd—"

Ian shook his head and grinned. "Father, recognize a

good deal when you see it."

With the major negotiations settled, we moved on to the less important ones—money. I convinced Ian to give Pete a major bonus, since he had worked so closely with James throughout the entire operation. "It was Pete's knowledge of geology that directed James to the mother lode."

I wanted Pete to enjoy the freedom I suddenly had, to go where he liked and do whatever he wished to do.

Ian agreed. "I had already decided to do that this afternoon when he showed up here at the house with all the mine's books. One glance at the records, and I knew the fine work was not done by my brother."

Since I'd decided to go to California rather than Massachusetts, we all agreed I should allow Ian to buy me out. Tomorrow we would take the train to Steamboat Springs and sign all the legal papers in front of a notary public. I would then board the train for California while the two men would remain in Steamboat Springs until the eastbound train arrived the next morning.

Mr. McCall stood and extended his hand to help me to my feet. Hesitantly, I took it. My nerves were still raw from his earlier threats. "I am sorry, my dear, for coming on like a bull seeing red. My son is right. I'm accustomed to speaking and everyone jumping to carry out my will. Please forgive me."

I nodded slowly. "I suppose I could have been a bit more demure, as your son would have put it. He once told me I'd make some man a fine wife if I weren't so impetuous and opinionated."

Ian laughed. "My brother said that?"

I nodded, a teary smile teasing the corners of my mouth. "I will keep my word, Mr. McCall. I won't deprive you of your grandchildren, Jamie or CeeCee, I promise. And who knows—by fall, I might be ready to move into that Cape Cod cottage I had never heard of before yesterday."

The older man pulled me into his arms, giving me a hug worthy of a Rocky Mountain grizzly. "You're a good daughter, Chloe Mae. Remember, you always have a place with us."

Early the next morning Jamie, CeeCee, and I visited each of our friends in town to say goodbye. When I returned to the Joneses' place, Pete met me at the gate. The children ran ahead of me inside the house.

Anger darkened Pete's eyes. "What is the idea, trying to pay me off for my friendship?"

I stopped and stared. "I'm not paying you for your friendship with me or with James. Where did you get that idea?"

"Ian told me you suggested—"

I interrupted. "I suggested he give you a bonus as the faithful manager of the Renegade Mine who handled everything after the accident, paying all the miners and closing the books. That you have also been our dearest friend has nothing to do with that! I'm insulted you would think that I would—"

"I'm insulted you would think that I would—" We looked at each other and laughed. "Friends?"

"Friends."

"I don't like having you and the children travel alone to California," he admitted.

I walked up the steps and leaned against the porch railing. "We'll be fine, I'm sure. Do you know what you're going to do now or where you're going to go?"

He stood at the base of the steps. "I'm going to stay around here until Otis comes to trial. After that, I might go see my mother in Oregon." He kicked the bottom step with the toe of his boot. "Your brother-in-law's generosity will allow me to complete some unfinished business in San Francisco."

"Really? You'll look us up, won't you? I'll give you Joe's address."

Pete nodded. "I'd like that."

Minutes later, Ian, Mr. McCall, the children, and I were on our way to Hahn's Peak in a borrowed sleigh. As we passed the VanArsdales' place, I saw the living-room curtain move. I waved, hoping either Ula or Noah had seen me. In Hahn's Peak we went directly to the station and boarded the train for Steamboat Springs. Bittersweet memories haunted my mind.

CeeCee fell asleep with her head in my lap. Jamie sat beside his grandfather, staring out the train window. I wondered if his thoughts were similar to mine. I longed to reach across the aisle and comfort him. But I knew that if I did, my tears would start flowing and never stop.

In Steamboat Springs we finished our business quickly. As I wrote my name, Mrs. Chloe Mae Spencer McCall, the finality of the moment overwhelmed me. Suddenly, it was as if I were letting go of the last of James. I gulped back my tears and signed the last paper.

We left the legal offices and walked to the depot, CeeCee bouncing along on Ian's shoulders. We cried when we parted, everyone but CeeCee. She was getting irritable from missing her afternoon nap. Jamie and I waved until the train crossed the wooden trestle at the west end of town.

During the next several days, we fell into a comfortable routine of sleep, play, food, stories, and sleep, play, food, stories. The last day, as we sped out of the mountains and across California's Central Valley toward San Francisco, one of the older passengers told tales about the masked bandit Black Bart.

"He robbed twenty-nine trains in all without firing a shot. Imagine the authorities' surprise when they unmasked him, and the fierce outlaw turned out to be a mild-mannered pharmacist from back East somewhere." The excitement I felt inside I could see reflected in Jamie's eyes.

As the train pulled into the Oakland station, the sun was setting. Jamie was the first to spy the bay. But I was the first to spot Joe. He was standing at the edge of the platform intently watching the faces of the deboarding passengers. The tall kid with the feet too big for his body had filled out into a solidly built, fine-looking young man with a mustache and trimmed beard.

When I tapped on the window, he looked up. His eyes widened, and his face broke into a grin. I motioned for him to meet us at the forward door to the car. After Jamie helped me collect CeeCee and her collection of toys, we joined the line of passengers eager to disembark.

Instead of waiting patiently for us to get off, Joe jostled his way onto the car through the rear door. "Chloe! Chloe Mae Spencer, er, McCall, let me take a look at you." He strode down the aisle toward me.

I set CeeCee and my luggage in an empty seat with the command to stay put. "I'll stay with her, Mommy." Jamie stepped out of the aisle.

"Thanks, son," I called over my shoulder as I squeezed through the crowded aisle toward my brother. When I reached him, he swept me off my feet into his arms. Dizzy with joy, I squealed, laughed, and cried—all at once.

"Would you look at you, little mama! I can't believe my eyes." He squeezed me tighter and whirled about in a circle. My shoes clattered against the armrests on the aisle seats. People were pointing and laughing.

"Put me down, you big galoot." I pounded playfully on his chest. "Put me down."

He threw back his head and laughed. "Make me, little sister! It feels so good to hug you, I may never put you down."

Behind me I could hear CeeCee's thin wail. "Mama. Mama!"

I glanced over my shoulder. "You will if your niece gets wound up into a frenzy."

He looked around me, then slowly lowered me to my feet. "Your daughter . . ." The awe in his voice brought on more tears. I wiped them on my sleeve. By this time the car had emptied, except for us, the children, and a smiling porter.

Joe moved past me toward the waiting children. He knelt down in the aisle beside CeeCee. "Oh, sis, she's beautiful, the spitting image of you. Will she come to me?"

I stepped behind him. "CeeCee, this is your Uncle Joe."

With the gentleness he reserved for his most skittish fillies, he said, "CeeCee, may I give you a hug?"

The little girl's face broke into a dimpled grin. "Daddy?" she asked.

I inhaled sharply. Joe blanched and glanced up at me. I waved my gloved hand. "Don't worry. She's been doing that a lot lately."

He nodded and stood. "And you must be the incredible Jamie I've heard so much about." Joe solemnly shook Jamie's hand. "Welcome to California, pardner."

Jamie smiled up at my brother. "She's told me all about you too."

"Oh, no!" A look of mock horror filled Joe's face. "I'm in trouble now."

Jamie laughed. "No, most of it was good."

Joe looked back at me and arched his eyebrow. "Most?"

I cuffed him playfully on the arm. "If you'll help me with CeeCee, Jamie and I can get all our lighter luggage. The trunks will be coming through in a few weeks. If you carry CeeCee and this valise, Jamie and I can manage the rest."

The porter rushed to me. "I'll take those, ma'am."

I smiled and nodded a thank-you.

Within minutes of arrival, I fell in love with Joe's ranch. It wasn't at all like our place in Kansas. The flat-roofed adobe house sprawled like a cat lying in the sun. My brother introduced us to his housekeeper, Maria Santana. The woman's warm, friendly smile made me feel immediately welcome. CeeCee took to her instantly.

"Maria," Joe asked, "would you take CeeCee and Jamie to the kitchen for a cool glass of milk and some oatmeal cookies?" The woman took the children's hands and led them away.

"Your rooms are down here." The heels of my shoes clicked on the cool red tile as I followed Joe to the entire left wing of the house he'd prepared for me and the children. "Maria's late husband's family came to California in the late 1700s from Spain. She has two grown sons who live in Los Angeles with their families, but she prefers to be independent. She grew up here on the ranch when it was owned by the Spanish don who built it."

He led me down an arched hallway and swung open a dark oak door. I stepped into a spacious bedroom that was more like a suite than a bedroom. It contained a dining table and two chairs, as well as a small sitting area in front of a gigantic whitewashed fireplace. I set my valise on the floor beside the bed covered in a red-and-gold jacquard spread.

"Chloe, mi casa es su casa. In English that means, My home is your home. Jamie's room is next door." He touched my cheek tenderly. "It's so good to have you here. I've been so lonely since . . ."

"I know. I understand. Oh, do I understand. But that's all in the past. We're here together, finally."

His face darkened. "Don't worry about money. If you or the children need something, just ask, all right?"

I laughed. "Joe, if I keep my head on straight, I will never have to worry about money again. So, please, I know your business is on its first legs, so let me help out with the expenses."

He studied my face for a moment while I straightened his collar. "I mean it, Joe. I have more than enough for three lifetimes."

"I can't take any of your money."

I picked up my valise and walked to the door.

"Hey, where are you going?"

I glanced over my shoulder and reached for the door latch. "Either I pay my own way, or the children and I are going to a hotel."

Joe heaved an exasperated sigh. "Can we talk about this tomorrow morning?"

In response to my nod, Joe said, "You haven't changed, have you? But now I'll leave so you can start unpacking."

After Joe closed the door behind him, I looked around the room. I unlatched the leaded-glass window and gazed out at a stone fountain in the center of a quiet courtyard. Around the fountain grew strange plants separated by red tile walkways.

I strolled out into the garden. I sat on the edge of the fountain and let the cool, clear water trickle through my fingers, soothing my travel-frayed nerves.

The Sunday after we arrived in California, we had visitors. Jamie had gone for a ride on one of Joe's geldings, and I'd just put CeeCee down for her afternoon nap when Cy Chamberlain and his wife Pamela, along with Phillip and Phillip's fiancée, Abigail Muldaire, arrived in Cy's shiny black surrey. I immediately recognized the Morgan horses with whom I'd once shared a stable car.

I followed Joe out of the house into the spring sun to greet our guests. As the foursome stepped out of the elegant carriage, I ran up to my two old friends to shake their hands. Instead, they each gave me a hug. Abigail, Phillip's fiancée, tittered nervously, while Pamela, Cy's wife, arched her eyebrow disdainfully.

Cy introduced me to his wife. "Chloe is the midwife I told you about. I'm sure she'll be willing to help deliver our child when the time comes."

The woman's tower of ebony curls didn't move a hair when she extended a limp gloved hand. She smiled in a half-lidded fashion. "How charming."

I shook her hand with the enthusiasm of a Colorado miner. "It's nice to meet you too, Pamela. I've been eager to meet the woman who captured Cy's roguish heart." I turned and grinned at Cy. But by the grim lines around Pamela's mouth, I knew better than to inquire about the birth of the child she was carrying.

Phillip gently took my elbow, turning me toward his fiancée. "And this is Abby, Abby Muldaire. And, Abby, I'd like you to meet Chloe Spen—excuse me, make that, Chloe McCall."

Abby smiled shyly as she extended her hand to me. "I've been eager to meet you, Mrs. McCall. Since Phillip learned you were coming to California, he hasn't stopped talking about you for a moment."

Pamela sighed dramatically. "Cyrus, how long will you keep me standing here? Please find me a chair."

"Of course, darling." Cy took his wife's arm and led her toward the open door. Joe took the woman's other arm.

This lady's just like Gladys's friends; are all high-society women like that?

Phillip took Abby's and my arms and led us toward the house. "I am so sorry to hear of your loss, Mrs. McCall," Abby said.

"Yes," Phillip echoed, "let me add my condolences to that of my fiancée."

"Thank you both. Being here with Joe has eased the loneliness." I choked back a sudden rush of tears. *Will I ever be able to graciously accept people's mention of James's death? Does it ever become easier? Does the pain ever stop?*

We joined Joe, Pamela, and Cy in the parlor, where Maria was already serving cool lemonade.

Cy turned to his wife. "Did I ever tell you about the day I spent with Chloe, traipsing all over Chicago looking for a nurse?"

Pamela's lips curled into an insipid smile. "Many times, dear."

He either ignored or missed the sarcastic edge in her voice. "Chloe, whatever happened to your beautiful long hair? At the Grange socials I used to try to figure out just how long it was." Catching himself, he added, "Not that it isn't gorgeous the way it is right now."

I laughed nervously. *If this guy expects his wife and me to become friends, he's going about it all the wrong way.* "Soon after James and I moved to Columbine, Colorado, our cabin caught fire. My hair went with it. Now, I'm spoiled by the convenience of shorter hair, so I keep it this way."

Cy made matters worse. "Well, it's absolutely beautiful, isn't it, Pamela?"

The woman forced a small smile. The tension of the moment was broken when Jamie burst into the room. "Mama, guess what? Miguel is teaching me to throw a lasso."

When he noticed the guests, Jamie became suddenly shy and stood behind my chair.

Phillip smiled at the embarrassed boy. "Hello, Jamie, remember me? I visited your home in Kansas."

Jamie nodded solemnly. "You're the man who made my daddy mad."

Phillip started, I choked on my lemonade, and the others looked amused, waiting for an explanation.

I touched a linen napkin to my lips. "What Jamie means

is, Phillip's visit prompted James to, uh, propose marriage."

A series of *oh's* filtered around the room.

"How romantic," Abby cooed.

Phillip then asked Jamie questions about what sub-
jects he liked in school and what he wanted to be when he
grew up. When Jamie admitted he wanted to be a physician, Phillip asked, "Do you think you'll be a better
physician than Chloe, your stepmother?"

Jamie shook his head and rested one hand protectively
on my shoulder. "Oh, no, Mama's the best because she
really loves people. She says I need to get as much knowledge as possible, but that all the knowledge in the world
can't make me a doctor unless I love people."

Cy glanced at me, his eyes filled with respect. "It sounds
like you have quite an admirer, Chloe."

I reached up and patted Jamie's hand. "I wouldn't trade
my son for all the diamonds of Africa."

Phillip lifted his glass toward me. "Ah, what about for
the teeming millions of China? Of course, living in San
Francisco, we have 40,000 or so of them, at least at the last
count."

"I haven't seen Chinatown yet, but I did see a few of their
homes. It's so sad, so many living in hovels not fit for
animals."

Pamela clicked her tongue. "My dear Mrs. McCall, those
people choose to live like animals. They wouldn't know how
to live any other way."

"Really? If your assumption that they don't know any
better is correct, perhaps they need a teacher."

Pamela rolled her eyes toward the ceiling as if to say,
"Oh, really! How naive." Condescendingly, she continued,
"They're dirty little thieves and beggars. It's not pleasant
seeing them about everywhere you choose to go."

The scowl on Joe's face was signaling me to keep quiet,

but I could feel my Irish rising. "We can't exactly blame them for being here. If I remember my history correctly, the shipping, railroad, and mining barons of San Francisco brought them here—and not too willingly either. Isn't that where we get the term *shanghaied?*"

"Well, yes, of course, but I can't be held responsible for that." *No, but I'll bet your daddy and your granddaddy can.*

Pamela examined the carefully manicured nails on her left hand. "After you've been here awhile, Mrs. McCall, you'll feel differently."

I lifted my chin and looked down my nose at the daughter of San Francisco's finest. "I certainly hope not. I can't help but wonder what you and I would be like if suddenly our money and fancy homes were gone. What if we were forced to walk in their moccasins for a day?"

"Their sandals, you mean?" Phillip sneered.

Unto the
Least of These

To say that Cy's wife Pamela left a bitter taste in my mouth for San Francisco's high society would be mild indeed. After the foursome left Joe's home, I sputtered for hours about the arrogance of the woman. Joe listened without saying a word.

Frustrated with the increasingly bemused look on his face, I asked, "What are you thinking?"

"I'm thinking it's good to have the old Chloe back." He strode to one of the parlor's tall arched windows and gazed out at the green pastureland across the roadway. "Since you've arrived, I've felt like we were both playing roles, careful to say and do only the right thing, afraid we might offend each another."

I straightened my spine. "Are you saying I'm offensive? If anyone is offensive . . ."

Joe turned and laughed. "No, no, not at all. I'm saying I like seeing the fire back in your eyes. Knowing the numbness hasn't penetrated through to your soul gives me hope."

I ran my hand over the sofa's leather armrest. "I don't think I understand."

"It's been so long since I've felt any emotion at all." Joe buried his face in his hands a long moment. He looked up and continued, "I'll admit having the children around has helped. They show me I can still smile. But to have you passionately defend people you don't even know—it's almost like the old days, before the bad times."

"Oh, Joe, I love you so much." I rushed across the room to his side. Tenderly massaging his shoulders and back, I said, "It's the children who have forced me to return from the land of the walking dead. Also remember, my loss is different from yours. My anger is focused on a person. I know who to blame." I swallowed hard and continued to work out the knots in my brother's neck.

"I can leave it in the hands of the law to mete out justice. I suspect you are blaming yourself and the entire world for your loss. That anger has anesthetized the rest of your other emotions."

We talked into the night, crying, laughing, and sharing old memories, both of our days as children and the years since leaving Pennsylvania. Finally he admitted exhaustion. I yawned. "There will be other evenings to talk."

He took my hand and lifted me to my feet. "And I'm so glad. I hope you decide to make this your permanent home."

Smiling sadly, I replied, "No home is permanent on this earth, dear brother."

He nodded slowly and walked me to my room. "Good night, Chloe."

"Actually, good morning," I replied.

The summer flew by at an incredible speed in spite of the relaxed pace of ranch life. On what would have been James and my third wedding anniversary, I received a letter from Pete that tore away my mask of acceptance and self-control.

"I hate to have to tell you this, but Otis was found not guilty, for lack of evidence. The sheriff and I suspect that he paid off the men whom you confronted in the saloon. They denied knowing or hearing anything. And the judge wouldn't take the word of a half-breed Indian!"

I couldn't believe it. I gripped the letter in my fist. The envelope fluttered to the floor. *Freed? Lack of evidence?* My head spun. I closed my eyes, afraid I might pass out.

"No, no, it can't be, Lord!" I shouted. My voice echoed off the high, open-beamed ceiling of my bedroom. "That's not fair. You promised justice! Where is the justice in allowing the man who killed my husband to profit from his dastardly deed?" I looked about frantically. I had to escape. I wanted to run, run as far as my strength would allow.

I crumpled the letter and threw it to the floor as I dashed into the garden. But I found no peace. I ran to the kitchen, where Maria was baking bread with CeeCee, her little helper.

"Maria, do you know where my brother is?"

By the look of concern on her face, I knew she'd heard my anguished cries. "In the barn, ma'am."

I leaned on the edge of the table to steady myself. "Would you mind watching CeeCee while I go find him?"

"Why, no, ma'am, she's no trouble at all. Is something wrong? Can I help?"

I shook my head vigorously. "No! No one can help. Thank you anyway." I turned and fled the room.

Joe wasn't in the barn or the stables or at the corral. Miguel, the ranch foreman, pointed toward the east. "He left with Jamie a few minutes ago for a ride to the hills. He wanted to check the fencing along the creek."

"Miguel, is there a mount I could ride, one not too frisky?"

The foreman grinned. "Mr. Joe told me the day you arrived that if you asked, you could ride Curry over there."

At the sound of her name, the mare snorted and tossed her mane. "Fine, could you help me saddle her, please?"

"I can do it, ma'am, while you go change clothing, I'm afraid your skirts might spook her."

I glanced down at my dress. "Oh, yes, you're right. I'll be

back in a minute."

He waved. "I'll have her waiting for you by the hitching post."

A few minutes later I was riding pell-mell down the dusty road. Poor Curry's energy gave out long before my anger. Breathing hard, she slowed to a trot. I patted her neck. "Good girl."

I allowed my body to absorb the rhythm of her gait and erased my mind of all thought until I felt as serene as the golden hills that surrounded me. When I got back to the ranch, Jamie came running from the stable. "Where did you go, Mommy? Miguel said you looked upset when you left. Uncle Joe and I were worried."

I dismounted and turned the horse over to the waiting foreman. "I'm fine, son. I just needed to get a little fresh air."

When we sat down to eat supper, no one spoke of my distress. It wasn't until I was putting CeeCee to bed that I realized I hadn't finished reading Pete's letter. But when I went to look for it, it was gone. The child watched as I scrambled on my hands and knees, looking under the giant bed, the dresser, and the chairs.

"Did you see Mommy's letter on the floor and put it somewhere?" I asked.

The child shook her head, her eyes round with fear.

Behind me I heard Joe clear his throat. He held the paper out to me. "Is this what you are looking for, Chloe?"

I leapt to my feet and snatched the letter from his hands. "How dare you read my personal mail! You had no right!"

He reddened. "You're right, I didn't. But when Miguel told me how upset you were and Maria confirmed his story, I came to your room to try to find the reason and found the letter discarded on the floor. I know it's no excuse. I am sorry. It won't happen again."

Why do you have to be so nice about it? I wanted to scream at you—I have to scream at someone. I burst into tears. Joe put his arm around my shoulders and patiently held me until I'd sobbed myself dry.

To the frightened little girl cowering on the bed, Joe said, "CeeCee, your mommy's feeling unhappy right now. I'm going to take you to Jamie; he will read you a bedtime story while your mommy and I take a walk in the garden."

After he returned, Joe led me through the double doors and over to the fountain. "Let it go, Chloe. Take your own advice and let it go. There's nothing more you can do." I started to cry again. "Chloe, leave it in God's hands."

I pushed him away roughly. He staggered, catching himself from falling into the fountain. The bitter bile in my throat reflected in my voice. "It's been in His hands all along—and look how much it's helped!"

"Come on, Chloe, these are your words. You're the one with the faith that God works everything out for good for those who love Him, right?"

I shook myself free. "Stop it! Stop it! I don't want to hear any more platitudes!"

Joe took a deep breath. "Did you read the part in the letter where your friend says he'll be arriving in San Francisco tomorrow and wants to see you? Who is this friend?"

I stopped. "Here in California?"

"Yes. So who is this man?"

I rolled my eyes skyward. "Joe, are you going to do this with every man who comes in and out of my life for the next fifty years? Honest, Pete's just a friend—James's and my best friend. Because if you are, I—"

"No, I promise," Joe chuckled, "to be suspicious of your male friends for only the next forty-nine years, OK? So why is he coming to San Francisco?"

"How do I know? You're the one who read the letter."

"He didn't say, except that he had business in the city. He

volunteered to take Jamie back East for you since he has to make the trip himself."

The awful thought of Jamie leaving me pushed all others from my mind. It was almost time to keep my promise to Jamie's grandfather. Just a few nights before, when I was tucking Jamie in for the night, he had asked me when he would be leaving. I put him off, saying I hadn't found anyone I trusted enough to accompany him. Now that excuse was gone.

The next morning all of us went to meet Pete at the train station. I paced the platform, restless and anxious. I spotted him and waved as he deboarded. Jamie shouted and dashed toward our friend. Pete waved back, then turned to help a beautiful dark-haired young woman down the steps. She smiled up at him as he placed her hand tenderly on his arm. I swallowed my look of surprise and rushed forward to meet him.

He gave me a hug, then hugged CeeCee and Jamie. Joe introduced himself, and the two men shook hands. I saw the woman nudge Pete. "Oh, yes, sorry. Faith, this is Chloe McCall, the wife of my best friend. She's the one who shot and butchered a buck elk by herself."

I blushed. Joe looked at me through startled eyes.

Pete laughed. "Did you tell him about that?"

"No, I haven't gotten around to that tale yet."

Joe rolled his eyes in disbelief. "What else can you tell me about my wild and wooly sister?"

Pete scowled. "Oh, you've only heard the half of it." He turned toward the woman. "And these are her children, Jamie and CeeCee. By the way, Faith is my wife. Thanks to your brother-in-law's generosity, I could afford to go back to Oregon and propose."

Faith broke into a dimpled grin. "And I accepted."

After a round of congratulations, Joe invited them to

stay at the ranch while they were in the area.

Pete shook his head. "I've reserved the honeymoon suite at the Palace Hotel. Of course, once the desk manager takes a look at us, he might cancel our reservation. Besides, I have an appointment at the attorney general's office in Sacramento to clear up that old business I told you about, Chloe."

I glanced toward Pete's shy bride. "Are you going with him, Faith, to Sacramento?"

"No, ma'am."

I glared at Pete. "You can't leave her alone at the hotel. I'll come back in the morning to take her to the ranch while you're gone. I'll have a delightful time telling her all about your nefarious past."

He grunted. "She knows the worst."

The next two days Faith and I had a lovely time getting acquainted. She confided that Pete's reason for going to Sacramento was to clear up charges of assault and battery leveled against him when he was a student in law school.

"He and a group of other students were playing cards one night when he accused the son of a wealthy shipping magnate of cheating. The boy became angry, called Pete a 'no good, lyin' Injun', and took a swing at him. Pete intercepted the punch with his left arm and simultaneously punched the big-mouthed fellow in the jaw with his right fist. Unfortunately, the boy fell back against the corner of a desk." She paused a moment.

"The man is paralyzed to this day. Unfortunately, the boy's father paid off the witnesses to say Pete provoked it. Knowing it was the word of a half-breed against big money, Pete disappeared in the Sierra Nevada."

"Poor Pete." I thought of my proud, compassionate friend. "And then he had to go through similar humiliation at Otis Roy's trial."

She smiled. "It was Mr. Roy's trial that convinced Pete to stop running. When he inquired whether the authorities were still looking for him, he found out that the charges against him had been dropped. Two of the students confessed to lying to the authorities." Faith took a deep breath. "Now Pete wants to go back to Connecticut to apologize to the man he injured. Your husband showed him that happiness is in letting go of your hate and anger. Pete is even making room in his life for God again."

My husband James? I never knew. James always found it difficult to talk to anyone of his faith in God. *But of course, he would have felt many of the same hurts after Mary died as I'm feeling now. How foolish I must have sounded, advising him in my blissfully naive way, to forgive and move on past the pain.*

When Pete returned from Sacramento, he was eager to be off to Connecticut. So by the end of the week, I found myself tearfully waving goodbye to my son. Feeling the haunted expression in his eyes reflected in my own heart, I'd recited all the platitudes—how fast the school year would go, how much he'd learn, how much fun he'd have meeting his cousin, Ashley. But neither of us was convinced.

I sank into depression during the following weeks. In desperation, Joe suggested I find something to occupy my mind. "Get out of the house. Go help at the downtown missions or something."

"I can't leave CeeCee."

Exasperated, he growled, "I'll hire a nanny if necessary. Two days a week. Think about it. You always wanted to go as a missionary to China. So here's your chance— Chinatown!"

"No, no, I couldn't do that."

A week later, at breakfast Joe announced that he was taking me on the city tour he'd promised when we first arrived. "Maria has packed us a picnic lunch and has volunteered to watch over CeeCee while we're gone."

A flicker of excitement stirred me enough to hurry me to my room to change into a more appropriate gown. I slipped into a forest-green gabardine with a cream-colored cotton plissé bodice, one of the dresses Gladys had insisted I buy in Denver. It hung loosely from my shoulders, revealing how much weight I'd lost since James had died. Pinning the bodice as tight in the back as possible, I slipped on the matching bolero jacket and checked my handiwork in the mirror. *Not good, but definitely better.*

Joe took me to Telegraph Hill overlooking the city, then to the Presidio, a United States military base. We ate our lunch down by the piers, where I fed most of my sandwich to the greedy gulls. Later we drove past the elaborate mansions on Nob Hill, then through the section of the city called Chinatown. Though parts of the district were typical of other cities and mining towns I'd visited, some were worse than I could have imagined: little children, dressed in rags that barely covered their nakedness, begging in the streets. Young girls of no more than thirteen selling themselves to drunken sailors. Old women hobbling along the street carrying burdens twice their size. Wasted, hollow-eyed opium addicts littering the doorways of paper-thin shacks.

Joe waved a hand toward the squalor. "Around here, a man can be murdered for the price of a bottle of whiskey. Shanghaiing is still common practice."

I turned toward my brother. "I know why you brought me here, but it won't work."

He smiled and pulled on the reins. The horses and wagon stopped in front of the only brick building in the area. The sign over the door read "The China Mission."

"Back in the seventies, a woman came to San Francisco from Baltimore as a missionary. She started this mission and preached her warnings against the sins of the city, but no one listened. Angry and frustrated, the woman told the people they would be destroyed by an earthquake; then she packed up and left town."

He helped me from the carriage. "Her helpers are still running the mission. Come, let me show you."

"An earthquake?"

"Oh, yeah, there've been a few since I've been here, but nothing as serious as this woman predicted, I assure you."

He led me inside the small entry, where we were met by Ida Jane Burns, a tall, angular woman with a severe limp. Joe introduced us. "My sister is a midwife. She's very interested in your work here. On her trip West, she visited the famous Hull House in Chicago."

The woman's eyes widened with admiration. "The Hull House," she whispered reverently. But that was her last whisper and her last reverent word. She guided me through the operation, her words coming at Gatling-gun speed. By the time we said goodbye, Ida Jane Burns had elicited from me a promise to volunteer two days a week.

As hard as I tried to be angry with Joe, I couldn't. I felt stirrings inside similar to those I'd experienced that day in Chicago with Cy and the day at the grange hall in Shinglehouse.

When Joe arranged with neighbors to have their daughter care for CeeCee while I was in the city, Maria threw a tantrum.

"Do you not trust me with your daughter?" She folded her arms across her chest and glared. "Have I done something wrong that you would feel it necessary to ask another woman to care for her?"

I shook my head. "Maria, I didn't want to impose. You do so much around here."

"Well," the woman huffed, her dark eyes snapping with anger, "it wouldn't be an imposition."

"Maria, I'd much rather have you taking care of her anyway. She likes you and knows you. I'll have Joe cancel the other woman."

"Good!"

I was surprised to find out how much I enjoyed the break of going into the city every Tuesday and Thursday, especially meeting and treating the people. I could only imagine what Pamela Chamberlain must have thought when Joe told her. She'd never know how much her obnoxious opinions were responsible for my decision to work there.

When Cy's daughter, Phoebe, was born in October, Joe and I went to take them a gift, a pearl-white knitted afghan I'd made. The woman barely extended us a welcome, tossing the gift on a table ladened with engraved silver baby spoons and cups and plates and rattles; dresses of Belgian lace and imported Irish linen; silk coverlets from the Orient, and Scottish woolen blankets embroidered with blue birds and daisies.

Pamela languished on her divan in her satin dressing gown, describing the excruciating pain she endured and the fact her figure would never be the same again. Lifting a limp hand to her forehead, she begged exhaustion. On the way to the elaborately appointed nursery to see the child, Cy assured us that Pamela did have a terrible delivery. "She was in labor for eight hours or more."

To myself I said, *For a first baby, I'd say she was mighty lucky!* After allowing us one glance at the infant, the hired nurse shushed us and hurried us out, lest our visit overstimulate the baby's digestive system.

As we stepped out into the carpeted hallway, Phillip bounded up the stairs to meet us. Cy apologized. "Chloe, I need to talk with Joe about some business. Would you be offended if I turn you over to Phillip for a few minutes?"

"Of course not."

Phillip volunteered to show me the atrium. Once alone, surrounded by a forest of lush tropical plants, Phillip paused beside a potted fern. "I've decided to break my engagement to Abby."

"Oh, I'm sorry to hear that. She's a very sweet young woman."

"Well . . ." He ran the fingers of one hand over the fern's delicate fronds and leaned closer to me. ". . . it wouldn't be fair to marry her if I'm in love with another woman." He took my hands and drew me to a nearby wrought-iron bench. Reluctantly, I sat down beside him. *I don't like where this is going.*

"Remember when you said, 'another time, another place'? Well, this is another time and another place."

"Phillip, first of all, I'd think long and hard before I gave up a woman as gentle and sweet as Abby. But if you really don't love her, then, yes, you should dissolve the engagement."

He leaned forward eagerly.

"Wait, I'm not finished. I might have totally misunderstood, but if you're doing it because you think you love me, then forget it. I have no intentions of marrying you—or anyone else."

His face fell a moment, then brightened. "Just give me a chance. I can change your mind."

I was shaking my head even before he finished speaking. "No, Phillip, our timing is still off. I have a lot of healing to do before I'd even consider such a proposal. I'm sorry."

Hearing voices in the parlor, we stood up. "I won't give up, you know."

"I wish you would."

Two weeks later, Cy told Joe that Phillip had broken his engagement. Abby had returned, in tears, to her home in New Orleans, while Phillip took a train to New York City on family business.

A letter from Jamie arrived a week before Thanksgiving begging CeeCee and me to come to Boston for Christmas.

"I miss you so much, Mama. I hate the school. The teachers are strict and sometimes mean. But I do love biology. Mama, you would love it too. I'm learning all about animals and plants. I've looked ahead in the book and read about the human body and how it works. I like astronomy too. I can't wait to see you and CeeCee again. If you and CeeCee come for Christmas, I will show you the stars and tell you their names."

I planned to stay in Boston for a month. Joe asked Cy to arrange for CeeCee's and my passage in one of the public luxury Pullmans that the Union Pacific had added to the line. But the night before we were to leave, CeeCee complained of an earache. By morning the earache had developed into a head cold. Sending the telegram saying we couldn't come was a most difficult thing to do.

January and February passed in a continual light drizzle. By March, I would have welcomed a rousing snowstorm. With April, the sunny days returned, partly because spring had arrived and partly because Jamie would soon be coming home.

Ian and Jamie arrived in California two days before CeeCee's third birthday. I couldn't believe how much Jamie had grown. We combined the celebrations, inviting Cy, his wife, and their daughter to the party. Pamela begged off.

Cy apologized for his wife. "I'm sorry, Chloe, but Pamela hasn't been feeling well. She might be pregnant again."

"It's perfectly all right, you know that. I'm just glad you could come."

Six weeks later I was surprised to find Cy at our front door, his team of matching Morgans tied to the rear of a rented carriage. His eyes empty, his face drained of color, he entered the house like a walking corpse.

"Cy, what's wrong? What's the matter?" I took his arm and led him into the parlor. He sat down heavily on the sofa.

"Pamela and her mother—" His voice broke. He started again. "Pamela and her mother took Phoebe and left for a Swiss health spa. Pamela said she needed a European cure. I'm afraid she went to have an abortion."

"Oh, I'm sorry. Did she say when she'd be back?"

He shook his head.

"It must be lonely in the huge, empty house. Can you stay here a few days to pull yourself together?"

He shook his head again. "No, I'm heading East on business. Actually, I've arranged to travel for Standard Oil for a few months, and I want to board my horses with Joe. I know he loves them almost as much as I."

"He's out with Jamie right now, checking fences, but his foreman is down by the stables. Would you like me to send for him?"

"No." The man stared down at his hands. "Chloe, I've tried to be a good husband. I don't know what I did wrong. Pamela hates me, she honestly hates me."

"Oh, no, I'm sure . . ."

He ran both hands through his hair. "I am so afraid she won't come back to me and I'll never see my daughter again."

"Cyrus, I'm so sorry. I don't know what to say."

He looked up, his eyes filled with anguish. "What is there to say?"

Cy stayed the night at the ranch and left California the next morning.

Summer passed all too quickly, and it was time for Jamie to return to Boston. During the summer months he'd grown strong and brown working under the California sun. I could hardly believe he was the same little boy I'd met five years earlier, cowering in the corner of the seat on the train West. Joe arranged to have a friend of his, a judge who was making a trip to Washington, D.C., deliver Jamie to Boston.

Again, it felt as if my heart had been rent asunder as I stood on the platform waving until the train disappeared from view. My salvation was my daughter and my work. I found the midwifery classes Ida suggested I teach rewarding and exciting. My first class of four Chinese women and one Spanish woman all chose to volunteer time at the mission as payment for the training. With six of us trained to deliver babies, it was easier to keep up with the calls.

September, October—in California, I barely noticed the months passing until a letter arrived from Pete that jolted me to the toes of my boots. "Faith and I visited Columbine on our way back to Oregon. Everyone is fine and asking about you. Ula asked if you are seeing anyone. I told her that I didn't think so. . . . I don't know how to tell you this, except to just come out and tell you. Otis was the secret buyer of the Renegade Mine. He opened the mine, hit the mother lode, and sold the operation for millions. He is now stinkingly rich! Sometimes, life isn't fair, is it, dear friend?"

The feelings of hate I thought I'd put to rest resurrected their ugly faces, consuming me with anger and resentment. When I read the Bible, I saw Otis's face. When I knelt to pray, I imagined James's crushed body. When Joe insisted I attend a little white church a few miles from the ranch, I left the services with a devastating headache.

I knew the answers. I'd been through all this before. But knowing I should let go of my anger and actually letting go were poles apart.

Cy returned to San Francisco the last day of October. I was working at the mission when, without warning, he showed up. If he had looked haggard before he left, he'd aged ten years since.

Even though I was dressed in a cotton shirtwaist and gray woolen skirt, he insisted on taking me out to lunch at Delmonicos. At first, I refused. He was a married man and I a single woman. Then, considering the mental state he was in, I agreed.

After we ordered and our food arrived, I took a bite of my watercress sandwich while he idly stirred his bowl of French onion soup. "How have you handled it so well, Chloe, losing your husband?"

I took my time chewing my sandwich, searching for the right answer. Finally I decided on honesty. "I'm not sure I have. Recently I learned that my husband's murderer got rich off the incident."

"Then you can understand my anger. I am furious with Pamela for taking Phoebe from me. And for taking the life of our second. I don't think I can ever forgive her."

I closed my eyes. *What must it be like being betrayed by your marriage partner? How devastating.*

Cy toyed with his soupspoon. "I have no doubt but that the woman's seeing other men. She's inferred as much. I'd love to wring her wretched little neck and toss her body into Lake Geneva."

I nodded, knowing all too well what my hate for Otis was doing to me. *I can't help you; can't you see that? I don't have the answers to solve my own problems, let alone give you advice on yours. Stop thinking I have some edge on sainthood.*

Yet, the man's eyes pleaded for help. To refuse Cy would be like refusing a drowning man a life preserver. "Cy, do you have a Bible at home?"

He shook his head.

"The best help I've found has been through God's Word." I felt like such a hypocrite, but I continued anyway. "Romans 12:19 says, 'Avenge not yourselves, but rather give place unto wrath: for it is written, Vengeance is mine; I will repay, saith the Lord.' "

"That's easier said than done."

"I know, but let's be honest. Our hate isn't hurting Pamela or Otis. They're both living in decadent bliss. We're the ones being destroyed."

He reached across the table and placed his hand over mine. "You're right. I think I'll pick up a Bible at one of the bookstores here in town this afternoon. Maybe I can come out to the ranch and study it with you sometimes?"

A warning alarm I'd come to trust since becoming a widow rang in my head. I shook my head. "That wouldn't be wise, Cy."

He studied my eyes for a moment, then drew back his hand. "You're right. But I still promise to begin studying."

"It would help if you started attending a church that preaches the Bible. After James and I lost everything in the fire, we gained an incredible amount of strength from our brothers and sisters in Jesus." I paused. A smile edged the corners of my mouth. "Maybe I'll take my own advice."

He paid our bill and helped me to my feet. "We can still be friends, can't we?"

"Absolutely!"

Letting Go

I fidgeted as the dressmaker pinned the last pleat in the skirt of my new rust-brown wool suit. I tugged at the front of the jacket, examining the braid on the cuffs, shoulders, and front of the jacket. "It has to be perfect, Sarah, absolutely perfect."

The dressmaker laughed. "It is important that your mother-in-law like you, yes?"

"Yes. She's never met me or my daughter. But more important, I want my son to be proud of his mama. He's used to proper Bostonian women wearing the latest fashion."

CeeCee and I planned to leave for Massachusetts the day after Thanksgiving. Joe had given Maria the week off so she could visit her sons in Los Angeles, so Joe and Cy helped me bake the pumpkin pies for Thanksgiving dinner while CeeCee drew a picture of a turkey for the middle of the dinner table. Being alone in the city, Cy had invited himself to the ranch for the holiday.

The next morning, Cy and Joe saw CeeCee and me off at the station. As I boarded the special Pullman car, the old familiar stirrings returned. *Will I ever tire of riding the rails?* I glanced down at my daughter. Her eyes danced with a similar excitement. She'd always been a bundle of energy, but lately, she'd added new meaning to the word *energy.* I chuckled to myself. *Maybe after traveling with a three-and-a-half-year-old . . .*

The McCalls proved to be gracious hosts during our stay. They provided plenty of time for Jamie and me to tour the city together. Though Mrs. McCall wasn't exactly warm, I got the impression she was being as friendly as her personality would allow. Dad McCall, on the other hand, spent many evenings chatting with me in the study. I had the feeling he thought of me as a link to his son. He even asked me if I needed funds. I laughed. I'd barely touched the money I had.

After I confided in him the news about Otis Roy, Dad McCall observed, "You still sound so angry, dear Chloe."

A tear trickled down my cheek. "I'm trying, honest."

"You'll never know real peace until you give your burden over to God. I've had to learn that many times over since the accident."

I tightened my lips into a thin line. "It wasn't an accident. That's the problem."

He looked at me and smiled. "I know; it wasn't an accident. It's just easier for me if I refer to it that way. Next summer, when Jamie returns, would you mind if my wife and I come for a visit?"

I smiled in surprise. "I'd love it."

A bemused smile wrinkled his face. "I'm not sure I can convince her to make the trip, but she has talked about visiting the Putnams in Denver. And we do have friends in San Francisco, so who knows?"

"I'd really like that," I assured him.

I visited Drucilla and Ian, though Drucilla acted as if she preferred to put our friendship in the past. This hurt. We'd gotten so close in Kansas. But she'd returned to her former life, filling her place as a charming matron in the Boston/Newport crowd.

Christmas at the McCall mansion was as extravagant as

it had been at the Putnams. I could see subtle changes in Jamie that disturbed me. He was becoming used to demanding and getting his own way. *We'll have fun working on that next summer.*

The night before CeeCee and I left for home, Mrs. McCall, Sybil, as she insisted I call her, was playing patty-cake with CeeCee while I packed our trunk.

Suddenly, without warning, she asked, "Are you seeing anyone?"

I looked up from the trunk. "Excuse me?"

"I said, Are you keeping company with a special man?"

I cleared my throat. "Sybil, I loved your son very much. I can't imagine replacing him."

"Who said anything about a replacement? People aren't replaceable. So, are you?"

I shook my head vigorously. "No."

"Well, you should. This child needs a father, and you need a husband."

I laughed nervously. "She has my brother Joe. And as for my needing a husband . . ."

Mrs. McCall pursed her lips. "I just want you to know that Dad and I have talked it over, and we think it's time. We won't be insulted."

"Well, thank you—I think."

Saying goodbye to Jamie didn't hurt as badly this time as it had before because I knew I'd see him in six months' time.

My next stop was Shinglehouse. I had tried to read between the lines of Ma's and Hattie's letters, hoping my father had softened in his anger toward me. But when CeeCee and I arrived at the station, all the family except Pa was there to meet me. When I asked about him, Ma averted her eyes and mumbled, "He had to make a special trip to Pittsburgh for the company."

Saddened and hurt, I didn't mention him again during

my stay. The biggest surprise was to meet Stanford Raleigh, their boarder. Stanford, a big, jolly man of thirty-five, taught science at the Shinglehouse high school. Within minutes, I knew he adored Hattie, and she him. And it would be only a matter of time before they both knew it.

When we said goodbye a few days later, I knew it would be a long time before I returned. My mother knew it also—I could tell by the way she clung to CeeCee. As I put on my bonnet and buttoned my gloves, Ma hugged me.

"I've missed you terribly, Chloe. When you left, I was devastated. But I'm proud of the woman you've become. And believe it or not, I think your father is too."

I smiled wryly. "Hmmph! He hides it well."

"Give him time. Give him time. As you know, some things take longer than others to heal."

I nodded. "And some things never heal. Will he let it heal?"

That question, I realized, applied to me as well. *Am I any different from Pa? Reason or not, are hate and forgiveness the same for everyone?* As the wheels of the locomotive clicked over the three thousand miles of track, I asked myself, again and again, the same questions. By the time I reached San Francisco, I had the answers and felt ready to move on. *Pa, you may be happy wallowing in your swamp of anger, but it's not for me. I'm getting on with life.*

With the arrival of 1904, I attacked the problems at the mission with a new vigor. In January, when I read in the newspaper that the wealthy mineral king Otis Roy planned to build a palatial mansion on Nob Hill, I brooded for a day, but then with God's help, I let it go. By spring I noticed with barely a twinge the frequent mention of him and his social life in the paper.

Cy had taken an interest in the mission, raising thousands of dollars from his wealthy friends. He showed up regularly to see how things were going, to be certain Ida and the rest of the staff had everything they needed. And each time he visited, he talked about Pamela. Yet, as painful as the ongoing separation was for him, I could see healthy changes taking place. His old confidence returned. And with the confidence came a new peace I'd never before seen in him.

Jamie's return to California announced the beginning of summer for me. I cut back on my days in the city to spend more time with him. My fears about his grandparents spoiling him dissolved. For back on the ranch, he was the same good-natured, caring boy he'd always been. But now, we had new topics to share. I loved riding out with him to watch the sunset, then staying to see the stars come out. He knew so much about the heavens that I actually found myself envying the opportunity he had to learn so many things. By the time he left for Boston in the fall, we'd become friends, as well as mother and son.

The fall passed quickly. With Cy's help, Ida and I had established three more missions in different parts of the city. I spent a day in each, teaching classes in midwifery and child care to immigrants. I attended a few of the women's suffrage meetings and was even asked to speak, but CeeCee, the mission work, and my involvement with the little country church near the ranch consumed most of my energy.

An emerald green silk gown in the window of a tiny dressmaker's shop on Market Street brought back such warm memories of James and Hays that I bought it on impulse to wear to a Christmas party Joe insisted I attend with him. I'd allowed my hair to grow longer than usual after Jamie said he liked it long. Piling the curls high on my head and fastening them all in place with a set of silver combs Joe gave me as an early Christmas gift, I studied my face in the mirror. *You're looking about as good as you can for a twenty-three-year-old widow and mother of two."*

The strains of waltz music met us as we arrived at Hiram Duffield's grand estate, bringing back memories of the New Year's party in Denver. *Will those old memories ever give me peace?* Even after several years, James was in my thoughts wherever I went.

In the brightly lighted foyer, an English butler took our wraps and announced us to the Duffields. After ingratiating myself to these two strangers, I hissed to Joe, "Why was it so important that we attend this party? I don't know a soul." When I turned to catch his response, he was strolling toward the opposite side of the room, where a young woman smilingly watched him approach.

"Who in the—?"

A voice behind me said, "Well, fancy meeting you here." I turned and found myself facing Phillip.

"Phillip?" My mouth dropped open. "When did you get back to California? Cy said you were finishing your law degree; is that true?"

He grinned, preening himself ever so slightly. "I have the sheepskin and the scars to prove it. Would you like to dance? Or would you prefer to find someplace where we don't have to talk above the music?"

I grinned. "Personally, I could use some food. I'm famished."

He laughed. "Leave it to you to say the unexpected!" He escorted me across the crowded ballroom floor and into the dining room, where a thirty-foot table groaned with food of every kind. We filled our plates and snaked our way to a sitting room off the main dining area.

After I settled myself on a yellow-flowered chintz sofa, Phillip pulled up a chair across from me. We laughed and talked throughout the evening. "Cy has told me all about your mission work in Chinatown. Obviously, part of your dream has come true after all these years. Let me ask you a question, if the borders of China were opened today, would you still go?"

I thought a moment of CeeCee and of Jamie back in Boston. "Yes, I think I would, if that's what God wanted me to do."

He shook his head, disbelief in his eyes. "God? A little impractical. I mean, according to my brother, you're a woman of substance now."

A devilish twinkle flashed from my eyes. "I've always been a woman of substance, haven't I?"

"You know what I mean."

I shrugged. "Wouldn't you go to Africa if you had the chance?"

A trifle bitterly, Phillip responded, "I wish life were so simple."

"I like to think that it can be."

He took a sip of punch. "You're good for me, Chloe, do you know that? Would you consider going with me to an art exhibit at the Palace Hotel on Tuesday?"

My thoughts bounced around like marbles in a schoolboy's lunch pail. *Date? Do I want to keep company with a man again? I admit I enjoy Phillip's company, but can there ever be anything more?*

I tilted my head and smiled. "I'd like that."

"Good. Shall I drive out to the ranch for you?"

I shook my head. "I'll be at the Chinatown mission in the morning; you can meet me there."

During the evening, Joe found us and introduced the young woman he'd abandoned me for as Elizabeth Jordan, the daughter of a language professor at the university. "Beth can read seven languages and speaks four fluently. I met her at a horse auction, where she and her father were looking for a trusty gelding to pull their buggy."

I liked the cheerful, sparkling woman instantly. We chatted for a few minutes; then the two of them drifted off to be alone. As they disappeared into the milling partyers, I spied a face I'd hoped to never again see—Otis Roy. He stood near the archway, where the hostess had hung a sprig of mistletoe.

A groan escaped my throat, and I blanched as a look of recognition passed between us before he disappeared down the hall.

Phillip touched my arm attentively. "What's wrong, Chloe?"

I folded my hands tightly to keep them from shaking. "I just saw the man who killed my husband."

"Here? Are you sure?"

I turned a steely gaze on him. "I'm sure."

"Are you going to be all right? Do you want to leave?"

I nodded yes to both questions and stayed rooted on the sofa while Phillip went to tell Joe he was taking me home. Out of the corner of my eye, I saw a pair of black boots standing beside me. I looked up, my face a frozen mask. "Mr. Roy, I heard you were in town."

He put his thumbs in his tuxedo cummerbund and rocked back on his heels. "And I, you. I've kept track of you, you know."

"Why?" I frowned.

"Because the only people left who can hurt me are you and that dirty Injun."

I stood to my feet. "Your manners haven't improved with your fortune, have they? You're as crude as ever." I arched my brow. "And as cowardly, I suppose?"

He grabbed my arm, digging his fingernails into my flesh. I tried to shake free, but he held on, glaring into my eyes.

Through clenched teeth, I said, "Mr. Roy, take your filthy hands off my arm this instant."

"Make me," he snarled through his bushy beard.

Phillip grabbed Otis's wrist and squeezed. "I believe the

lady asked you to unhand her." Otis winced with pain and let go.

Phillip narrowed his eyes threateningly. "I never want to see you touch this woman again. Do you understand?"

Otis shifted his gaze between Phillip and me before he noticed the curious looks of other party guests who had gathered around. Uttering a feral growl, Otis turned and stalked from the room.

The encounter left me so shaken that I refused to answer Phillip's questions. When he stopped the carriage in front of my brother's house, Phillip asked, "Are you going to be all right?"

Turning toward him, I said, "Otis Roy has wreaked havoc on my past happiness. I refuse to allow him to do the same with my present and future. I'll be fine."

Satisfied with my answer, Phillip said good night and promised to meet me at the mission at noon the following day. I spent the next few hours reading the Bible promises that had seen me through the worst of times.

By the next day, I'd put the experience behind me and was able to enjoy myself at the art exhibit with Phillip. Three more outings followed. Besides taking a buggy ride through Golden Gate Park, Phillip and I celebrated the arrival of 1905 with a quiet dinner at an out-of-the-way restaurant. The third was a day-long excursion to see the big trees.

When I returned that evening, Phillip paused at the door long enough to give me a gentle kiss on my lips, the first we'd shared. Suddenly the door jerked open. The icy tone my mild-mannered brother used with Phillip startled me. It must have surprised Phillip also, for he excused himself right away, saying he'd have to hurry to catch the last ferry back to the city.

The moment Joe slammed the door behind Phillip, I planted my hands on my hips. "OK, what's going on? I've never known you to be that impolite—and to a friend!"

"A friend," Joe growled. "He's no friend of mine."

I couldn't believe what my brother was saying. "What are you talking about?"

Joe led me into the parlor, where we sat down in the two chairs by the fireplace. "Chloe, you know I would never interfere in your private life. And I am glad you are beginning to socialize again. But Phillip Chamberlain is not the man you think he is."

"What are you talking about?" I couldn't believe the deep frown that still clouded his face.

"Cy came to visit tonight."

"So?" There was nothing unusual about a visit from Cyrus Chamberlain.

"He came to talk with you about his brother."

I felt the heat rising inside me. *What's going on?*

"Cy says Phillip is married and has an infant son in Baltimore."

"What?" I jumped to my feet. "I don't believe you."

"It's true. He showed me a photograph of the three of them together." Joe stood and reached for me, but I brushed his hand aside.

"Why didn't Cy tell me sooner?"

"He said he wasn't aware the two of you were seeing each other until today. As Phillip was leaving the house this morning, he mentioned the excursion to see the big trees. When Cy objected, Phillip told him to mind his own business."

The memory of the kiss on the front steps brought a blush to my cheeks. To make it worse, I'd actually enjoyed it. "I-I-I feel so foolish. I should never have let down my guard. What Cyrus must think of me!"

"He thinks the world of you. Why do you imagine he came all the way out here to warn you?"

"Well, I wish he'd told me to my face instead of telling you!" I marched down the hall to my room. Slipping into a nightgown, I fell to my knees. "Oh, dear Father, I am so sorry. I didn't know Phillip is a married man. I feel so dirty, so used."

On Monday I busied myself at the mission, trying to forget Phillip's betrayal and my embarrassment. Around eleven that morning Phillip showed up, hat in hand. As he walked into the small parlor I used as a classroom, I stood and faced him, my head erect, my back ramrod straight, my lips tightened.

"Before you say anything," he began, "let me apologize. I planned on telling you at the art exhibit, but I just couldn't find the right moment to bring up the subject. And one thing led to another, and it became more and more difficult."

"Bring up the subject? A wife and a son—and you couldn't find the right moment to tell me?" I stared at him in disbelief. "Phillip, you are a cad and a bounder! I've never been so disappointed in another human being in my entire life."

"But look at it from—"

"I'm not finished!" I continued. "You betrayed your vows to your wife, your honor as a father to a son. You desecrated our friendship beyond repair."

"Chloe, I always intended to tell—"

Fire blazed in my eyes. "You kissed me! You had no right to do so!"

He shrugged apologetically. "I-I lost my head for a moment."

"And you lost my trust forever."

"Chloe, please. I'm only a man."

"No, Phillip, you wear a man's clothing, and you speak with a man's voice, but a man, a real man would never behave in such an ungentlemanly fashion." I quivered with fury. Ida passed by the doorway, her eyes wide with questions.

Impatience flashed in Phillip's eyes. "Are you finished?"

"No, Phillip, we're finished."

He strode to the doorway, then paused and turned. "Tell me, would there have been any hope for us, if I, uh, hadn't married—"

I gasped at the man's audacity, then laughed aloud. "That's something you'll never know, will you?"

I turned slowly and walked to the bare window that overlooked one of Chinatown's filthiest back alleys. Phillip's question carouselled around in my brain the rest of the day. That evening when I recounted the story to Joe, I admitted I didn't know the answer.

A crooked smile appeared on his face. "It's a moot point, don't you think?" Joe always did have a way of going for the kill.

The meal over, Joe disappeared into his study while I read a bedtime story to CeeCee. After James's death, I continued the practice of having a little worship together each evening. It reminded us that we were still a family, and we both enjoyed our special time together.

CeeCee's bedtime prayer included Jamie, her grandparents, and the new batch of kittens out in the barn. After tucking her into bed and kissing her good night, I put on a woolen sweater, grabbed my hairbrush, turned down the light, and stepped outside into the courtyard. This was my special time to be alone, to review the day and to make things right with God.

A winter moon highlighted the California laurel and oleander shrubs. Removing the combs and pins from my hair, I dropped them into my skirt pocket. The curls tumbled down onto my shoulders and back. After running my fingers through the locks of hair, I began to brush.

One, two, three, four, five. It's getting long again, I thought as I counted the strokes. *I probably should at least trim the ends. Eleven, twelve, thirteen, four—*

I heard a knock at the front door and the sound of male voices—Joe's and Cy's. *I don't want to see him now.* I rushed toward my bedroom door. As I reached for the handle, Cy stepped into the garden and called my name.

"Chloe, don't go. We need to talk."

I paused. *It isn't Cy's fault his brother behaved so despicably. That doesn't make me feel any friendlier to him. Don't shoot the messenger . . .*

I laughed and turned. "Cy, what brings you out here at this time of night?"

He hurried over to me. "Two things. First, please forgive me for not alerting you sooner about Phillip. But I honestly didn't know the two of you had been seeing each other."

His eyes searched my face for my reaction. Cy followed me to the stone bench. I sat down, but he remained standing with one foot on the end of the bench.

"It's not your fault. I do wish you'd told me directly, however. It was humiliating to learn it from Joe."

"I'm sorry. You're right."

"Well, imagine how it felt to have my—"

"You were right; I was wrong."

"Oh." *Does he have to be so nice about it?* "You said something about a second reason for your visit?"

"Yeah, uh, I received a letter today from Pamela. She's demanding a divorce so she can marry a Russian count."

"Divorce?" I tried to remember if I knew anyone who'd ever done such a thing. No one came to mind.

He straightened and strolled over to the fountain. "I know I have no right to come to you with my problems. But we've been friends for a long time." He turned toward me. "I don't love Pamela any longer. I haven't for some time now, especially after acquaintances returned from visiting Paris, where they saw her several times with her count." The anger in his voice shifted to despair. "I can't give up

Phoebe. I must have my daughter back. What can I do? What would you do?"

I exhaled sharply. This was a problem I'd never even imagined, let alone faced. "Whew, I hardly know what to say." I was stalling for time. "The first thing I think I'd do is head for Europe and get my child back. Even in that decadent society, a court of law would frown upon a marriage partner's infidelity. It would be worth a try, wouldn't it?"

He dropped his head. "I think you're right. I'd never forgive myself if I didn't at least try."

Cy walked over to me and took my hands in his. "Thank you again for being such a good friend. And I again apologize for the pain and embarrassment my brother caused."

I smiled wryly up into his shadowed face. "More embarrassment than pain, I assure you. We weren't that close."

He looked down at my hands. "I'm glad."

Gently I withdrew my hands from his. "If there's anything I can do to help with Phoebe . . ."

"Thank you. Right now, all I can manage is one step at a time."

I patted his arm and headed toward the parlor door. "I've been there before; I understand."

We entered the well-lighted parlor, where Joe waited. Cy glanced toward me and smiled. "Oh, did I tell you that Phillip sent for Jenny, his wife?"

"No, but be sure to tell your brother how eager I'll be to meet her when she arrives."

Cy frowned. "You won't tell her about—"

I laughed aloud. "Of course not. I just know how difficult it is to adjust to a new home and new friends. Nothing more."

Cy left for Europe two days later. A week after his departure, Jenny arrived with Phillip's son, Andrew. Joe invited them out to the ranch for a welcoming dinner. I responded to the timid woman as I would to a tiny brown wren lost in a hurricane. She acted intimidated by Phillip's every word and glance. Hungry for a sympathetic face, Jenny latched onto me immediately, in spite of her husband's attempts to keep us apart. *As if I'd wound her to get even with him! What a pompous jerk!*

During the next few months, Jenny started dressing like me, combing her hair like mine, and volunteering to help at the mission on the same days as I. I didn't mind, but Phillip made it clear, at every opportunity, that he did.

One morning Jenny didn't arrive at the mission on time. Later Phillip stalked in. In front of Ida, he informed me that his wife would no longer be assisting at the mission. "I do not wish to have my son exposed to the contagious diseases circulating through this neighborhood."

Ida nodded. "That's fine. Be sure to tell Jenny we'll miss her, and we'll be sorry to lose her help."

Following Ida's cue, I added, "You know, Phillip, Jenny has a gentling influence on the people with whom she works. She's a real jewel of a person."

Pointing his finger directly in my face, he almost shouted, "You stay away from Jenny. I don't need you meddling in our affairs. I don't need you inciting my wife to defiance."

Inciting Jenny to defiance? "I don't know what you're talking about." I sucked in a smile. *Jenny? Defiant?* In my wildest imagination I couldn't picture the meek little woman expressing any opinion of her own, let alone defying anything her husband might decree.

"You know. You know, all right. Next you'll have her out in the streets parading for the right to vote!"

"The right to vote?" I was more mystified than ever. "I never—"

"I mean it. Stay away from Jenny!" He turned on his heel and stormed out of the building.

I looked at Ida. "What was that all about?"

She shrugged. "Ya got me."

The Tremors Begin

Mrs. Isabelle Chamberlain rocked San Francisco's high society like a major earthquake. Cy returned from Europe with his three-and-a-half-year-old daughter in one hand and his divorce papers in the other. The pain in his eyes revealed the devastation in his soul. He brought along his mother to help care for the child until he could find a suitable nanny, after which Mrs. Chamberlain would return to her husband in Shinglehouse. By the looks of the possessive grandmother, I wondered if an appropriate nanny could ever be found and if poor Mr. Chamberlain would be forced to transfer to the California office in order to once again enjoy connubial bliss.

The woman greeted me with the friendliness of a badger protecting her cubs. I longed to assure her that I was not after her precious son—or any other man, for that matter. However, the same could not be said for the single and not-so-single women of Nob Hill. Hardly a week passed but that Cy's name was linked with one well-heeled beauty or another.

Cy continued to support the mission program, stopping in often to see how things were going. He said we were his little getaway, a haven where he didn't need to play the role of young corporate financier.

The week before Jamie arrived for summer vacation,

Hattie wrote that she and her schoolteacher were engaged to be married in the fall.

"I wish you could be here as my matron of honor. Of course, I'll ask Myrtle. Don't tell Myrtle, but you were my first choice. Oh, Chloe, I never dreamed it would happen for me. I gave up hope long ago; after all, what farmer could afford to marry a crippled wife? Fortunately, my Stanford is a schoolteacher."

With Joe dating his Beth, and now Hattie about to marry her schoolteacher, I couldn't imagine life any cheerier. I realized I would need to find my own place before long. Newlyweds don't need a widowed sister in the house. Perhaps in the fall. In the meantime, I'd relax and enjoy the summer with Jamie and CeeCee.

The P.S. at the bottom of Hattie's letter stirred hope in my heart. "I caught Pa studying the photograph you sent of you and CeeCee at Christmastime. And the other night, he mentioned you and her in his prayer at the table. You can thank my Stanford for that."

Thank Stanford? OK. To whatever or whomever was responsible, I am eternally grateful.

Maria and I fretted the entire week over Jamie's arrival. We both wanted everything to be perfect. While in the city, I visited a small bookstore on Market Street and bought him a book on the planets and stars, complete with illustrations.

Joe and Beth accompanied CeeCee and me to the station the afternoon Jamie was scheduled to arrive. They watched as I paced the length of the platform and back again. I glanced at my watch, then strode over to the bench where they sat. "The train's late! Can you believe it? I thought the Union Pacific prides itself on being on time."

Joe laughed. "Your watch is fast. They still have five minutes before their reputation is ruined."

I shook my head and tapped my foot impatiently. "Go

ahead and laugh. I don't care."

"That's good." He laughed again. Beth tried to hide her grin.

"You two are incorrigible. Wait until your son is coming home after being away for nine months!"

Beth blushed, and my brother gulped in surprise. "Aren't you jumping the gun a little here? We're not even married yet."

"You will be. Take it from your big sister, you will be."

The arrival of the train ended that conversation.

Eagerly, I pressed to the front of the crowd and scanned the windows of the passenger cars for Jamie's face. No sign of him. *What if he missed his train? What if he's stranded somewhere between here and Denver?* I knew he'd made it to the Putnams' house, for he'd sent me a telegram.

I watched the passengers deboarding: a middle-aged matron carrying two hat boxes and a Pekingese puppy, a silver-haired man in a bowler hat and business suit, a blond young man in his early twenties. Then I saw him. While the tall gangly body clothed in a school blazer and trousers didn't fit my memories, I recognized the eyes. My son was almost a teenager. I rushed to him. "Jamie, oh, Jamie, it's good to see you."

Stiffly, he hugged me and introduced me to the blond young man. "Mother, I want you to meet Thaddeus Townsend. He's a junior law student at Harvard. His parents live in San Francisco."

I shook hands with the young man and glanced at the crowd. "Are your parents here to meet you, Thaddeus?"

He smiled and shook his head sadly. "Probably not. The last I knew, my father was in Los Angeles on business, and my mother was doing the grand tour of Europe. She's supposed to be home by the end of the week."

I threw a glance toward Joe. "Well, you'll stay with us until they return—as payment for bringing my son Jamie safely to California, of course."

The young man laughed. "James's grandfather took care of that, Mrs. McCall. Now if you'll excuse me, our butler is supposed to be in this crowd somewhere. Nice meeting you."

I threw my arm around my son and hurried back to where Joe and the others waited. "It is so good to have you home, Jamie. I've missed you so much."

"Where is CeeCee?" He'd no more than asked the question when she burst between two women's skirts, demanding to be picked up. Laughing, he swung her into his arms. "I don't believe you. You've grown like a stinkweed!"

"A stinkweed?" CeeCee pouted. "I'm not a stinkweed."

Jamie sniffed the child's hair, then her face and neck. "No, I guess you're not a stinkweed, more like a persimmon."

"I'm not a persimmon, either. I'm a little girl."

In the carriage ride home, I asked, "Maria asked me to ask you what you want for breakfast tomorrow morning, Jamie. Your favorite, johnnycake?"

He turned solemn eyes toward me. "Mother, would you be offended if I asked you to call me James instead of Jamie?"

I paused a moment. "I-I guess not. After all, it is your name." *But, like it or not, you'll always be Jamie to me.*

During the next few weeks I discovered many changes in the boy teetering on the verge of adolescence. When Cy brought me home one day from the mission, Jamie glowered. When Cy came for Sunday dinner and later asked me to go for a walk with him, Jamie asked Cy where we were going and when we'd be back.

As we walked, I tried to explain. "He's being protective of me. He doesn't understand that we're just good friends. He's at the age where he thinks men and women can only have one type of relationship." I smiled into Cy's grim face.

"I'm sorry. I hope he didn't make you uncomfortable. Actually, I think it's kind of touching."

"Touching!" Cy jammed his hands into his pockets and picked up the pace.

I talked with my son about Cy's visits. "We've been friends for a long time. He's lonely since his divorce. Be nice to him for me."

Jamie glowered, but said nothing.

Cy and my son established an uneasy truce that lasted throughout the summer. And considering that Cy's visits were becoming more and more frequent, it was a strain. The few times Mrs. Chamberlain and little Phoebe came along, I had the distinct impression that she and Jamie had instinctively joined forces.

When it came time for Jamie to head back East to begin his freshman year at the prep school, I made arrangements for Thaddeus to accompany him.

At the station, my son took my hands in his and stared into my eyes. "Mother, you won't do anything stupid while I'm gone, like marrying this Chamberlain character, will you?"

"Jamie, oops, I mean, James, don't be ridiculous. Cy and I are friends, that's all." I clicked my tongue. "Where do you come up with these ideas?"

The boy didn't let go of the subject. "Just promise me, you won't marry him,without telling me first."

I sighed. "Fine, I promise. Does that make you feel any better?"

"Yes." He kissed me and hopped on the train.

In September I received a letter and a postcard. The postcard from Jamie reminded me of my promise, and Hattie's letter described her wedding day and her subsequent move into a cottage in town.

"We went to Niagara Falls for our honeymoon. The

enclosed photograph was taken by the falls." Loneliness tugged at my heart as I studied the smiling couple in the photograph. *How can I be so happy for Hattie—and yet so envious?*

Being around Joe and Beth didn't make it any easier. And unfortunately, James's concern over Cy's attentions planted a thought in my mind that hadn't previously been there. Always before, we could talk like a brother and sister, but now I found myself tongue-tied and awkward when we were alone. And if I found him looking at me, I would blush and turn away. Immature behavior for a widow of twenty-four.

Hattie's letter must have prompted Joe and Beth to set a date for their wedding—Thanksgiving Day. They announced it at a special dinner at her parents' home in the city. She invited the Chamberlains as well, since Joe asked Cy to stand up with him. Beth, an only child, asked me to be her matron of honor, and she wanted CeeCee to be the flower girl.

When we returned to the ranch that night, Joe assured me he wanted me to stay at the ranch after the wedding. When I demurred, he said, "Well, I hope you will at least stay until Beth and I return from visiting the folks back East. Maria will be heartbroken to have CeeCee taken from her the same time I leave."

I laughed. The round little woman adored the child.

During the weeks preceding the wedding, Cy and I found ourselves thrown together at every dinner party and social event until the local gossip columnists started speculating about us in print. One evening, after a party given in Joe and Beth's honor, Cy offered to take me back to the ranch so I wouldn't have to wait until Joe could leave.

A pathway of moonlight glistened on the choppy waves of the bay. A cool breeze whipped my skirts about my ankles as Cy and I stood at the railing on the ferryboat.

"Isn't it beautiful?" I whispered, watching the waves lap the side of the boat.

"Yes." His voice caught in his throat. "It is."

I gazed over at him. He wasn't looking at the waves; he was looking at me with unspoken questions in his eyes, holding me captive.

"Cy? Is something wrong?"

"No, nothing." He turned his face toward the water.

I persisted. "Did I say something? Did I do something?"

He leaned his elbows on the brass railing, his hands extended out over the water. "No, I was just remembering."

"Remembering? Tell me, what did . . ." I studied his profile in the moonlight, his straight aquiline nose, his deep-set brown eyes, his strong, stubborn chin.

"I was remembering the night in your brother's garden when I apologized for Phillip's rude behavior. Your hair flowed down around your shoulders like a silken cape, shimmering in the moonlight. I'd never seen anything so lovely." He turned slowly to face me. "Even my anger at Pamela couldn't sully the moment." He touched my face gently.

"I-I don't know what to say."

"What is there to say?" He turned back toward the water. "So much has happened since our day together in Chicago. We're not the innocent children we once were."

"You're right." I inched closer to him. My arm brushed against his sleeve. "Neither of us can go back in time or remove the scars, but we can and should go forward."

"Are you saying—Oh, Chloe, I can't. I know how much you loved your husband." He stared down at the water rushing by the side of the ferry. "It was different for Pamela and me. Ours was a marriage of convenience, not love. In the beginning, I honestly convinced myself that I loved her."

"I'm sorry."

"Let's walk." He tucked my arm in his and led me along the empty boat deck. "Right now, it seems like you and I have everything going against us. My mother, your son, my divorce, your love for James—is there any hope?"

I tilted my head and smiled up into his sober face. "Are you giving up without a fight?"

He stopped and stared at me. "Excuse me?"

I smiled again. "Are you quitting without a fight? You know, a faint heart never won a fair lady, so says Miguel de Cervantes, anyway."

"Are you saying there's hope for us?"

"I don't know. I guess that's up to you."

A tiny wry smile formed at the corners of his mouth. "Do you want to give us a try?"

"Do you?"

He turned, and we started walking again. At the rear of the ferryboat, we could see the lights of San Francisco shimmering on the bay. "I'm not sure."

Not sure? Wonderful, I've misread his signals and made a fool of myself. How stupid can I get!

When he tried to tilt my face toward his, I pulled away in embarrassment. "Hey, what's wrong?"

I shook my head. "I'm sorry. I misunderstood. I guess the moonlight got to me."

"No, don't misunderstand my hesitation." He captured my face between his hands. "I value your friendship more than you can ever imagine. I don't want to mess it up by falling in love."

After all he'd been through with Pamela, I could understand his hesitation. And with the loneliness I'd been experiencing since Hattie's wedding, I realized that I probably did misread his signals.

"Cy, I agree with you. You're too important to me as a friend to risk losing. Let's just let things continue as they are, all right? Friends?"

He smiled. "Friends." He bent down and placed a gentle kiss on my lips. When he touched his lips to mine a second time and then kissed my eyelids, my throat constricted with emotion. I remained suspended in time as he took my hands and kissed each finger tenderly. "Friends," he whispered, his voice strangely ragged.

For a brief moment, we stood engulfed in a magical world of our own. But a blast of the ferryboat horn above our heads returned us to reality. After docking, we climbed back in Cy's carriage and headed for the ranch.

Half a mile before the turnoff to the ranch, Cy brought the horses to a stop. He kept both hands on the reins and stared straight ahead. "Chloe, where do you and I go from here?"

I swallowed hard. "As an old friend once told me, 'Take life one step at a time.'"

He flicked the reins, and the carriage moved forward. "I'm not sure I can do that."

"Do we have any choice?"

As Joe and Beth's wedding date approached, it was obvious to both Cy and me that one step at a time was the only way to survive the wedding folderol as well. I took time off from my mission work to go for dress fittings. Though the wedding was to be held in the Jordans' parlor, it would still be a major event of the season. I also helped throw a bridal shower for Beth and helped her shop for her trousseau. Plus, I still had a five-year-old daughter who needed love and attention. All of this put Cy's and my relationship on hold.

The morning of the wedding, Miguel took CeeCee and me to the Jordan mansion in the buggy. Goddard, the Jordans' butler, met us at the door. The doors and staircase were bedecked with garlands of flowers. The parlor where the wedding would take place had been emptied to make room for the Jordans' guests, since the Chamberlains, Maria, Miguel, and I were Joe's only guests.

"This way, please." The butler led us up the gaily festooned staircase and to the master suite, where Mrs. Jordan was waiting for us. The woman gushed, "I'm so glad you're here on time. Come, I'll show you the room where you can change later for the wedding."

She led us into a bedroom swathed in red velvet—red-velvet bedspread, red-velvet upholstered armchairs, red-velvet draperies, red-velvet flocked wallpaper, red Persian carpet. If potted palms had grown in red, Mrs. Jordan would have had those too. However, she had to settle for the common green variety. CeeCee's and my dresses hung on the outside of the rosewood chifforobe. I set my white kid purse and gloves on the dressing table.

Mrs. Jordan placed her hands on CeeCee's shoulders and called to one of her personal maids. "Cora, please take little CeeCee down to the kitchen for a small bowl of vanilla ice cream while her mama and I help Elizabeth get ready."

CeeCee looked questioningly at me.

I nodded. "It's OK. You go along. I'll see you a little later."

The child took the maid's hand and left the room. The woman smiled apologetically. "I didn't want her to upset Elizabeth in any way. Brides are often so excitable."

I thought, *The only one around here easily excited seems to be you, my dear.* But I just smiled and followed the woman down the hall.

Mrs. Jordan swept into her daughter's room with the delicacy of a locomotive. And I followed in her wake.

"Chloe," Beth squealed, "you're here. I've been wondering all morning when you would arrive."

I laughed and undid my bonnet. "You told me one o'clock, and one o'clock it is. Now, what can I do to help you get ready?"

"Toss your cloak and bonnet on the bed and come brush

my hair. It will give us a chance to talk before the hair-dresser arrives. Mama, why don't you see how Daddy's coming along."

Mrs. Jordan started to protest, then thought better of it. "I'll be back in ten minutes with Nadine to do your hair."

Beth thanked her, then returned her attention to me. "I just wanted to tell you that I agree with Joe about you and CeeCee staying at the ranch. He told me how you were thinking of looking for your own place. It's not necessary."

I picked up her silver hairbrush and studied the etchings on the back. I closed my eyes to blot out the bittersweet memories. *Dear James.* I'd never forget the joy on his face the day we returned from our honeymoon, and I found the silver dresser set with my initials engraved on the back. It was as if I were suddenly transported to the lavender-and-rose bedroom in Kansas. I could see the rosewood head-board so clearly. I could smell the atomizer of lemon-verbena perfume sitting on top of the dresser. I saw our reflections, James's and mine, in the dresser mirror. From a distance I could hear someone calling my name, but I ignored the sound. The voice persisted.

"Chloe, Chloe, are you all right?"

I staggered a moment and opened my eyes.

Beth, her chestnut-brown hair hanging loose down her back, stared at me through the dressing-table mirror. "Are you all right?"

I smiled weakly and nodded. "I'm sorry. I'm afraid I was woolgathering. Weddings do that to me, I guess."

She touched my arm tenderly. "It must be difficult, losing your husband. Joe told me about losing Cathy, and they weren't even married. Do you ever get over it?"

"It gets easier with time." I smiled, drawing the silver-handled brush through her tangled hair. "I try not to think about it, but every once in a while it all comes back. I've learned to depend on God as my source of strength to get through those times."

Beth watched my face through the mirror. "Do you think you'll ever fall in love again?"

I chuckled. "I've told half the world I wouldn't, but, uh, well, I've learned it's wise to let God lead out in those things."

She smiled. Two deep dimples dotted her perfect complexion. "Cyrus Chamberlain wouldn't have anything to do with your, uh, modified position, would he?"

I blushed and tugged a little harder at one tangle.

"Ouch!" She grabbed her head and laughed. "You have a mean streak in you, Chloe Mae McCall."

I tapped her scalp with the back of the brush. "That's what big sisters are for, to make little sisters behave."

She grabbed my wrist. "Before you take another whack at me, answer my question. Is there any hope for the two of you?"

I sighed and stepped back. "Cyrus has suffered a lot of pain from his divorce. In some ways, I think a divorce hurts even more than the death of a marriage partner. At least I know James never rejected me."

She released my wrist. "You didn't answer my question."

I pulled the brush through her shiny locks for a moment before replying. "It's the only answer I have right now."

When Mrs. Jordan burst into the room with the famous Nadine, hairdresser to European royalty, I went to my room to dress. *Why a successful European hairstylist would come to San Francisco to ply her trade makes no sense.* I unfastened the buttons on the back of my dress and stepped out of it. Tossing it on the bed, I switched into the silk ecru undergarments that gave the peach attendant's gown, as Mrs. Jordan's dress designer explained, its "whisper-soft, ethereal aura."

I sat down at the dressing table and unfastened my hair. Removing my brush from my purse, I brushed my curls until they shone. Next I fastened the peach-dyed feather and rhinestone concoction on top. After carefully combing each curl around my finger, I let them cascade down my back. I added a few corkscrew curls around my face and examined the masterpiece. *It will do.*

Cora arrived with CeeCee in time to help me ease the peach silk gown over my hairdo and shoulders. As she buttoned the pearly buttons up the back of the dress, I tugged at the neckline and bodice. "Does this have to be so low? The dressmaker promised to do something with it."

"Ma'am, I think if you let me." The maid adjusted the gown so the full mutton sleeves began off the shoulders. "See. It's higher now. And here—" The woman reached under the bodice facing and pulled out a triangle of lace that matched the lace scallops along the hem. "This goes across here. See? Perfectly modest."

Not for a woman who's used to wearing collars that fasten right beneath her chin! I tugged at the sleeves and neckline in front of the mirror. Grudgingly, I had to admit the dress was modest and did look quite fashionable.

I helped CeeCee into her dress, combed her curls into ringlets, then fastened them on one side with a giant matching bow. Following, a quick spray of Gardenia from the atomizer on the dressing table, and we hurried to Beth's room.

She stood looking out the window, watching my brother and Cy arrive in the Chamberlains' carriage. The delicate gown of Venetian lace over satin trailed on the floor behind her. She glanced up at me. The lace-covered, wide-brimmed hat with a cluster of bows at the back shaded her blush.

"He's so handsome. I do love him, you know."

I hugged her, careful not to dislodge her hat. "I know, and I wish you both a long, happy life filled with dozens of fat and laughing babies."

She blushed again. "And you'll be there to deliver every

single one of them, won't you, sis?"

"You bet."

She leaned forward and whispered, "Have I told you how much I'm going to enjoy having you for my sister?"

I nodded. "At least a dozen times—today."

The moment dissipated as Mrs. Jordan bustled into the room. "It's time, darling. All the guests are in place. Shall I tell the organist to begin playing?"

Beth stretched her arms toward her mother. "Mama, I love you."

The woman reached in a concealed pocket at the side of her dress and withdrew a lace-edged linen handkerchief and dabbed her eyes. "I know, darling, I know."

The wedding ceremony came off as rehearsed. I concentrated on the minister's words in order to hold at bay the memories of James's and my wedding in our Kansas parlor.

"Please repeat after me. I, James . . ." *No, no, not James. This is Joe's day, remember? Joe's and Beth's.*

"I, Elizabeth Anne . . ." As Beth repeated her vows, I felt Cy watching me. I glanced down at my flowers, then slowly turned my face toward him. He smiled. A wave of shyness overcame me. I smiled. He looked at the preacher; I did the same.

". . . For better or worse . . . in sickness and in health, till death us do part . . ." *Till death us do part.* The words resounded in my head throughout the rest of the service and the reception. Before I realized what was happening, Cy was hurrying me and CeeCee to the waiting carriage while the bride and groom bade farewell to their friends at the house.

Later, the three of us stood on the railway platform waving goodbye as the train pulled out of the station. I sniffed into my lace hanky. "It seems like we're always saying goodbye to those we love."

Cy picked up CeeCee in his arms, placed his arm about

my shoulders, and led me to his waiting carriage. "Mother asked me to bring you over to the house before I take you back to the ranch tonight. Is that all right with you?"

Surprised, I agreed.

He set CeeCee down on the rear seat, assisted me into the buggy, then climbed in after me. "Tomorrow, she's taking Phoebe to meet my father in Chicago, where they'll celebrate Christmas together."

"Really? I didn't know that. Why aren't you going?"

He pursed his lips. "Well, to be honest?"

"To be honest."

He took a deep breath. "I was hoping to spend at least part of the holiday with you and CeeCee. Am I being too presumptuous?"

I grinned teasingly. "I don't know, are you?"

He drew the carriage to a stop at the foot of Nob Hill, wrapped the reins around the brake, and glanced into the back seat.

"Sh," he whispered, "she's sleeping. Poor little kid. She's tuckered out." He placed one arm behind me on the back of the seat. "Chloe, I'm serious about this, about us. No jokes, no playing games. I need to know if you think there's any hope for us to share more than our friendship?"

Like a splash of cold water in the face, I sobered. *Not now, Cy. Don't ask me to make any decision this afternoon.* We hadn't talked since the evening on the bay. After such an emotion-packed day, my nerves were raw and unprotected. *Chloe,* I argued with myself, *be honest. Do you really think tomorrow will be any better? You've been avoiding this moment for weeks now.*

"Should I take your silence as a yes or no?" he asked.

"Neither. I need time, time to think."

"How much time?"

"I don't know," I wailed. Passersby glanced toward the carriage at the sound of my voice. I repeated myself in a whisper. "I don't know."

He flicked the reins, and our carriage entered the stream of late-afternoon traffic once more. The Morgans climbed the hill with ease, coming to a stop in front of Cy's home. As Cy helped me from the carriage, a groom rushed out to care for the horses.

CeeCee awakened and asked where she was. After helping her out of the carriage, Cy took my arm and led me up the steps into the massive three-story gray-and-white house, complete with bay windows, gingerbread trim, and a turret. My daughter ran ahead and leapt on the porch swing.

He paused at the door, his hand on the knob. With his free hand, he tipped my chin upward. "Will this help you make up your mind?"

I put my hand to my mouth and shook my head. "No, Cy, not in front of—"

Gently, he took my hand and touched it to his lips. At the instant his lips touched my hand, the front door flew open. "My, my, it sure took you long enough to get here after the reception," Mrs. Chamberlain exclaimed. "Was the train late departing?"

Though her sudden appearance ended the kiss, Cy held my fingers within a breath of his lips. "No, Mother, the Union Pacific was right on time, as usual."

Breathless, I glanced past Cy at my daughter. She'd been so busy swinging she hadn't noticed the exchange between the three adults. "CeeCee, come inside. Phoebe's waiting to see you."

The biggest surprise, Mrs. Chamberlain's change of attitude toward me, became evident to me as the evening progressed. Always before, I suspected she still thought of me as the daughter of an employee. This time, she treated me with respect.

Phillip and Jenny arrived with their son Andrew in time

for a late dinner. I'd seen them at the wedding but had avoided any direct contact. Now avoidance was impossible. Phoebe's nurse took the children to the nursery while the adults gathered around the carefully appointed table. Phillip glowered throughout the meal. When his mother asked what was wrong, he claimed to have a headache and left the table for the study.

After dessert, Cy led me into the parlor. The two Mrs. Chamberlains excused themselves from our company. "I need to nurse Andrew," Jenny whispered. "And Mama Isabelle wants to say goodbye, since she'll be away for a while. You're welcome to come with us if you'd like."

I thanked her for the invitation, but declined. "CeeCee and I need to be heading back to the ranch soon."

"Oh," Jenny cried, "not until I come back downstairs. Promise?"

"OK, I promise."

"It's been so long since I've seen you."

"Yes, it has."

I watched her skip up the stairs after her mother-in-law. "She's such a pretty little thing, and as sweet as they come." I turned and smiled at Cy. "Not a stubborn bone in her body, I imagine."

He strolled slowly across the room toward me. "And tell me, do you have stubborn bones?"

I arched an eyebrow. "You can be certain of it."

"Hmm." He paused in front of me, taking my hand and examining it. "I like your stubborn bones."

"And my Irish temper?"

He brushed his hand through the cluster of curls cascading down my back. "To match these red curls?"

"Absolutely."

"Should I consider myself forewarned?"

"Forewarned and forearmed." *Till death us do part.* The words rang in my head again. I blanched.

Concern filled his eyes. "Is something wrong?"

I nibbled on my lip. *Lord, are You trying to tell me something here? All right, till death it is. But You'll have to close the door of my memories of James. I can't do it.*

I shook my head slowly. "I never answered your question." I swallowed hard.

His face grew serious. "Are you prepared to answer it now?"

"I think so."

"And . . ."

"Be patient," I scolded gently. "This is difficult for me."

"Be patient? I can't breathe. How long can a man go without breathing?"

I laughed nervously. "I think, if you're ready, I am too. But we've got to take this step slowly, for both of our sakes. Neither of us wants to make a mistake the second time around."

"Oh." He exhaled sharply. "I was so afraid I'd rushed things. I was so afraid you'd spook and run."

"I'm not a filly who spooks and runs. I'm a mature woman who must consider, not only her future happiness, but the happiness of two children."

"Take it slowly, right—for both of us." Then, without warning, he grabbed me and kissed me, a short, hard kiss, much like a schoolboy would give his twelve-year-old sweetheart.

"You call that slow?" I giggled.

From the open doorway, a cool, calm voice said, "Am I interrupting anything here?"

Terror at Sunrise

I froze at the sound of Phillip's voice. Cy looked past me. "Not a thing, brother." Cy slid his arm possessively around my waist and turned me to face his irate brother. "Come right on in. Mom and Jenny will be right back. They went upstairs to feed Andrew."

A sardonic grin formed on Phillip's face. "So, you picking up where I left off?"

I gasped, and color flooded my neck and face. In a growl, Cy responded, "If you are smart, Phil, you won't say another word."

Phillip snorted, turned on his heel, and left. "Cy," I whispered, "please take me home right now. I'll go get CeeCee while you arrange for the carriage."

"Wait. Don't let my brother ruin—"

"Please, take me home." I ran up the stairs and into the nursery. The nurse and the two little girls looked up from their storybook in surprise. "CeeCee, say goodbye to Phoebe and thank her for a nice time. We're leaving. Where's your coat?"

The nurse handed me the child's light-blue woolen coat. I stuffed the child into it, then hurried her down the stairs. As I passed the Chamberlains' startled butler, I said, "Please, give my regrets to Mrs. Chamberlain for leaving so suddenly. Tell her I wish her a wonderful holiday in

Chicago with Mr. Chamberlain."

As we emerged from the house into the damp November evening, the horses and carriage rounded the edge of the three-story house. CeeCee eyed me curiously as I hustled her down the steps and into the back seat of the carriage. I hopped into the front seat before Cy could help me. "Let's go."

As the team started clopping over the cobblestone streets, I leaned back against the padded leather seat and closed my eyes. "Chloe, what is this all about?" Cy demanded.

"I'm sorry. Suddenly I felt so cheap, like a Barbary Coast trollop on Saturday night."

"Why? Surely you weren't surprised at my brother's sarcasm." Cy snorted derisively. "He just had an acute attack of pride and jealousy, that's all. We're bound to see a lot more of that since he is family."

I fidgeted with the buttons on my white kidskin glove. "Maybe this isn't such a good idea."

"What?"

"Our seeing one another socially."

"I've never heard of anything so foolish in my life!" Cy flicked the reins over the backs of the horses. "Now, we've got a good chance at a solid, loving relationship. And, brother or no brother, I won't let Phillip destroy it. And I won't let you destroy us before we even begin."

By the time we boarded the ferryboat, I decided Cy was right. I'd overreacted to an inevitable situation. The sensible thing to do now was to put it behind me.

When we reached the ranch, Cy helped me carry CeeCee into her bedroom, then waited in the parlor while I changed her into her nightgown and tucked her into bed. Turning out the lights, I closed the door and tiptoed down the hall to the parlor. Cy stood as I entered the room.

"Can I make you a cup of hot tea?" Though I had less time to collect and dry herbs than I did in Colorado, I still kept a supply of the best-tasting varieties on hand. "How about cinnamon clover?"

"Sounds good." Cy followed me to the kitchen. He sat down at the table while I heated the water in the kettle. "On Christmas Eve there will be a special candlelight service in one of the churches in town. Would you and CeeCee like to attend it with me?"

"That sounds lovely." I brought two cups and saucers to the table. "Cy, I know so much about you, yet I know so little, especially about your belief in God."

A look I couldn't interpret spread across his face. "What do you want to know?"

Where do I start, Lord? "Do you believe in God, that He exists? Do you believe that He died for us?"

Cy pursed his lips for a moment. "Yes, to questions one and two. I don't know, to question three."

I thought about his answers a second, then continued. "Do you believe God directs our lives if we let Him? Do you believe He loves us?"

"You want the truth?"

I nodded.

"You might not like it." He took a deep breath. "My parents took me to Sunday School as a child. When we moved to Shinglehouse, we stopped attending. I guess history would prove a man named Jesus was crucified in Jerusalem." He leaned forward, his elbows on the table. "Whether that Jesus is any more a God than Confucius or Buddha or Mohammed, I'm not sure."

A thousand arguments popped into my head. I wanted to show Cy by sound logic that my Saviour was indeed real, that He came as God to save me, and that He loves me and directs me every day. Then I remembered how I fell in love with the Saviour. "Cy, do you still have that Bible?"

He nodded.

"Will you do me a favor?" Again he nodded. "Before we go

to the Christmas service, would you read through the books of Matthew, Mark, Luke, and John? Before you start, will you promise to ask God to open your mind to the words you will read?"

Cy frowned. "I've never put much stock in hell-fire religion."

I shook my head. "You'll get no hell-fire preaching here. Think of the four books as four biographies of the same man, much like you would read about Abraham Lincoln or George Washington."

Reluctantly, he agreed. After a second cup of tea, he left for the city, and I raced to my room, fell on my knees beside the bed, and prayed.

We attended the Christmas Eve program together. CeeCee sat enchanted by the glowing candles surrounding her. And I'd never seen the story of Jesus' birth so beautifully depicted. We had arranged for CeeCee and me to stay with the Jordans overnight. The next morning, Cy took us out to eat Christmas dinner at a quiet little restaurant near his place.

We spent the rest of the day with the Jordans opening presents around the Christmas tree in the parlor and singing Christmas carols. Cy left, promising to pick me up at one the next afternoon to take me ice-skating. Memories of racing my brothers across Honeyoye Creek filled me with anticipation. Mrs. Jordan volunteered to take CeeCee to Golden Gate Park to ride the year-round carousel.

The Mechanics' Pavilion, a huge barn of a building, covered an entire block. As well as ice-skating, the high-vaulted building was used for roller-skating, the annual Mardi Gras Ball, indoor circuses, and boxing matches. The poster we passed on the way into the hall advertised an upcoming fight between "Philadelphia" Jack

O'Brien and Bob Fitzsimmons.

After Cy, who'd never worn a pair of skates, laced me into mine, he cast a jaundiced eye at his own thin-bladed boot. "I'm supposed to be able to stand up on these?"

"Of course." I leapt to my feet and clomped across the splintery wooden floor to the ice. After testing the sharpness of the blades, I skated about in circles. "See, it's easy."

"If you say so," he said skeptically.

Leaning against the brass rail separating the ice from the spectator stands, I called. "This was your suggestion, remember?"

I skated away, whirled about, and swooshed back as he stepped off the wood onto the ice. His left blade touched the ice first and slipped out from under him. Cy caught himself by grabbing the rail. When he followed with his right foot, it did the same. Again he clutched the rail for support.

I skated backward, giving advice as he turned and wobbled in place. "Walk along the rail until your feet grow accustomed to the blades."

"I can't do this, Chloe." His feet slipped out from under him again, and he swung helplessly around the rail before sitting down on the ice with a thud. "Is this a rite of passage in the Spencer family?"

"No, why?"

He scrambled to his feet. "Your brother used to come skating every Sunday night last winter."

I laughed. "My little sister Ori learned to skate before she turned five."

He massaged his left hip. "Sure, it was easy for her; she didn't have so far to fall."

By the end of the evening, I'd weaned Cy from the rail. "Next time we come, I'll teach you to pair skate," I promised.

"Who says there'll be a next time?" Cy grumbled.

On the way back to the Jordans' that evening, Cy drew

me close. "I had so much fun with you this afternoon, Chloe. One of the best things about you is you make me laugh. I'd almost forgotten how to laugh, and you brought it all back."

During the weeks that followed, we spent as much time together as possible. With Mrs. Chamberlain and Phoebe back from Chicago, I often stayed in the city after one of our outings. Sometimes I brought CeeCee along; other times, she stayed at the ranch with Maria.

Whenever Cy and I were together, we talked. We discussed the corruption in the city government. We debated the push for local fisheries to unionize. We argued the right for women to vote in the next state election. We laughed over the newspaper headlines that quoted a Benton Harbor, Michigan, preacher as saying the city would be destroyed by an earthquake in the month of February.

When I said it might not be a laughing matter if it really happened, Cy told me, "You're thinking like an easterner. Do you realize there have been four hundred seventeen earthquakes recorded in the city during the eighty years they've been recording quakes?"

Whenever he could get away from the office, Cy came down to the mission, where he wielded paintbrushes, moved furniture, drilled nine- and ten-year-olds on their times tables. Anything that needed to be done, he did. While we didn't talk religion, I watched him become a happier, gentler person. One evening after we'd spent the afternoon scrubbing down the fifty-year-old iron cookstove, Cy blew a strand of hair away from his forehead and said, "You know, it really is true, when you help others, you feel good inside, kind of clean and new."

I grinned and dabbed at a spot of charcoal on his nose.

He looked down at the spot cross-eyed. "Well, almost clean, anyway."

Joe and Beth arrived home from their honeymoon on the last day of February—bringing CeeCee presents from our parents. When I asked, Joe confided he'd seen evidence that Pa was softening toward me. "I think he's ready to let bygones be bygones."

Near the end of the month of March, I knew I cared enough for Cy that I needed to write to Jamie as I'd promised. As I sealed the letter, I tried to imagine how upset he'd be when he read it.

The highlight of March was our visit to the Japanese Tea Garden at Golden Gate Park. We strolled along pathways lined with blossoming cherry trees before Cy suggested we sit on a stone bench near the pagoda. "You're so quiet today. Is something wrong?" he asked.

I'd been thinking about an article I'd read in the morning paper on an open house held by Otis M. Roy and his new actress bride to show off their brand new mansion. The columnist described the expensive paintings in the parlor, the stunning diamond-studded mirrors on the dining-room walls, and the crystal chandeliers in the ballroom, imported from some Austrian count's castle.

"Is something wrong?" Cy asked a second time.

"No, I don't think so." I told him about the article. "For the first time, I can honestly say the bitterness is gone from my heart. I feel nothing but pity for him. He will never find genuine peace and happiness, no matter how many Austrian chandeliers he imports."

Cy looked puzzled. "I don't understand."

"A few months ago, I realized I'd lost sight of an eternal truth I'd discovered years ago. I began praising God in all things. It took away the bitterness; it can take away your bitterness too, Cy."

He gazed across the garden. "You mean Pamela?" he asked softly.

"Yes."

April in San Francisco didn't have the dramatic charm of springtime in the Northeast, but the charm it did have came in the form of mild blue days and gardens filled with rhododendrons, azaleas, and primroses. The evening of the seventeenth, Cy and I went roller-skating at the Mechanics' Pavilion. This was a sport we learned on "equal footing," as Cy put it. Neither of us had previously roller-skated.

Around nine that evening, we returned to Cy's home to find Mrs.Chamberlain flustered. "Oh, I'm so glad you're here. Mrs. Caxton, our neighbor, has gone into labor. She can't reach her family doctor. He went to hear that Italian opera singer Enrico Caruso perform in *Carmen*." Mrs. Chamberlain wrung her hands nervously. "I told her you are a midwife. You will help her, won't you?"

"Of course, I will. Where is Mr. Caxton?"

"He is trying to locate another doctor."

Cy opened the front door for us. "Should I come along?"

"If we need you, we'll call."

Relieved, he closed the door behind us. A quick examination suggested that Mrs. Caxton was having false labor. While Mrs. Chamberlain rummaged through the woman's pantry for comfrey tea, as I instructed, I made my patient as comfortable as possible. Once the tea was brewed and served, I suggested Mrs. Chamberlain go home, as the baby probably wouldn't arrive for some time.

When the young Mrs. Caxton finally fell asleep, I lay down on her brocade lounge chair and dozed a bit. At last Mr. Caxton returned with a physician. His examination of Mrs. Caxton led him to the same conclusions I had come to—that the baby would not be born that night, and perhaps not for another week or two. The doctor suggested that I stay the rest of the night—just in case.

Mr. Caxton paid the doctor, then stepped across the hall to sleep in another bedroom. Around five o'clock, I awakened with a kink in my neck.

My patient was sleeping soundly, so I stepped out on a second-story balcony and gazed down at the sleeping city and inhaled the sweet aroma of springtime. Somewhere in some rich man's stables, a horse whinnied, then gave a shrill cry of alarm. *The poor creature sounds terrified.*

I returned my attention to the bay and the lights of Sausalito and Belvedere on the other side. *Maybe I should try to get a few more hours of sleep.*

I turned to go back inside when I heard a deep rumble, like the sound of a runaway locomotive, coming from the south. I shook my head in disbelief. We were several miles from the railway station. I leaned over the edge of the balcony, trying to see what might be making such a racket at this hour.

I froze at the sight. The street below was rising and falling like the waves of the ocean. Before I could run, the shock waves slammed me against the wall of the house, only to have the floor slip away beneath my feet. I found myself face down, clutching a small rattan mat with my fingernails. Around me, I heard the crash of breaking glass and the groaning of straining masonry. A distant church bell gonged. Other bells scattered around the city joined the frenzied concert. Struggling to my knees, I watched in horror as the city skyline danced to the death knell of the church bells. The earth rolled with two- and three-foot high waves, toppling towers, brick walls, and masonry foundations. Dust plumes puffed into the early morning air.

After the shaking finally stopped, I staggered to the doorway and paused to calm myself, wondering why the bells continued to toll. Suddenly, from every direction came a new sound—the deafening roar of caving roofs, collapsing buildings, and tumbling chimneys joined the still clanging bells.

At a crash behind me, I stumbled inside to find Mrs. Caxton clutching her pillow and weeping. Her brick chimney lay in a heap at the foot of her bed. I helped her into a dressing gown before her terrified husband lifted her into his arms. I followed him down the stairs and out into the street.

Most people fled their homes regardless of their attire. One dazed man stood in the middle of the street with his face lathered and a shaving brush and razor in his hands. Cy, his daughter, and his mother hurried out their front door right before a second tremor hit. I staggered toward Cy but fell to my knees before I reached the picket fence. The rumbling noise swelled to a thundering crescendo, held it a moment, then suddenly stopped.

Throughout the tremor, no one cried out, not even in a whisper. Except for a chimney falling or roof crashing in the distance, the eerie silence continued several more seconds until broken by a soft, ominous sound—the gentle hiss of escaping gas.

I scrambled to my feet and hurried to Cy. He squeezed my hand as the four of us joined the swarm of people fleeing their homes. Suddenly I remembered Ida; the first place she'd go after such a tragedy was the mission.

"Cy, stop!" I commanded. "I've got to go to the mission. Ida's going to need my help treating survivors."

Conflicting emotions filled his face. "You can't go there alone, and I can't take you, not with my mother and daughter needing me."

I touched his arm gently. "It's all right. I understand. You take your mother and Phoebe to Joe's and tell him I'm safe and well. I'll be home as soon as the emergency is over."

He shook his head. "I'll come back for you as soon as possible. You and Ida will need all the help you can get." He looked at the parade of terrified people rushing down the hill. "I'd feel a lot better if you'd come with me."

I caressed his unshaven cheek. "You know I can't. Now, go, take Phoebe and your mother to safety."

He kissed my lips firmly, then disappeared with his mother and daughter into the hoards of people racing down California Street toward the ferryboat docks.

Gathering my skirts in my hands, I ran to the next corner. *Stockton, that will take me to Chinatown.* I paused and glanced up at the four- and five-story buildings lining the narrow street, then down at the street. People were clambering over piles of bricks, plaster, and other building rubble between me and my destination. Taking a deep breath, I prayed, *Lord, be with me. If it's Your will, keep those building erect until I reach the mission.*

As I straggled my way down the street, I saw a woman about my age leaning against a wrought-iron gate, holding a squirming toddler under her one arm. Her other arm hung at an odd angle from her body.

I have to help. Speaking soothing words to her and the child, I ripped the ruffle from my petticoat and made a sling for her broken arm. She told me her name was Janet and that her husband was in Sacramento on business. Once Janet's injured arm was protected, I took the child from her. "Come with me. I'm heading for the mission off Dupont. They can help you."

The woman nodded, but I suspected she didn't understand where I was taking her. Hoisting the child onto my hip, I grabbed Janet's good arm and dragged her down the street.

At the end of the block, we were stopped by a wall of white-faced people staring down the street. Billowing black smoke drifted into the air over the lower sections of the city. *Fire! If this crowd panics, we'll be trampled!*

"Come on!" I shouted, plunging into the crowd and dragging the dazed woman behind me. Even as we crossed the intersection, other fires suddenly flared up in the morning sky. I wondered why I couldn't hear the fire bells clanging and fire wagons rushing to battle the blazes.

We cleared the intersection and continued scrambling down the street. My side ached; I longed to stop and rest, but I knew Ida needed my help.

The young mother fell to her knees, crying and begging me to leave her there. "No," I cried, "it's just a little farther. You can make it."

"I can't, I can't," Janet wailed. "I just want to die."

"Well, you'll get your wish if you stay here. See how wobbly those walls are. One little aftershock and they'll come down on your head. Now, come on." The child in my arms whimpered.

She shook her head. "Take my child. I need to rest; then I'll follow you."

I turned to leave when two men standing nearby grabbed Janet by the arms. She screamed with pain before I showed them how to help her without putting pressure on her broken arm. For the first time, I noticed he was wearing a top hat, a tailcoat, his underwear, and a pair of stockings, dress shoes, and spats. The man on the other side of her wore a red-and-white striped nightshirt. His bare feet were bleeding from the broken glass in the street.

We stumbled past an old man clutching a small dog in his arms and staring helplessly up at a building whose interior stood totally bared to the world. People peered over the edge of what had been their apartments, gazing down into the rubble below. For a brief moment, I considered stopping to help. But I knew if I did, I would never reach the mission.

When we finally reached the mission, we were met with a pile of rubble, and the surrounding buildings were in flames. I spotted a policeman herding people away from the area. "Tell me, where did the woman go who operates this mission?"

He gestured over his shoulder. "I sent everyone from the area to Golden Gate Park. The military is setting up an emergency hospital there."

"Golden Gate Park?" *The park is on the other side of the city.*

"There's another emergency facility at the Presidio, as well as one at the Mechanics' Pavilion. Your friend might have gone there."

Overwhelmed by the enormity of the disaster and the distance to help, I stood in the middle of the street. *The Mechanic's Pavilion would be the closest shelter.* By the look on Janet's face, I knew we had to reach safety soon.

Crude litters covered the floor of the Mechanics' Pavilion, where Cy and I had so recently roller-skated. Bright red, blue, and yellow streamers still dangled from the rafters. The men eased Janet to the floor, and I handed her the toddler. A young priest was caring for the injured and the dying.

"I brought some patients for you." I glanced around at the crowded conditions. "Obviously, you have enough already."

He straightened and smiled. "They started coming soon after six this morning when two doctors from the hospital across the street broke down the doors. I just got here myself ten, fifteen minutes ago."

"What hospital across the street?"

"The Central Emergency Hospital collapsed on most of the staff and patients." He pointed in a sweeping arc to the suffering people. "These are the survivors. There's very little water, and all we can give is first aid."

"I'm a trained medical worker. Where do I start?" He directed me to the medical personnel already at work. More injured arrived all the time. I worked alongside the harried doctors and nurses with fifty or more other volunteers. I turned the last of my petticoat into bandages after only half an hour. To ease the shortage of bandages, I asked women who were total strangers to donate their petticoats. Even in the press of wounds to bandage and the injured to comfort, I managed to pray for strength and for God to send me where I was needed the most.

The answer to my prayer came in the form of a wagon load of injured Chinese women and children, none of whom spoke English. The driver, a white-haired grandfather, collapsed in the doorway of the Pavilion. When a doctor and a nurse tried to carry him inside the building, the people exploded into an uproar. Even amid pain and death, prejudice sprang up. I walked closer to hear what was happening.

The doctor tried to reason with the mob. "The man is dying. He needs help. So do these women and children. You can't turn them away."

An aristocrat, still dressed in his opera-house finery, drew a pistol out of his satin vest pocket and aimed it at the doctor's head. "We mean business, doc. Those yellow skins have no place here with white women and children."

The doctor turned toward his ragtag staff. "I can't just let them die outside our doors."

The young priest gently eased the pistol from the angry man's hand. "I understand that the authorities are directing the injured to Golden Gate Park for medical help."

I stepped forward and told the doctor that I was from the China mission and understood a little Cantonese. Relieved, he asked, "Will you tell these people they need to go to Golden Gate Park for help, that we have no more room?"

With halting Cantonese and numerous hand gestures, I told the women what the doctor said. A young woman holding twins replied. I turned to the doctor. "She says no one knows how to drive the wagon."

The doctor asked for a volunteer. The angry faces turned away in embarrassed silence.

I shook my head in disgust. "I can drive them, doctor. I've been handling horses since I was a kid."

"Are you sure?" He ran his fingers distractedly through his disheveled shock of black hair.

I turned to the priest and a second man, who'd recently been one of the loudest protesters. "Load this old man in the back of the wagon." Without giving him time to decline, I climbed into the driver's seat and grabbed the fallen reins.

The priest waved and called, "God go with you, child."

I smiled and shouted, "Giddyap!"

Unsure of the most direct route to the park, I headed the animals in the general direction, only to have the street barred by a flaming inferno. Army troops marched down the center of the next street, forcing people onto the sidewalks. And the third block was jammed with terrified pedestrians fleeing the other two blocks. I cracked the whip above the horses' heads. The panicky horses leapt forward. Before us was confusion and disorder. The people were using any means of transportation they could find. Women pushed baby carriages loaded with lamps, clocks, clothing, even a mounted moose head, down the middle of the street. Trunks scraped across the cobblestones as men struggled to save the contents. I swerved to avoid hitting two dazed women aimlessly wandering across the street. They were still dressed in their satin party dresses. As I slowed to avoid a live electric wire dancing in the street, a businessman held up a fifty-dollar bill.

"Take me with you."

I looked at the crowded wagon and shook my head. "No room." When he tried to drag an elderly woman off the back of the wagon to make room for himself, two other women shoved him to the ground. We passed people straggling toward the park, carrying phonographs and empty bird-cages.

After backtracking a number of times, we finally reached the park. A policeman directed me over to one section of the park where a first-aid station for Asians had been setup.

I immediately volunteered my services. Around me wild rumors flew. Eager to hear news that might pertain to Cy, I eavesdropped on every English conversation possible. Looters had been shot. The ferries and the ferry dock had burned. The Call building was destroyed. The prisoners in the city jail were running loose in the city.

As more people arrived, they brought even wilder tales of massive destruction the length of the California coast, a tidal wave washing New York City into the sea, Chicago ablaze from the same quake. Prophets of doom walked about, declaring that the end of the world had come, that God had come to judge and destroy the wicked. I thought of Jamie and wondered if he were safe. I thought of CeeCee on the other side of the bay. She would be in much more danger than Jamie in Boston. Then I thought of Cy, his daughter, and Mrs. Chamberlain. I glanced at my watch. The hands had stopped at seven-thirty.

Was that seven-thirty this morning or seven-thirty tonight? Cy, where are you? Are you safe? Did you make it across the bay to the ranch? Oh, please, dear Father, don't let anything happen to him too. I couldn't stand losing a second husband. A second husband? He's not my husband!

With the throng of people casting about in confusion, I didn't hold out much hope of him finding me anytime soon. The night sky glowed a hazy red. I'd seen the ravenous flames. I'd seen buildings crash to the street. I'd seen the looting, the drunkenness, and violence. Anything could happen out there tonight.

I pushed myself to keep busy, to keep from thinking. It

wasn't difficult, with all the injured people clamoring for attention. The light and stench of the fire continued throughout the night. Exhausted from lack of sleep and famished from hunger, I curled up beneath a rhododendron bush and fell asleep.

Reaching Out in Love

Tortured nightmares interrupted my few hours of sleep. At dawn, Lin Po, one of the teenage girls from the mission, awakened me with a bowl of watery lukewarm noodles. It was the first food I'd had since returning from roller-skating at the Mechanics' Pavilion. I thanked her and ate greedily.

Throughout the morning I bandaged wounds, comforted crying children, and set broken bones, all the while scanning the horde of passing faces for Cy and Ida. Late that afternoon, I was cleaning glass shards out of an elderly woman's feet when Lin Po ran toward me shouting, "Missy, missy. My friend, Kim Li, having baby. She needs you."

I tied off the woman's bandage and jumped to my feet.

"She's over there." I followed Lin behind a hedge where thirty women stood side by side in a tight circle. Lin spoke in Cantonese to the women, and they parted enough to let me through, then closed the circle behind me. On the ground, a young woman of sixteen writhed in silent agony. An older woman cradled Kim Li's head in her lap. I looked about the circle. "Lin? Lin?"

The women let Lin into the circle. "Lin, can you translate for me?"

The girl nodded, her eyes wide with fear.

"Ask Kim Li if I may examine her."

Lin spoke softly to the frightened mother-to-be. Kim Li nodded and allowed me to determine the baby's progress. Like military sentinels, the women maintained the circle of privacy throughout the next seven hours until Kim Li produced a baby boy.

When I handed the squawling infant to its grandmother, Lin poured a bowl of water over my hands. Another woman offered me a bowl of rice. I shook my head. "Thank you, but I'm too tired to think of eating." I staggered over to my rhododendron bush, curled up, and again fell asleep.

Suddenly I was awakened by someone vigorously shaking my shoulder. "Missy, Missy," Lin cried. "Two men come, ask for you. My mother send me to tell you."

"Two men?" I leapt to me feet. "Which way did they go?"

She pointed west. "Toward Japanese Tea Garden."

I thanked her and took off running, leaping and dodging the bodies of sleeping refugees. I ran from campfire to campfire, asking about the two men. Sheer grit kept me going. If I didn't know better, I would have believed someone was playing a giant game of hide-and-seek with me. I rounded the pond where picnickers rowed boats on Sundays and collapsed against a tree. I couldn't run any farther. Then I heard a familiar voice in the darkness.

"I know she's here somewhere. That Chinese lady was very definite about it."

"The woman might have her mixed up with someone else. And who knows how much English the poor lady understood?"

I pulled myself up and called out, "Cy, Cyrus Chamberlain, is that you?"

"Chloe? Chloe, where are you?"

"Over here by the boat dock. Where are you?" Relief flooded through me.

"Joe and I are across the pond from you," Cy shouted, his voice echoing off the boathouse.

"Is everyone all right? Is CeeCee frightened?"

"Everyone's fine. CeeCee and Phoebe are having a great time together. Stay where you are; we'll be there in a few minutes."

I paced back and forth in front of the boathouse, hoping that Cy and Joe were hurrying. Suddenly hearing footsteps running up behind me, I whirled around and dashed in the direction of the sound.

"Cy, I love you," I called.

A man burst through the trees, looked at me strangely, and continued running. My face flushed. I was thankful the darkness hid my embarrassment. The next time I heard racing footsteps in the shrubbery, I waited until I saw a face before declaring my love.

Cy swept me into his arms, burying my face in his shoulder. "We've been looking for you since last night. When I saw what had happened to the mission, I was afraid I'd lost you forever. Oh, Chloe, don't ever leave me."

Tears ran down our faces unchecked as we clung to one another. Joe considerately strolled down the pathway a few yards to give us privacy while Cy led me onto the empty dock, where he showered my tear-stained face with kisses. "I have never prayed so hard as I've prayed during the last twenty-four hours. I know God answered my prayers. We could have walked right past each other in the darkness and never have known it."

A few minutes later Joe returned. "There must be thousands of people stranded here."

I sat down in the middle of the dock. "Twenty thousand, so the officials say." Cy and Joe joined me. "I delivered a baby this evening. Imagine bringing a life into such a chaotic situation." I told them about Kim Li and Lin Po. Then I recounted my journey to the park. When I told them about my stay at the Mechanics' Pavilion, Cy stopped me.

"Did you know the pavilion burned? Almost no one made it out alive."

I thought about the young priest, the untiring doctors, Janet, her child. *Father, I could have been one of those victims. Thank You!* I heaved a grief-laden sigh. "What about you two? What took you so long to find me?"

Joe laughed. "We were conscripted by the military to fight the fires on Market Street."

"The Palace Hotel is gone, as is everything around it." Cy caressed my back and shoulders. "You won't believe Nob Hill. My place is gone, the Jordans', the Caxtons'—nothing's left. Remember Otis Roy's new mansion on the 'hill of the palaces'?"

I whipped about to face Cy.

He shook his head. "Completely consumed by fire. Mr. Dalton, my stockbroker, had a house across the street. Dalton said that when the military came to evacuate the area, Otis Roy broke away from the soldiers and ran into the burning house shouting, 'My gold! My gold.'" Cy ran his finger along my chin before continuing. "The man plunged into the flames only to have the roof collapse on him. All his paintings and imported furniture were destroyed too."

"How terrible," I whispered. "What a senseless tragedy."

Joe eyed me curiously. "I would expect you to rejoice, Chloe. Talk about justice! This is the man who killed James, remember?"

"I remember." I hugged myself to ward off a sudden chill. "But all I can feel for him is pity."

"It's like something out of a Shakespearean tragedy," Cy observed.

I leaned my chin in my hands. "Or the biblical story of Haman hanging on his own gallows."

Light from surrounding campfires reflected off the surface of the water. I rested my head on Cy's shoulder and silently watched the gurgling water, accompanied by groans in the night.

"I suppose you aren't ready to go home yet," Joe said.

"Probably not. There's so much to do here. These people need all the help they can get."

Cy leaned over my shoulder. "You know, we had a hard time finding you because you weren't at the main emergency station."

"That's because the Americans wouldn't allow the Chinese to stay."

Joe growled his displeasure. "When will people learn what it means to be humane? Can you use some more help?"

I nodded sleepily. "We sure can. Why? Are you volunteering?"

Joe, Cy, and I spent the next morning assisting at the first-aid station before returning to the ranch in the afternoon.

Some days later, Cy found Ida, who, along with other volunteers, continued to care for the Chinese refugees until they could care for themselves.

At home, a letter from Jamie awaited me. Too tired to open it, I ate some supper, bathed, and disappeared into my room to sleep for the next 36 hours.

I awakened at midnight famished. Finding Jamie's letter on the night stand, I wrapped myself in an ugly yellow chenille dressing gown that one of the ladies of Columbine gave me after the fire. I stuffed the letter in my pocket and padded to the kitchen. While I made myself a bowl of oatmeal, I read his letter. Most of it told of his classes and his eagerness to get back home.

The next-to-the-last paragraph drew my attention. "Mama, at first, I was angry at you over Cy. When I complained to Grandma McCall, she told me I was being selfish and childish to keep you from marrying again, if the man was decent. (And I guess Cy is decent enough.) She said I would grow up, fall in love, and marry one day, leaving you all alone. I've thought about it and decided she's right."

The last paragraph produced tears and laughter. "Mama, there's this cute blond girl named Anna, the headmaster's daughter. I think she likes me." I stuffed the letter back in my pocket and walked to the stone bench in the garden to eat my lumpy cereal.

The sky was overcast. I didn't notice Cy sitting on the other side of the fountain. "Ah, what yonder maiden doth before mine eyes appear?"

I jumped, and my spoon plopped into the cereal. "Cy! What are you doing out here at this hour?"

"I could ask you the same thing, but I won't. What if I told you I've been sitting here all week waiting for the princess to emerge from her tower room?"

I snorted. "I'd say you were either totally mad or lying. Which is it?"

"Alas, my love . . ." He stood and strolled over to my side of the fountain and sat down beside me. ". . . I must confess. My presence is purely accidental. I came out for a bit of fresh air before retiring for the night."

I laughed and poked him in the ribs with my elbow, then offered him a spoonful of my cereal. "Here, it's good."

"Yech! Even my mother can't get me to eat that stuff."

I finished the oatmeal and set the bowl on the tile floor beside the bench. "It is so peaceful here, after Golden Gate Park."

Cy linked his hands over one knee and leaned back. "It sure is. I've appreciated Joe and Beth inviting my family and me to stay here until we can decide where to go from here."

"What do you plan to do?"

He nodded. "I sent a telegram to the home offices, but I

haven't received a reply from the big man yet. He may want me to return to New Jersey to file a full report."

"Oh." I didn't like the thought of him leaving California. *So much can happen. So much needs to be settled between us.*

He eyed my ill-fitting mountain of a dressing gown. "My, that's an attractive garment."

I adjusted the collar about my neck. "It is, isn't it?"

He cleared his throat, not certain whether I was joking or serious. "Sure is pretty out here tonight."

"Sure is."

"Have you ever seen such a beautiful moon?"

I gazed up at the cloudy sky, then at him. I caught the slight elevation of one side of his upper lip.

"It sure is. And just look at all those stars, like diamonds on silken velvet."

He chuckled. "Are you going to agree with everything I say tonight?"

I cast him a teasing grin, nodding slowly.

His smile broadened. "Really?"

Again I nodded.

Staring into my eyes, he asked, "Are you being serious?"

I nodded.

"Then, will you marry me?"

Without hesitation, I nodded once more.

He grabbed my shoulders. "Are you serious?"

I lifted my eyes to meet his. "I already answered that question earlier."

I waited patiently as he studied my face. "You are serious. You really will marry me."

"Sh . . ." I touched his lips with my index finger. "You ask too many questions."

He inhaled sharply. I leaned forward and sealed my answer with a kiss. When he finally realized I was serious, his face glowed with joy. For the next hour we held hands and talked, occasionally stealing a kiss. He told me about the crush he had on me way back in Shinglehouse. I couldn't believe I never knew it.

"It lasted one entire summer. From my third-story bedroom window, I would watch that pretty little freckle-faced redhead skip out of the library with stacks of books. What did you do with them all?"

I tilted my nose toward the sky. "I read them, of course."

"All of them?"

"Uh-huh." When we were too chilled to sit on the stone bench any longer, Cy waited on the sofa in the parlor until I ran to my room to change into something more appropriate. I returned to a barrage of questions.

"How soon can we marry?"

"Where do you want to have the wedding?"

"Where would you like to go for our honeymoon?"

"When shall we tell the children?"

There was no end. I had no answers, especially to the one unspoken question I'd wondered about for months.

"Cy, you've never talked about your reaction to the Bible-reading assignment I gave you before Christmas."

"I haven't mentioned it because I didn't want you to think I was giving you a line." He stared down at the floor, then straightened. "I no longer doubt Jesus was who He said He was. But I don't understand about this born-again stuff."

I explained to him that being born again means you ask forgiveness of your sins, and you give yourself to Jesus to work His will in you. I found a Bible in Joe's library and read him the story in Acts of Paul and Silas and the jailer. "Paul said, . . . 'Believe on the Lord Jesus Christ, and thou shalt be saved.'"

"That's it?"

"That's it. The hard part comes in trusting God with everything—the good, the bad, and the impossible."

He leaned his elbows on his knees. "I've spent the last four months studying and praying. I know how important it is to you that we be like-minded in this. After working side by side with the other volunteers at the mission, most of whom were professing Christians with nothing material to gain, I knew that's the kind of person I wanted to be and the kind of person a woman like you deserves to marry."

All my doubts were laid to rest. As to the time, place, or situation of our marriage, it didn't matter. Cyrus and I had a firm foundation on which to build our love. We talked until the first golden streaks of daylight appeared over the spring-green hills behind the ranch.

At the breakfast table, we announced our engagement. After a moment of stunned silence, everyone babbled at once. Joe leapt from the table to congratulate Cy and to kiss me. Beth squealed with delight. "I've been praying for months this would happen."

CeeCee danced around the room. "I get to be a flower girl again." Suddenly she stopped midstep. "Mommy, can Phoebe be a flower girl too?"

"I think that would be a good idea, don't you, honey?" I smiled at Cy. He looked startled. That's when I realized I'd never before called him honey.

Mrs. Chamberlain folded her hands together in front of her face and cooed, "Isn't this romantic? Oh, dear, there's so much to do. And where around here will you be able to purchase a suitable gown for the ceremony?" Horror swept across her face. "Where will you hold the ceremony? Everything is chaos in San Francisco. And on this side of the bay, well . . ." She rolled her eyes toward the ceiling. "Need I say more? Oh, poor Cyrus, he won't be able to be here!"

I started to explain that we hadn't actually set a date, when the woman leapt to her feet. "Of course, you'll get married in Baltimore at my parents' estate. That way, your family, as well as ours, can attend. It will be the event of the season."

Cy smiled at me and rounded the table to where his mother stood. "Mother, Chloe and I haven't yet discussed any of this. But we'll consider all your suggestions." He kissed her cheek. "I promise."

I liked the respect he showed his mother, tender, loving, yet self-confident enough to make his own decisions. If the way Cy treated his mother was any indication of how he'd treat me, I was encouraged.

A number of events decided the time and date of our wedding for us. First, Thaddeus Townsend's father came to tell us that he and his wife were sailing for Europe. And since Thaddeus would be going with them, he would not be able to accompany Jamie to California. Then Mrs. McCall wrote and asked if I could bring CeeCee East for a visit. The day the home office telegraphed Cy to return in June for a conference, I also I received a letter from my mother.

"When your father read your note regarding your up-coming nuptials to Cy Chamberlain, he said, 'I wish we could be there.' He talks about you often and studies the photographs of you and the children. I hope this news will bring you joy as you prepare for your wedding day. With love, Ma."

After reading the letter, I went to find Cy. He was saddling one of Joe's riding mares.

"Hi, honey," I called. "Are you going anywhere special? You want some company?"

He stooped to tighten the horse's belly band. "Sure, come on along."

"OK, I need to change into a riding skirt. Meet me out front." Since coming to California I'd adopted a riding outfit consisting of a chambray blouse, a split riding skirt of tan suede, and matching boots. When I bounded out of the house, Cy was waiting by the hitching post. CeeCee and Phoebe waved from the veranda, where they were having a tea party with their favorite dolls.

We cantered across the pasture toward the hills overlooking the ranch. The spring-green grass was fast turning to summertime gold. When we reached the ridge, I asked if we could stop and rest awhile. We dismounted and secured the animals to a small mandrone tree, then sat on a rock outcropping overlooking the valley.

"Cy, I've been thinking about your mother's idea to get married back East. Maybe it isn't such a bad idea."

"What do you mean? You want to get married at my grandmother's estate in Baltimore?" He eyed me as if I'd taken leave of my senses.

"No, not exactly. But we could get married in Shinglehouse. Hattie says the new community church has lovely stained-glass windows."

He slipped his arm about my waist. "Are you sure you want to do this? Give Mother an inch, and she'll be incorrigible."

I laughed. "On the other hand," he continued, "we wouldn't have to wait until I get back from New Jersey, would we?"

"Nope. And if we all went back together in the private Pullman, we'd have adequate chaperonage. Could you arrange to get the company car out here in the next couple of weeks?"

He nuzzled my neck. "Oh, I think I could manage somehow."

I had one last bombshell to drop. "Remember I told you how Mrs. McCall is eager to have CeeCee visit? The dear lady would be delighted to have CeeCee to herself while we spent a week at my cottage on Cape Cod."

"James's cottage?"

I turned slowly to face him and met his gaze. "Our cottage, as soon as we're husband and wife. Will you find it difficult to accept that I own land and am comfortably set?"

His brown eyes studied mine for several moments. "No, I don't think so."

In a low, nervous voice, I said, "You'd better be sure."

The tender smile he gave erased my fears. "Chloe, when I promise before God to love you for better or worse; for richer or poorer; in sickness and in health, I will vow to love you and all the extras you bring with you—CeeCee, Jamie, your former husband, your previous in-laws." He slid one arm around my shoulders, and we walked along the crest. "Memories that don't include me, even wealth I didn't provide. And I know you will promise the same to me. It won't be easy blending our pasts in order to build a new future, but with God's help, we can do it."

Tears sprang into my eyes. I cleared my throat. "Did I ever tell you about the VanArsdales, in Columbine? They'd both been previously married. Yet I've never seen such a happy couple." Ula's and Noah's faces sprang up in my memory. "They were totally dedicated to one another. Noah once told me that the secret to their happiness was a three-way partnership—Ula, God, and him."

Cy stopped and turned me to face him once more. "I want that kind of marriage, Chloe, more than anything else in the world."

"Me too."

A bit hesitantly Cy asked, "Would it be out of line for us to ask God to become our partner before we're actually married?"

"I don't see why."

Silently, we dropped to our knees. Clasping hands and gazing into one another's eyes, we prayed together. Haltingly, Cy thanked God for me and for our growing love. He asked God to come into our relationship and to bond us together.

I choked back my tears as I prayed that all Cy's wounds be healed, that the hate and anger we'd both suffered would be turned to joy and love, drawing us closer together. I'd loved James with all my heart, but at that moment, I'd never felt so close to another human being as I did to Cy. After I said amen, he whispered in a voice raspy with emotion, "Let's pray together like this often."

Once we announced our wedding date to the family, the event took on a life of its own. Everything fell into place like a giant hand was overseeing the details. It was decided Joe and Beth would travel back with us in the company Pullman, since Phillip and Jenny had left for her parents' place immediately after their home was destroyed in the earthquake.

Mrs. Chamberlain insisted I shop for a wedding gown in Denver. Because that would give me a chance to spend a day or two with Gladys and Phineas, I agreed. I wrote letters to Pete and Faith in Oregon, to Gladys, to my parents, to Ula, to Aunt Bea, and to Mrs. McCall. After telling them about our earthquake experiences, I gave them the good news of our engagement and wedding plans. I received letters back almost immediately, wishing us happiness. All were eager to play their roles in our scheme. While I felt sad that Pete and Faith would not be able to attend, I was grateful that he approved of my decision to remarry.

On June 3 we boarded the Union Pacific for the long ride east. As the wheels beneath the luxury Pullman clattered along the tracks, memories, like the pages in a photo album, flickered by—Hangtown, Virginia City, Salt Lake . . .

It looked like all of Columbine had turned out to meet our train and wish us well during the short stopover in Steamboat Springs. Ula pulled me aside. "He's a good boy, I can tell. I'm happy for you."

When the train whistle blew, I hugged her and climbed on board to continue our journey. In Denver, Gladys and

Mrs. Chamberlain vied for CeeCee's attention. They both agreed, however, on my wedding dress, a lavender silk gown with horizontal lace insets on the skirt. Matching lace, like a pointed shawl covered the shoulders, bodice, and neck. The gathered silk sleeves narrowed at the elbow, where lace flared loosely to the wrists.

I tried it on and turned slowly in front of the full-length mirror. One glance, and I was in love. The lavender tones brought out the natural blush in my cheeks and deepened the red in my hair. I glanced at Beth and asked, "What do you think? Do you agree?"

She smiled and whispered, "Just this once, but don't tell anyone." I also purchased appropriate dresses for CeeCee, Ma, Ori, and Hattie. I could only hope Ori's, Ma's, and Hattie's dresses would fit properly. Mrs. Chamberlain bought hers and Phoebe's.

We stayed overnight at Aunt Bea's place in Hays. Reluctantly we said goodbye in the morning. Though we didn't stop over in Chicago, Cy and I did watch the city lights come on at sunset from the Pullman's observation deck.

A drizzling rain couldn't dampen my spirits as the train pulled into the Shinglehouse station. I pressed my face to the window, eager to catch the first glimpse of my father. My daughter stood beside me.

"There they are." I pointed to the cluster of people standing under the eaves of the station. "There's Grandma Spencer, Aunt Hattie, Uncle Stanford, Cy's daddy, Aunt Myrtle, Uncle Franklin, Ori, Amby . . ."

When Myrtle's son waved, the little girl laughed and waved back. The conductor had barely slid the steps into place when I bounded from the Pullman car, bare headed, hat box in hand.

"Ma," I called, running into her arms. I was immediately swallowed up by my laughing, chattering relatives. But the one I longed most to see was nowhere in sight. Disappointed, I turned toward Ma, who was hugging CeeCee.

"Mother?" She read the pain in my eyes.

A look of confusion crossed her face. "What is it?" Suddenly her face brightened. "Oh, he's here. He just went to check the schedule. He's been driving poor Franklin crazy for the last hour." She stood on her tiptoes to peer over the heads of the crowd. "There he is, coming out of the depot."

I whirled about and spied my father. When our eyes met, he froze in the doorway. Emotion welled up in my throat; my eyes swam with tears. Cy gave me a gentle push. Timidly, I started toward my father.

Arriving and departing passengers hurried past us, occasionally blocking our view. But always after they passed, our eyes connected once again. My family grew silent as they watched me walk toward my father. I heard my daughter ask, "Is that my grandpa?" Someone shushed her.

Pa took a few slow steps toward me. The rain drizzled in my face, pasting my wet hair to my forehead. I didn't care. After eight years, Pa and I stood three feet apart, face to face, and neither of us spoke. Slowly, he held out his arms to me. A sob escaped my lips as I stepped into his embrace.

"Oh, Pa, I've missed you so much." I didn't try to control the tears that mingled with the raindrops moistening his jacket lapels.

His arms tightened around me with a fierceness that matched my hold on him. He buried my face in his shoulder. "Chloe girl, you are so beautiful. I am so proud of you."

I pulled away. "Pa, I'm sor—"

"No, you've apologized enough over the last eight years. Now, it's my turn. I'm the stubborn old goat, as your mother puts it, who needs to say I'm sorry. I've been such a fool." He swiped at the tears streaming down his cheeks. "I've let the pride of a bunch of dead Spencers keep us apart. Can you ever forgive me?"

I nodded slowly, then again melted into his arms, once more his little girl. With one hand he brushed my wet, matted curls from my face. I sobbed from the joy of the moment, from the sorrow of all those wasted years, from relief that the pain separating us was finally over. He held me for several seconds.

"I know I don't deserve it, but can you find it in your heart to allow me to give you away at your wedding to Cyrus Chamberlain?"

I laughed and cried at the same time. "I'd like nothing more. I'd planned to ask you anyway."

Reluctantly we strolled over to join the rest of the family. Cy's eyes glistened with emotion as he kissed me on the cheek and drew me to his side. "Sir," Cy addressed my father, "I'd like to request your daughter's hand in marriage."

My father grinned and sniffed back his remaining tears. "It's a little late for that, don't you think? And if I denied your request, would it make any difference?"

Stunned, Cy cleared his throat. "Well, sir, we really would appreciate your . . ."

It wasn't until that moment I realized how much I'd missed Pa's belly laugh. My father threw his head back, making the station platform ring with his laughter. "Hasn't my daughter taught you anything about the Spencer sense of humor? Welcome to the family, son." The two men shook hands.

Mrs. Chamberlain called to Cy, "Are you ready to go home, son? Or will you be staying with the Spencers?"

"I'll be there in a minute, Mother." Cy kissed me and promised to be out at the house first thing in the morning to take me to a meeting with the community church pastor. "What time should I arrive?"

"I'll be awake." I gestured toward my family. "I probably won't sleep at all tonight."

He laughed and kissed me again. "Until tomorrow, my sweet."

My prediction was right. We spent the rest of the day and on into the night talking, laughing, and crying. The family sat spellbound as I told them about the events of the earthquake.

Around midnight, Myrtle and her family left. That's when we took a break and put the younger children to bed. When I came downstairs from tucking CeeCee into my old bed, the group had moved to the kitchen table, where Ma was serving hot tea and sweet rolls. Four hours later, Pa, Stanford, and the boys went to do chores, leaving Ma, Hattie, and me. Ma begged exhaustion and left. My sister and I were still talking when the men returned from chores. I did catch a few hours of sleep before Cy arrived.

By the time we left the parsonage, it was arranged that the wedding would be held one week from Thursday. I immediately sent a telegram to Jamie, so he could be present for the ceremony. What I didn't expect was for the entire McCall family to attend, including Drucilla and Aunt Bea.

"I thought it was high time I got back to see my kin," she explained. She hadn't mentioned a word about the possibility of her taking a trip East when we stopped to see her the week before.

The morning of the wedding, Cy's relatives, including his brother and family, arrived from Baltimore. Stanford, Myrtle, and her husband, Franklin, spent the morning decorating the church with baskets of daisies and pink roses while Hattie and I puttered around upstairs in our old room, chatting and giggling like teenagers. Ma and Ori spent the morning making nosegays for each of us to carry.

I whispered a prayer of thanksgiving when Ma and the others put on their dresses for the wedding—we had not had to alter any of them, they had fit perfectly. When Joe pulled up with the family carriage to take the women to the church, I kissed each one goodbye. CeeCee was adorable, bouncing down the stairs in her pink organdy dress, white stockings, and white patent-leather high-top shoes.

I watched from the upstairs window until the family carriage disappeared from view, only to be replaced with the Chamberlains' splendid carriage. Mr. Chamberlain had offered to have Ross, his driver, pick us up in the Chamberlains' shiny new horseless carriage, but I declined, preferring a quieter, more traditional form of transportation.

As I buttoned my white kid gloves at the wrist, my father called from the base of the stairs, "Chloe, the Chamberlain carriage is here."

"Thanks, Pa. I'll be right down." My father and I hadn't had time to be alone to talk since I arrived. So when Cy and I made transportation arrangements to the church, I requested that Pa and I ride alone.

Taking one last look in the mirror, I adjusted the spirals of curls wreathing my face and pinned on a wreath of white satin ribbon and honeysuckle. *One step at a time, Lord. You've led us this far. Please continue leading us.* I thought of Cy's serious, concerned face, and my jitters were replaced with confidence.

Reaching for the lavender satin slippers Gladys had insisted on buying for me, I slipped them on. At the top of the stairs, I took a deep breath, straightened my shoulders, and walked slowly down the stairs. When I reached the bottom step, my father lifted my gloved hand to his lips and kissed my fingertips. "Have I told you how proud I am to call you my daughter?"

My eyes misted. "You're going to make me cry. Then my eyes will be red and puffy for the ceremony."

He chuckled, tucked my hand in the crook of his arm, and escorted me to the waiting carriage. There was so much I wanted to tell him about James, about Cy, about Noah, about Pete, but now wasn't the time or the place. My sadness dissipated when I realized there would be time. Now that the wounds could heal, there would be plenty of time.

The carriage rattled over the rutted road I'd traveled so often in my childhood. I'd come full circle, even to marrying a hometown boy with my father's approval. Pa patted my hand. "Relax, Chloe girl."

I looked down at my clenched fist and laughed. "I'm nowhere near as nervous as when I married James. I guess it's because Cy and I are starting out differently."

"Because you've both been married before?"

I shook my head. "No. We've vowed to one another to keep God as the third partner in our relationship. You wouldn't believe the difference that decision has already made."

"I'm proud of you both. And I envy you. It sounds like you are a lot closer to the Lord than I."

A mist of sadness enveloped me. "I've had a lot of opportunities to exercise my faith. After James died, I didn't see how I could keep going. But I made it through. Every step of the way, God has sent some faithful servant to guide me through the darkness." I swallowed hard. "Isn't God's love remarkable?"

My father cleared his throat and sniffed. "I'm learning. Thanks to Stanford and Hattie, and now you, I'm learning."

The carriage stopped in front of the gray stone church, and Pa and I walked up the pathway. As the outer doors swung open, Pa took a deep breath and squeezed my hand. "Here goes," he whispered.

We climbed the stone steps and entered the vestibule. Ori and Phoebe waved and giggled. CeeCee hugged me around the waist. "Mommy," she whispered, "you're beautiful." I bent down and kissed her.

Hattie came up to me. "The mothers are already seated. The men are coming in from the side room, see?"

I looked through the oval window in the swinging door and smiled as Jamie proudly took his place beside Joe. My eyes shifted to the pale face of my bridegroom, standing straight and tall in his dove gray suit. I stepped back to let the attendants open the doors. Ori and Hattie entered to Beethoven's "Ode to Joy."

When the first chords of the "Wedding March" sounded, Pa disentangled his arm from my fingers, reached into his pocket and pressed something into the palm of my hand. A twenty-dollar gold piece sparkled up at me. I started in surprise; then tears sprang into my eyes. "No, you already gave me mine, remember? It was lost in the tornado."

He smiled and tapped the tip of my nose with his index finger. "The coins are mine to give." He picked up the gold piece and slipped it inside the palm of my glove. With a twinkle in his eye, he whispered, "But don't think you're going to get another—no matter how many men you marry."

"Pa," I scolded, slipping my arm in his, "behave." He smiled, straightened his cravat, and ushered me to Cy's waiting arms.